Arc of the Universe

A Novel

Nikki Alexander

ISBN: 979-8-9927262-0-6 (paperback)
ISBN: 979-8-9927262-1-3 (ebook)

Published by Strawberry Tree Books
Interior layout by Gecko Edit

For my mother

"The arc of the moral universe is long, but it bends toward justice."

Dr. Martin Luther King, Jr.

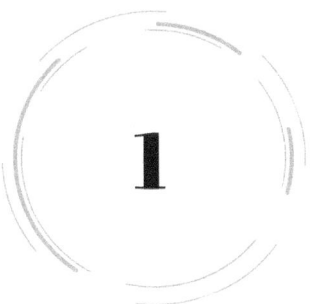

1

THEY HAD the technology to launch astronauts from planet Earth into space, to travel 140 million miles to an experimental colony on Mars, and yet, today of all days, her heel had broken. She didn't need to wear heels—at nearly six feet tall, Carrie bemoaned any reminder of her height, let alone footwear that would make her stand out even more in a crowd. But it was an auspicious day, and after some resistance, she had been talked into a kitten heel.

Mistakenly. Screw those death traps, anyway.

She sat in a small conference room on the fourth floor of the Project Mars headquarters building, one leg crossed over the other, clutching the offending shoe. She wore heels so infrequently that it had probably disintegrated from old age. She'd bought them ten years ago, back in 2022 when she'd first started teaching. It had seemed right, for her first day as a law professor, to dress the part: tweed blazer, neatly pressed slacks, a silly pointed-toe slingback heel. When she stepped behind the lectern, embossed with the twisted stems of Briar University's signature crest, the outfit instilled confidence. She looked the part. She had the academic credentials. Ornately framed diplomas from prestigious universities lined her office walls, and the knickknacks on her desk had been freshly unpacked from a two-year Harvard fellowship. She lasted a full week in those heels before realizing it was stupid; all she'd ever cared about was helping her students understand the contours of the law. She could do that in sensible footwear.

Her phone buzzed with a text.

All good? Kim had written. Carrie immediately dialed.

"Not all good," she whispered to her best friend, although she was alone in the little conference room.

"What happened? The press conference hasn't even started yet. I've got the livestream pulled up on my computer now."

"You convinced me to wear heels, and now one has *snapped*," Carrie said. "Broken. Given up. Like me, if I have to hobble into that press conference in half an hour on one heel." Her bare toes felt obscene in the otherwise pristine conference room.

"I didn't tell you to wear heels," Kim said. "I dressed you in a silk blouse, Dior topcoat, and some pretty killer tailored striped pants, if I do say so myself, and I told you not to mess it up with your footwear choice. I swear, if you're wearing those beat-up shoes from a decade ago, Carrie Davenport..."

"I ... no. Yes. I've been busy, and ..." She sighed. Shifting from foot to foot for the last hour couldn't have helped the situation. Her insides felt like they had liquefied, until she was a sloshy little sack of flesh that could collapse at any moment. It didn't matter what she wore. In less than an hour, she would literally be stepping into the biggest professional opportunity of her lifetime, and no choice of footwear could change the impact it would have on her and, somehow, humanity.

Teaching brewed its own anxiety. In some of her larger classes she faced seventy students, who had all been college debate team champions or Rhodes scholars, or who had flown halfway around the world as Peace Corps volunteers. All staring at her, waiting for her to educate them on areas of the law that at times made no sense. At least there were text-books—compilations of cases meant to tell students exactly what they needed to know to understand contracts, or torts, or the US Constitution. This was different. Uncharted. Rather than students, there would be news reporters, heads of federal government agencies, and billionaires in the room. Her task wouldn't be to share her thoughts about a constitution written nearly two hundred fifty years ago but to write the very law itself. A thing both monumental and impossibly easy to mess up.

She blinked and looked at the phone screen. Thirty seconds had gone by without her saying anything—she'd been in her head again.

"Carrie," Kim said quietly into the phone, bringing her back to reality. "You can do this. Just breathe. You are truly the smartest person I know."

"I'm already screwing it up."

"No, you're not. Well, maybe a little bit, because those shoes were a fashion disaster from a bygone decade, but not academically. You were meant for this."

"God, I hope so." She had to get this right.

"Is there anyone who doesn't have the fashion sense of a one-eyed grandma to help you?"

"Hey! No—" She was interrupted as the door swung open, revealing a flash of red hair.

"Dr. Davenport!" Libby, the Project Mars communications director, offered her a dazzling smile, her brilliant white teeth practically reflecting the room. "We've got about thirty minutes until the press conference. Are you ready to go?"

Physically? No. Emotionally? Also no.

"Sure!" Carrie smiled and discreetly hung up on Kim, who could probably hear what was afoot anyway. "I'm just a little frazzled because the heel of my shoe broke a minute ago."

Libby glanced down at Carrie's exposed brown toes. "Oh, gosh! On press conference day! That's gotta be stressful. Not to worry, I'll put an aide on it." She tapped on her phone, and within moments a young woman appeared behind Libby in the doorway.

"You need something?"

"A pair of women's shoes. Size ten?"

Carrie nodded, her eyebrow raised.

"Where would I get that?" the aide asked, wide eyed.

"I don't know, but you have thirty minutes to figure it out. It's not rocket science." The aide scurried off.

Libby winked at Carrie. "I love making that joke. Everything else we do here literally is. Consider it handled."

Carrie tamped down her embarrassment at *this* having been her last-minute crisis; not how she'd discuss the legal ramifications of her work, but something so completely divorced from all the ways she normally shined. She looked at Libby, words escaping her.

"It's fine," Libby said, her gaze fixed on her phone screen as she typed out an email. The life of a communications

4

director. "I already know you're one of the most talented professors of a generation. When you're done with your work for us, everyone else will know that, too."

"That's kind of you. It'll be nice for the legal community to read the team's report."

Libby's gaze snapped back up to Carrie. "Not other lawyers. I mean the whole world."

Twenty minutes later, she rode the elevator up from the fourth floor to the very top, the button simply marked "A." The top floor of the towering glass headquarters building offered the kind of view only a billionaire could provide. From fourteen stories up, the surrounding landscape started to blur, until a hodgepodge sea of scrub grass and native plants coated the ground in an earth-toned carpet that sloped down to the blue Pacific beyond. To step out of the elevator, walk through the atrium, and enter the resplendent auditorium built entirely of frameless glass was to step into the sky itself. The white marble floors resembled clouds ushering the crowd directly to the heavens, and thin panes of glass were all that separated mere mortals from the gods above. Carrie wondered if the lightness the space evoked, the sense of possibility, was what the astronauts would feel on liftoff.

She wanted to puke.

When she reached the doorframe separating the atrium from the auditorium hall, she stalled over the sill, like an animal being led to slaughter. Her eyes squeezed shut, although she could still hear the raucous din of voices ahead pinging against the glass walls. *What a freaking massive crowd.*

Even with her eyes closed she couldn't ignore the way her heart threatened to pound right out of her chest. She would know approximately five people out of the hundreds that awaited. She just had to make it through today, and by tomorrow she'd be home in the comfort of her cozy wood-paneled office. Before she could make any effort to quell her anxiety, the tip of something sharp pressed into the small of her back.

"If you would keep walking, Ms. Davenport, I'd like to get settled on stage," said a clipped voice close to her ear. She turned and realized she'd been prodded—like cattle—with the brass-tipped corner of a leather padfolio.

She stopped herself before her eyebrows shot up in an incredulous stare and forced her lips to stretch into a tight, polite smile. Adam Kilpatrick barely spared her a passing glance before he brushed past her into the room.

"Doctor," she muttered under her breath for what felt like the millionth time.

Carrie took a deep breath and swept into the room. She tried to embody her professor persona, with the confidence and haughty stare that her young faculty assistant, Anna, had once said made her look downright scary; she strived for a cool academic tone no matter how much public speaking anxiety loomed within. About two hundred onlookers milled among the auditorium rows in advance of the press conference. They watched her back hungrily, on alert. Their eyes swept from the tight pull of her dark bun, her edges slicked back with edge control, down the expensive cut of the long topcoat Kim had insisted she wear. The reporters seemed fixated on the orange Project Mars lanyard around her neck, with its badge that meant she was *somebody*. The intensity of their scrutiny and the steady hum of conversation made the room around her buzz so palpably that Carrie's hands tingled. She stood in front of the rows of seats and spun in a circle, taking in the panoramic oceanfront view, the swarm of reporters, and a long panelist table with three black microphones on a pristine white tablecloth.

It didn't feel real, being there, at last. The initial phone call with Project Mars had been a hand yanking her from the warm burrow of peaceful reality into the cold air of the unknown. Before she'd gotten the call, she'd been preoccupied with wrapping up an academic journal article on how Eastern European countries had designed their constitutions. And now, as much as being thrust in the limelight made her toes curl, she was meant to step up to the low stage and sit behind the panelist table to discuss outer space.

Before her fight-or-flight instinct could fully kick in, a huddle of reporters parted, and she spotted Libby. The other woman waved her over to the stage.

"Dr. Davenport! We're thrilled you're here." For a second, Libby's eyes hovered on Carrie's shoes, and Carrie fought the urge to smile. She was wearing an early prototype of Project Mars's space sneakers, designed to streamline the bulky astronaut boot.

Carrie shook the petite woman's hand again, as though they had not just solved their own shoe catastrophe. Libby's long red curls bobbed as she spoke.

"Though I'm sure you've seen his name before, you probably haven't met Grant, our head of strategy for Project Mars." She gestured to a tall man standing next to her. "He oversaw the committee that selected you for the lead role, with Beau's input."

"Mr. . . . uh, Grant, it's a pleasure," she said, her voice sounding more authoritative than she felt. "I'm honored that you saw something worthwhile in my credentials. I won't let you or Project Mars down."

He nodded at her, his dark watchful eyes expressionless.

Libby perked up. "Please sit, Carrie, we have you here between Mr. Hughes and Dr. Kilpatrick."

"Oh, good, front and center," she said, hoping she'd kept all sarcasm out of her voice.

In the left chair sat a tall, lean man with feathery graying hair and with gold-rimmed glasses perched on his angular nose. Adam Kilpatrick stared ahead, avoiding her gaze, his hands resting on the leather padfolio he'd used only moments before to prod her into the room. To the right, a burly man chatted animatedly with an aide as he stood behind his chair, using a meaty hand to wipe a slight sheen of sweat off his forehead and into his wavy reddish-brown hair.

Carrie sank into her chair like the seat was her own insulated space suit, the last line of defense between her and destruction. She spared a glance at her phone to check the time. Ten minutes before they'd start. In her peripheral vision, Carrie caught burly fingers slipping across the starchy white tablecloth. She turned her head a fraction of an inch and watched as the hand wrapped around the miniature plastic water bottle that had been placed to the side of her microphone. Owen Hughes had seated himself and attempted a covert operation to co-opt her water.

"I'll be damned if these tiny bottles hold more than a sippy cup's worth of water," Owen grumbled. He had already guzzled and crushed in his large hand the bottle that had been placed beside his own microphone. "You don't mind if I . . ."

Carrie cleared her throat. "Oh. I suppose not." Her throat was so dry it was hard to swallow, but more pressingly her stomach churned as though it would forcibly reject whatever she drank. She evaluated Owen as he gulped and demolished her bottle of water, a few droplets clinging to his russet beard. Hell. If he was willing to brazenly take her water, she'd better woman up, too. She squared her shoulders and faced the auditorium door head on.

The sound of the reporters' clicking cameras ricocheted about the room in fits and spurts as new figures emerged from the steel door at the side of the auditorium. It started with Lois Riggs, the recently confirmed head of NASA and former International Space Station astronaut, and then celebrated astrophysicist Arthur Beck, and then the director of the United Nations Committee on the Peaceful Use of Outer Space, Simonetta Di Pippo. Carrie recognized, too, faces she'd seen on television, like the California governor. Then there were faces she figured only she and the fellow panelists would recognize, like the head of the American Law Institute.

A brusquely cleared throat snapped her attention back to her immediate environs. Beside her, Dr. Kilpatrick straightened his tie and spared Carrie a half glance.

"Can I assume, Ms. Davenport, that you'll speak about our plans to journey to Monticello to study some of Jefferson's lesser-known writings?"

Carrie sat straighter in her chair. This was her wheelhouse.

"It's Dr. Davenport," she told him shortly. "And no. While that's a part of our research, Jefferson is only one of the sources we'll—"

"It's B-Ball in the buildinggggg." With a collective intake of breath, the entire room's energy shifted, and a handful of onlookers began to clap. A short man in his early forties, clad in a form-fitting black sweater, dark jeans, and Air Jordans emblazoned with a blue P on the side, stood with his hands cupped around his mouth to announce his own entrance, his booming voice unconcerned with whatever had been transpiring in the room before his arrival. Beauregard Ball was a Southern billionaire entrepreneur and space fanatic. Subtle he was not. He had nicknamed himself "B-Ball" as a self-deprecating ode to the fact that he was, at best, five foot three, and by all accounts unathletic. He compensated for the nickname by owning the Seattle Sonics NBA team and funding the entire operation that had prompted the day's press conference.

A suite of aides with Project Mars lanyards gathered around Beau as he shook hands and made his way around the room, pointing at supporters and tilting his head back in laughter, at ease and in charge. He progressed from the auditorium door down the front row, and Carrie realized with a start that he was headed along a slow path toward the panelist table.

Within a few minutes of schmoozing, Beau reached Dr. Kilpatrick. His gaze flicked briefly to the name tent card, then up to Adam, who stared down his nose at Beau. Adam's only tell was a small drop of sweat that had beaded at his temple.

"How's it going, man?" Beau said, shaking Adam's hand breezily.

"Mr. Ball," Adam Kilpatrick said. "You've selected an excellent team to oversee the rules and foundational principles for your Mars colony."

Beau grinned. "I think so, too." He glanced over at Carrie, and she was surprised that he continued without looking down at her tent card.

"Carrie Davenport. I'm glad you're leading this project. I can't wait to see what you do for the colony, and I'm grateful for your service." His eyes pierced into hers, serious and intent in a way that did not match his easy drawl.

Her heart thudded heavily in her chest, and she found herself nodding. "You can count on us to get this done."

Beau laughed, his hyper-focus gone so quickly that Carrie wondered whether she'd imagined it. "I hope so. And Owen, man, Congressman Blake told me you're a sports fan. Let me know if I can hook you up with tickets to the next Sonics game."

Owen beamed. "Yessir. Hell, I could have afforded them myself if I had bought Perpetua stock back in 2005 like everyone told me to."

Beau drifted away, the same easy smile spread across his face. "Hindsight is twenty-twenty," he said, his arm already outstretched to shake hands with a crowd waiting just beyond the panelists' platform.

Carrie's eyes followed Beau as he continued to work the room. Before long, Libby cleared her throat. Beau pivoted from where'd he'd been demonstrating his new phone to a suite of reporters and addressed the room at large, his voice carrying even without a microphone.

"Right, okay, the press conference. Folks, this is a big freaking deal. I know we've wowed you with the technical specs, and last week we thrilled you with the NewGravity Z-4 Vectran space suits that we've got for our space-goers, but don't snooze on these folks from legal. Everybody's gotta play by some sort of rules. Check it out."

Apparently satisfied that he'd nailed the introduction of the country's preeminent constitutional law scholars, he plopped down heavily in the auditorium's front row and pulled up what looked to Carrie like original Tetris on his phone.

Libby, with a doting smile that could only mean she was well accustomed to Beau's antics, hastened to the podium.

"Thank you to the visionary founder and leader of Project Mars, Beau, for that excellent introduction. Now, for all our lovely members of the press here today, if you haven't been sleeping under a rock, you're well aware that Perpetua has been fortunate to grow from a tech startup in Beau's brother's garage to a trillion-dollar technology, aeronautics, and space company. For years, Perpetua has honed its ambitious plan to send one hundred carefully selected space-goers to Mars for an experimental two-year colony as a test for human settlement on the red planet. Despite what the social media gossipmongers might post on Lune, Project Mars is still on track to launch our experimental class in 2034. Yes, we're a private company, so you wouldn't think we'd have a panel of experts on government here. But we know that every group of people needs rules, and we hope the rules that govern these colonists will serve as the foundation for a greater, larger society in years to come. And with the contributions of our generous supporters"—Libby waved at a group of men clad in tailored suits near the front of the auditorium—"if all goes well, in only five years we'll be sending up our second colonist class, who will reside on Mars permanently. We don't take this constitution-making stuff lightly. It's our future. So, we've assembled a constitutional design team that will be researching and reporting on their design for the colony government in about six months. I'm here to introduce you to the incredible team that will create our colony's foundational principles." Libby grinned at Carrie. "Led by the inimitable Dr. Carrie Davenport."

The room exploded in flashing lights. The auditorium already glowed bright with the midmorning sun beaming through the windowpanes, but each camera click from the tumultuous crowd of reporters set forth a new firework show of light. Carrie beamed like she was posing for a magazine cover, then shook herself. She was a scholar. This wasn't a red-carpet debut. She tried to look steady and imposing, like someone qualified to write laws for the future of space.

"Dr. Davenport is a leading constitutional law scholar at one of the nation's top ten law schools, Briar University. She's the author of seven books and frequently consults with emerging democracies. She is joined by Dr. Adam Kilpatrick, esteemed theorist, historian, and Yale Law professor; and Owen Hughes, former pro-football player, Texas native, and longtime political consultant on Capitol Hill, affectionately known as 'the Peacekeeper' for his skill in bipartisan coalition building."

To her left, Dr. Kilpatrick cleared his throat and stared over his glasses at the audience, his arms crossed and eyes piercing as though daring anyone to challenge his place on stage. His red tie was cinched tight around his neck under a tweed blazer. On her right, Hughes let out a guffaw, like he was amused by the ruckus, and waved away the applause, his movement clumsy enough that Carrie worried he might hit her. She still wasn't sure what to do with her own limbs, so she gripped her thighs under the table and continued to half smile.

At least the crowd ahead didn't look half as large as the one for the space suit press conference she'd streamed last week. Laws were important, but boring, apparently.

"Libby!" A reporter with a dark buzz cut struggled to make himself heard over the crowd and the sound of Beau's game of Tetris two rows in front. "Will First Amendment rights like freedom of speech be protected for the colonists? Will they be able to speak out if something goes wrong, or are they bound to Project Mars corporate speak?"

"First Amendment rights? Hopefully not," Libby quipped. "I've had enough dealing with freedom of the press and rascals like you, Harry." Her bright-white teeth flashed as she grinned at him.

A tall South Asian man behind him stood. "For the team specifically, to what extent are you prioritizing international law versus American constitutional principles? Any response to the critique that focusing on American law will further whitewash the colony?"

Carrie exhaled. This was just like managing her classroom, when her students posed hard-hitting questions to philosophical dilemmas that had no right answer. This question, she knew, did have a right answer, even though there was nothing she could do to change the situation. The colony was going to be very white—about 95 percent white, she'd heard. Though the reporter didn't say it, as a Black woman and practically the only other person of color in the room, Carrie knew the question was for her. She could feel the entire room's focus shift to her.

"Thank you for your question," Carrie said, her voice even and, she hoped, confident. "We'll use United States law as a starting point because the initial colonists are American, and that's what is familiar to them. But by all means, we are considering every fundamental principle of justice and equity because there are areas where other countries truly excel over the United States—"

A deliberate cough to her left caused her to falter mid-sentence; when the voice began fully talking over hers, she petered out.

"Please forgive Dr. Davenport. The United States has one of the best and most developed legal systems in the world," Dr. Kilpatrick cut in, his tone deep and velvety. "No country has a better justice system. Of course we will rely on United States law."

If she could personally exile Dr. Kilpatrick to another planet, Carrie would have done it in a heartbeat. She had met Adam on two prior occasions, at academic conferences and the like, and it had been two times too many. His tone, confident and dismissive and smooth like he was a radio DJ introducing a song rather than dismissing claims of whitewashing, grated against her like sandpaper. Academia was her wheelhouse. She had not made it through four years at Duke, a law degree and PhD at the University of Virginia, a Harvard fellowship, and ten years of teaching at Briar to be talked over on an endeavor Project Mars had chosen *her* to lead.

"As I was saying, we'll be conducting a broad review," she said, cutting back in after Adam's interruption. "Our team will be reporting our initial findings in about six to eight months. Stay tuned for a summary on where we've landed on this around May 2033." Carrie finished in a friendly, upbeat tone that masked her rampant desire to bludgeon her new colleague.

"Excellent," Libby said.

The reporters asked a flurry of questions, ranging from serious to frivolous. The questions on the team's own qualifications had been easy, even if they'd made Owen squirm. Owen and Adam fielded other inquiries about their work while she bit the inside of her cheek, trying to remain calm.

"Dr. Davenport, if you wouldn't mind taking the lead on this one," said a voice from the side of the room. Libby had called on another reporter, who pushed chunky black glasses up her nose and smiled apologetically. "I hate to ask, but can you explain the consequences if this goes wrong? If the colonists don't get along and chaos ensues, they can't just return home. Any discord could lead to anarchy, destruction of valuable experiments, the discontinuation of the Mars program, or . . . I don't know. Death. How do you view that?"

I view it as freaking terrifying. When she'd gotten the call from the selection committee, her heart had nearly stopped. It was the culmination of everything she'd been working toward: her years of study, the chance to leave her mark in her field, and her hope to help shape the next generation. But how the hell was she supposed to do it? If she got it wrong, humankind's first attempt at living anywhere other than Earth would descend into chaos. The enormity of the task settled onto her shoulders with a new weight, like a lead blanket. The colonists would be living under a legal system that she designed. The country's bravest, most intrepid explorers would be guided by the very rules she created, conforming their behavior to ideals she set. And, more than that, the laws she wrote would apply not just to this initial group of one hundred but to a generation's worth of Mars colonists, if Beau's ambitions bore out. It was all on her—an introverted, divorced North Carolina professor from a South Carolina town that barely had any stoplights.

"We take our responsibility seriously. We will do everything in our power to research, reflect, and work as hard as we can to get it right," she said, her throat hoarse. For once, Adam did not interrupt.

"Everything will go perfectly!" Libby beamed. "Dr. Davenport is brilliant, thorough, and 100 percent focused on this mission. We've assembled a cohesive team that will work marvelously together. Let's move on from all this talk of death and destruction, please. We have time for one last question, so let's make it an easy one."

A twentysomething Project Mars intern stood. "Have you seen the viral video of the president dunking a plush replica of the Mars rocket vehicle into a hoop from across the Oval Office? Tell me there will be a law that makes viewing that level of swag mandatory for every participant."

Owen laughed, the same deep, chortling belly laugh from earlier. "We'll get right on it, son."

2

THE NEXT DAY found Carrie back home in North Carolina, rushing to make it out of the house and to campus on time. Her house, however, had better ideas. It only took a second to trip over the broken third-to-last step to the basement, and she lay curled in a ball on the faded green basement carpet for twenty minutes, questioning her choices. Her cell phone rang a few paces off from where it, too, had fallen. She cursed and stubbed her toe on the couch as she scrambled to her feet and struggled to catch the call before it went to voicemail. She let out a rough "Yes?" as she pressed the phone to her ear, checking first that the screen hadn't shattered.

"Well, that's no way to greet your old man."

"Daddy," she breathed into the phone. Her shoulders slumped in relief. Even though it had grown increasingly feeble in the last few years, his gruff baritone was still like coming home.

"Why do you sound out of breath?" he asked. She could almost picture his furrowed brow, a knowing, suspicious glare creasing the weathered brown skin around his eyes.

"Oh, nothing. I'm just searching for an old book down in the basement for my Comparative Constitutional Law seminar. I'm teaching on the difference between US and European federalism today, and there's a great example in one of the books I read back in law school."

"Uh-huh. You fix that broken step I've been getting on you about?"

She glanced at the step she had just tripped on minutes prior.

"It's on my to-do list," she said lightly. So what if it had been for two years.

"I know a fancy professor has got to have a big house, but why'd you pick one that was so old?" He had never understood why she had purchased a traditional Victorian fixer-upper instead of one of the new McMansions clustered together three miles from Briar's campus. "You don't even have Devon to help fix things anymore."

Not Devon again. "I like my house—"

"Oh, don't mind me," he interrupted. "You've been living in and loving that house for ten years. What I was really fixing to tell you is that I saw yesterday's press conference. The nurse came and set it up on a laptop for me, and there you were on the screen. My baby girl."

"You think I did okay?"

"I thought, there's the girl that's going to change the world. You always did have your head in a book, desperate to know everything that goes on in this big universe. Now your own name will be in history books."

She smiled and rubbed her knee, already aching from her fall. She'd have a bruise soon.

"Thanks, Daddy. Speaking of books . . ." She glanced at her watch. "I'm going to be late for office hours if I don't head out soon. I need to find this book and get to campus." She didn't add that half of the delay would be the mental energy it would take to push past Devon's boxes of junk in order to find her old books from law school. She wasn't angry enough to burn his things in the backyard, but she was tired enough not to call him to get his stuff.

"Alright, I don't want to hold you. I'm about to head down to the shop anyway. Marcel is picking me up."

"You're going down to the shop? Weren't you just there last week?"

"I want to make sure Jimmy has got everything under control. Make sure he's keeping all my tools polished and fresh." Thirty-five years running his own auto body shop, and after four years of retirement, he still couldn't let go.

"Be careful. Don't get near any of the fumes. Sit down if it gets hard to breathe."

"You don't have to tell me twice," he said. "You go on and save the world, now. I've got to get on if I want to beat Jimmy at a game of dominos before lunch." She heard him chuckle, and she was prepared to hang up when he jumped in.

"Carrie, baby? One more thing. Don't let those other professors get screwy with you. Remember who's the boss here." The line clicked before she could respond.

That afternoon, Carrie swept into class with all her usual force and aura of power, clutching Professor Tushnet's book on comparative federalism under her arm. The students couldn't have known that she'd risked a potential knee injury and a cloud of dust and emotional turmoil at the back of her basement to find it, but she was going to give them the lecture of a lifetime regardless.

Briar's campus filled Carrie with a sense of possibility. The university had been named for Henry Briar, who'd used two generations' worth of plantation money to invest in the steel industry and eventually created a school in his name. The money showed. Royal blue carpets lined the hallways of the main law school building, cream-colored columns supported tall, arched ceilings, and the lecture halls featured rich wood paneling and the newest projection technology. From the windows of her favorite lecture hall, Briar's famous rolling hills stretched out in full green display, dotted with trim brick buildings. The campus and the importance of her lecture instilled Carrie with a sense of purpose as she settled her leather laptop bag behind the lectern. A loud chorus of squeaking wooden chairs and shifting students snapped her gaze up to the room.

Most days, the forty-person lecture hall was nearly full. If not for the Calvin-Klein-underwear-model-turned-real-estate-lawyer Professor Havens, she would have had, to her great satisfaction, one of the highest class enrollment rates at the school. But today, not only did students fill every wooden seat but a group of around fifteen students she did not recognize had crammed themselves behind the last row of seats, leaning against the back railing. Carrie blinked, a rush of nervous energy setting her heart hammering. She wondered if she'd accidentally done something embarrassing that had gone viral, like walk to class without pants. She frowned at the crowd and looked down at her notes . . . and her legs, appropriately clad in dress pants. Maybe they all liked Professor Tushnet's work? Or European federalism? Students *had* once recorded her when she performed an original *Hamilton*-style rap rundown of *The Federalist Papers*. She glanced at her assistant, Anna, whose eyes were wide as her gaze darted from the crowd of students to the cramped seating chart she used for attendance.

Carrie took a deep breath. "I'm glad you're all here today," she said, her voice loud enough to reverberate throughout the room, even with the extra bodies. "Because what we're going to discuss today is fundamental. It's another chapter in our exploration of how similar legal concepts can look markedly different in other societies and cultures." Her strength grew, as if she'd been fasting and had finally consumed her first meal of the day. This was her passion, and it was her privilege to guide her students on this journey. Her voiced warmed and deepened with confidence.

Carrie swiped up on her phone, and a map of Europe flickered up onto the wall behind her. "So, this is Europe. I hope you've all heard of it before." She earned a couple of strained chuckles. "It provides us with some fantastic examples of other ways to structure a federalist government."

She spent the next half hour explaining the role of federalist systems in protecting diverse cultural identities, the history of federalism in the United States, and modern issues in the European Union, gesturing toward various areas on the map to make her point. When fifteen minutes remained, Carrie faced the room, which was still crammed with people all the way to the back rows, and crossed her arms over her chest, the navy fabric of her signature overcoat pulling at the shoulders. She took a wide-legged stance as she stared down the crowd.

"Questions?"

She pointed toward a dark-haired woman in the front row. Her hand had shot up like an arrow, her lips pursed in concentration. Carrie fought off a smile.

"Jennifer."

The woman exhaled in relief. "Great. Thanks. I was studying some of the American ideals of self-government that first gathered steam in the British Empire, and I couldn't help but notice how even those historical first notions are remarkably similar to our American ideals today. The whole idea of 'taxation without representation' was that people must consent, themselves or through their representatives, in order for laws to bind them. It seems to tie back perfectly to last week's discussion on how federalism can lead to the stability of a democracy like in the US."

Carrie tried to keep her face neutral and patient, fighting the urge to blurt "That's more of a comment than a question," though the words were poised on the tip of her tongue. She wondered if she'd been as transparent, back when she was a student, about her hopes for a letter of recommendation. Probably not. She'd always been shy, reluctant to raise her hand unless she'd obsessed over the question in her head before daring to share it out loud. Carrie didn't mind the gunners now that she was a professor, though. It gave her the chance to clarify and emphasize the important takeaways for those students who had missed a point in a moment of distraction.

"A valid point. There are striking similarities between historical examples and today. Across hundreds of years, people crave the same things: meaningful representation and freedom from arbitrary laws. Federalism allows for more layers of local government so representatives are more closely connected to their constituents." She scanned the room. "Anyone else? Other than Jennifer?"

Three hands toward the back of the room shot up. Carrie raised an eyebrow at the enthusiasm and skipped over two men standing at the back, leaning so far on their tiptoes that they threatened to topple onto the people seated in the last row. She called on the one who was seated, who at least had to be a student.

"Did you really get to meet B-Ball yesterday? Is he actually that short in person? Any chance he talked about the new FutureGen Perpetua VI high-speed rover vehicle?"

Carrie blinked. The swarm of activity and panic from the day before assaulted her like she had teleported back into the glass auditorium—the crowd of reporters assessing and judging her, the eyes of politicians and genius scientists scouring her, wanting to know if she was a worthy player in this history-making endeavor. The stress cut like a knife, even as she recognized the tremendous honor and duty.

"We're here today, Mr. . . ."—she glanced down at her seating chart—"Mr. Bynum, to discuss comparative federalism. I'm sorry to disappoint, but I don't have any juicy tidbits about yesterday's events." She paused, then cracked a half smile. "Except to maybe say that, yes, five four is a particularly generous description of Beau's height."

Quiet laughter reverberated through the room.

A young woman she hadn't noticed before, who'd parked herself on the top step of the lecture hall, stood and immediately raised her hand.

"Not about Beau?" Carrie cautioned.

The woman shook her head. "I'm curious . . . I'm in undergrad, so I don't know everything about the law, but it seems like a private company claiming part of Mars for its own personal compound has to violate some sort of international law. Is that at play here?"

Carrie was both stunned and heartened that interest had spread across campus like wildfire, all the way to the under-grad students. "It is," she said slowly, her voice warming. "But that's not my area of expertise—I'm not an international law scholar." She held her hands up in defense. "I can only imagine that Project Mars's diplomatic relations team has engaged in close conversations with NASA, the State Department, and international leaders. There's a treaty called the Outer Space Treaty . . . and yes, it's a real thing, ratified in 1967. It says no nation can claim part of another planet as its own. Obviously, Project Mars isn't a nation, and while NASA is working in collaboration with it, NASA hasn't officially endorsed it. Still, the law should apply to them as a US company. Here's the key: Project Mars has created a loophole for itself by saying that the settlement is technically 'open to all' and any nation can send folks up to its compound once it's established. Which is pretty easy to say when no one else has the capability to settle Mars yet."

"Sounds like a big loophole," the woman said with a raised eyebrow. "A massive, international law–breaking loophole."

"Indeed. You should go to law school and take them to court on it." Carrie glanced around the room as if hidden microphones would reveal a team of Project Mars observers ready to snatch away her position. "But maybe wait until I've drafted the constitution . . . and the check clears."

She was met with wry smiles and a nod from the woman. Carrie returned to her spot behind the lectern. "I'm joking, but in any event, your comment is spot on. In fact, what the team is crafting isn't really a *constitution*. I'm using that word because that's what most people know, but constitutions are for sovereign governments, and that's not what the colony is. A better word would be a *charter*, but that's decidedly less catchy. Thankfully, my job isn't to decide whether the colony is legal. It's to figure out, for whoever the colonists may be, how they should organize themselves."

Carrie wrapped up her lecture and stared at the students and onlookers shuffling out, lost in thought. The mystique around Project Mars hadn't eluded her. Every time she browsed online, some news article cropped up championing Beau and speculating what Perpetua would do next. They weren't operating in a secret lab. If the students' excitement was anything to go by, her work might as well be plastered on a billboard in Times Square. Struggling to ground herself, she clenched the laser pointer in her hand until the plastic creaked and buckled. The law, the very thing she studied and revered, would be in her hands.

3

THE GRAY GOTHIC buildings of Yale University loomed over Carrie as she stepped out of a black car in New Haven three weeks later. The narrow windows and dark stone archways, a bit tragic in cold, overcast November, looked nothing like the stately cream-colored columns and wooded surroundings of Briar's campus. Yet there was a sense of calm nonetheless, as she'd abandoned the swarm of traffic and commotion outside LaGuardia Airport for the two-hour journey north. She readily eased into this familiar environment, where students lugged backpacks full of heavy books and bulletin boards were plastered with ads for used futons and pop-up concerts.

She navigated her way to one of the law school buildings and ascended to the second floor. She double-checked her email—yes, room 233—and slid open the wood-paneled door to the conference room. As soon as the door opened, Carrie was hit with the sound of rumbling laughter. Two figures sat at an oval conference table. With one leg crossed over the other, Owen was slapping his knee at something

Adam had apparently said. Owen's brash laughter did not surprise her. What stunned Carrie most was to see the grin on Adam's face. She didn't know he could smile.

"Come in," Adam said, waving her forward. "Welcome to Yale. Owen got here an hour ago, so we've just been chatting about our undergrad days."

Owen waved her forward, too, with a meaty hand. "Good to see you, Carrie."

"Likewise," she said. "What's so funny about undergrad?" She set her leather tote on one of the empty seats and slid into the one beside it, her hand reaching for her laptop sleeve.

"I was joking about the final exam in my freshman political science course. I had a brain fart and mixed up the words *federalism* and *fascism*. I wrote a whole essay on the great American fascist tradition and how it's made our government so stable and strong. I'm shocked the professor didn't give me an F and refer me to the dean."

Carrie cracked a smile. "It wouldn't be the first time someone has confused the two. I've had to grade my fair share of painful essays, and I promise you, yours doesn't take the cake."

"I can't imagine they had a survey of various forms of government in your undergraduate courses, Ms. Davenport?"

Carrie gritted her teeth. "Believe it or not, the curriculum at Duke was pretty comprehensive." She opened her laptop, unwilling to meet Adam's gaze. "And please, call me Carrie." It would at least be better than his willful decision to ignore her PhD every time he addressed her. It wasn't that the title "doctor" mattered much to her. The term wasn't a great fit; in a medical emergency, the best she could do was explain the inner workings of the constitution. But she'd worked hard. And most people in her life recognized this, from the university to her students to her academic peers. Adam . . . didn't. Her twenty years of study and hard work were worthless to him, which rendered her and all she cared about equally worthless.

Owen leaned back in his spinning chair, the chair's back creaking under his long catlike stretch. "Well, I for one am looking forward to today. Get some real work done after all that pomp and circumstance."

Good lord, yes. They had to get this law thing right. The six-month deadline for their report loomed over Carrie's shoulder like a term paper she'd forgotten to write until the night before. She navigated to the file on her computer where she'd saved the agenda for their introductory meeting and double-clicked.

"You won't need to take notes, Carrie," Adam said in his low, silky baritone. "My secretary is here to serve as our scribe."

Carrie's gaze shot up. There was an entire person in the room she had not even seen. A pale mousy-looking woman with brittle brown hair and red glasses sat in one of the chairs ringing the edge of the room, a foot or two from the conference table. The woman flashed her a nervous smile, and Carrie smiled back kindly. Of course, Adam wouldn't think the woman important enough to introduce.

"It's great to meet you," Carrie said. "So, I thought we could start by—"

"Did you get the PDF I sent you?" Adam interrupted. "I think Thomas's work perfectly grounds us in the task before us and serves as an exemplary metaphor for our legal system."

Carrie paused. "What PDF?"

"I sent it this morning, to your email. Did you not have a chance to review it?"

"You mean while I was on the plane?"

Adam shrugged. "I thought you'd be preparing for our meeting. Apparently not."

Carrie reached deep into her soul, where the kindest, most patient part of her being resided. The part that would do battle with the urge to choke Adam by the very fabric of his tie.

"Your contributions are appreciated but perhaps geared toward a future discussion," Carrie said. "Today, we will be recapping what's required of us, discussing the timeline leading up to our six-month report, dividing up key reading materials, and determining whether there are additional scholars with whom we need to consult."

Adam sat silently, and Carrie glanced from him to Owen.

"Excellent plan." Owen nodded.

"Great," Carrie said. She flicked an image from her phone up to the blank sidewall of the conference room. "So. There's the launch vehicle and lander with room for a hundred participants. We know that the experimental class will be on Mars for two years, and then they will return to Earth so the Project Mars team can assess how things went. A year or so later, if all goes well, there will be groups of one hundred permanent participants launched every eighteen months for the next five years. And, barring no issues, that will lead to long-term human settlement."

Carrie paused but was met with only Adam's detached stare and Owen's enthusiastic nodding. She heaved an internal sigh.

"Alright. I think the goal here, then, is to design the best possible constitution *now* so there will be meaningful feedback after this experimental group. We can see if self-governing worked, and if they need fewer elected positions or a heavier authoritarian hand—whatever it may be—for the permanent settlement."

"Agreed," Adam said. "Although it's rather asinine to think we will have anything other than an elected democracy. Your openness to antirepublican government is befuddling, to say the least." He tapped a green marble pen against a yellow legal pad, a frown pressed between his eyebrows.

Carrie contemplated whether she knew a good enough lawyer capable of getting her off for murder. Unlikely.

Despite Adam's nagging, this first phase filled Carrie with creative energy, leaving her tingling from her head down to her toes. Adam seemed to assume that American democracy was the clear choice. In truth, it probably was the most fitting form of government for the colonists. But she'd spend the next few weeks learning everything she could, delving deep into various forms of government throughout history, so they could make an informed decision. While Project Mars had the ultimate say-so for major colony decisions, the colonists would be able to govern themselves for most day-to-day matters.

"Thank you for your input," she said in a neutral tone. "Let's switch to the agenda, then, so we can have actual material to debate." She projected a list of recommended reading onto the conference room wall, and the three divided up reading materials for two categories: theoretical writings on various systems of government and empirical studies on the relative successes of those governments. She would read everything thoroughly herself, of course, but couldn't possibly keep it all in her own head. Within the next week she planned to select a research assistant to take on a portion of the research and summarize the findings.

"Great. And finally, do we want to bring any other scholars into our next meeting? I think it would be good to show that we consulted with a broader range of political and legal experts."

Owens shrugged. "Adam's got the American legal history and political theory expertise, I have the practical down-and-dirty political know-how to figure out how they'll game this damn system we rig, and you're an expert on constitution-making. What more do we need?"

"I think people will balk if a small unrepresentative group of three doesn't show it has spoken with a more diverse—"

"No," Adam said. "Perhaps they can write white papers to assist or advise, but this effort should come from us. The founding fathers knew best, and the same principle applies here. A handful of experts are meant to guide the rest of the nation."

"I've written a book on constitutional conventions, and the trend across nations is that broad coalitions and buy-in are better at garnering support for the document," Carrie said.

"I read that book," Adam said. "While interesting, it was a bit of a . . . freshman attempt. I don't think it applies here." He looked at her with the awkwardness and detached sympathy of a doctor delivering bad news.

"I worry that your opinion may be underinformed. The peer reviews certainly did not find it lacking." It had, quite literally, been her freshman attempt at publishing, born out of research she'd done while in her third year of law school at UVA. But her advisor had called it a triumph, and the book had been cited in other scholars' work over seventy-five times. She still received emails from other academics praising her for the effort. She wouldn't let Adam denigrate it just to satisfy his ego.

Carrie shook herself off. "I'm pleased to be able to lead this project and pleased to welcome other voices down the line. That's all we have for today, and I look forward to welcoming you both to Briar for our meeting next month."

Owen closed his leather padfolio and slapped a hand on the cover. "To North Carolina it is. Hey, we could even go out for barbecue after. Spend some of this Project Mars money."

Carrie smiled. "Indeed." If only their next meeting could be years instead of mere weeks away. There was no rush to be back in Adam's presence. Her sense of foreboding was countered only by her sheer excitement for actually doing the work. The heady mix of emotions sent her stomach twisting, and it spurned a tiny knot of stress that lodged in between her shoulder blades, probably to stay.

Before her flight left LaGuardia early the next morning, Carrie spent the night in New York City. She took a cab to an Italian restaurant on the Upper West Side that evening, and even amid the crowd of people, Carrie easily spotted a woman with a sleek, pressed long bob and the smoothest brown skin imaginable. Her heart surged with love and emotion. Kim's dark eyes flashed as bright as the city skyline when she spotted Carrie. Kim stood and waved, and Carrie threaded her way through the restaurant to the table for two.

"Sorry, am I meant to bow? I'm in the presence of space

royalty. Pray tell, I'm so grateful my own George Washington has time for dinner with me."

Carrie snorted. Kim grinned and threw herself at Carrie, her tiny body hitting Carrie's hard. Carrie wrapped her arms tightly around her best friend, like she could squeeze the love out of Kim's body and soak up the support and stability she so desperately needed. She felt lost, and Kim was an anchor.

"Let me look at you," Kim said, sounding very much like a mother of three. "Yes, okay, that will do. Never saw an Ann Taylor blazer that didn't work for you."

"An artist surveying her work."

Meanwhile, Kim was dressed in a beaded couture dress that must've been featured on the runway at Fashion Week. Even when they had been college roommates, Carrie had worn the same blue Duke sweatshirt every day while Kim had worn the latest True Religion jeans with breezy Free People tops.

"How is the visiting professorship?" Carrie asked. "I hope these Columbia kids recognize they've borrowed George-town's best professor."

Kim scoffed, giving a "why are we talking about me right now?" face, but true to form was moments later deeply engrossed in the saga of a faculty meeting and her assistant's inability to follow a seating chart. "Anyway, Columbia is nice, but New York is colder than DC in the winter, which will wreak havoc on my pores."

"Even in the cold, you look like you could stop a train. The picture of calm and controlled."

Kim smiled. "Well. I miss my kids, I do. But a little peace of mind during the weekdays? Girl, I'm about to publish three articles this semester. I don't know what I'll do when I go back to DC next month."

Carrie nodded, although it was not much of a change. At home, Kim was Wonder Woman. She accompanied her sexy brain-surgeon husband to hospital fundraising dinners and managed her two-and-a-half perfect kids . . . three, really. Kim's middle child, Naomi, was Carrie's godchild and favorite ice-cream taste-test companion. Kim's children wore handsewn costumes to the school play and raked in the most cash at bake sales, and still, Kim routinely published in the country's best political science journals. Carrie had always watched, as if from behind a glass, as Kim lived a life Carrie could never have managed.

Devon was gone. And good riddance. They had met at a bar, a meet-cute so cliché it made Carrie cringe. He was a car-insurance salesman who pursued his real passion, a DJ gig, on the weekends, and he had sculpted a party lifestyle around his nine-to-five. Carrie had been flattered he'd been into her, had wanted to marry her. Her willingness to lean into their relationship, to let it happen for the sake of having *something*, had been the wrong call. It didn't take him long to realize who she truly was.

"Your face looks like a storm is brewing."

Carrie pushed away thoughts of Devon. "This Project Mars team is not easy."

"You mean Professor Snooty Face and Owen 'Never Met a Man He Couldn't Charm' Hughes?"

Carrie smiled despite herself. "Yes, the dream team. Owen is fine, even though I don't trust him to read a single thing. He's more of a practical, on-the-ground guy. He did some lobbying on the Hill for Project Mars a while back, and I suspect continuing to play golf with the PM folks didn't hurt in getting the gig. I'm mostly worried you'll have to bail me out of jail for murdering Adam."

"Let's be clear, Carrie. Adam hasn't published a paper in years. None of my undergrad students have ever gone to Yale Law and said, 'Gee, I can't wait to take a class with Adam Kilpatrick.' He's dry, outdated, and he's only here because they want a conservative white face to be the father of the law. We all know the real work is coming from you. And you're gonna crush it."

Kim wasn't entirely wrong. Right out of law school Adam had published a brilliant treatise on the American Revolution that had made him the darling of academia and helped him to quickly gain tenure. But years passed, and his creativity dwindled. Few published papers, few speaking invitations, each idea somewhat less novel than the last. She could sympathize with the relentless pressure to publish on top of teaching, giving guest lectures, serving on committees, mentoring students, and the like. But his fall from grace made him so . . . ugh. Insufferable.

Kim leaned in close. "Back, like, five years ago, when his wife was alive, word on the street was that they used to host these elaborate, intimate dinner parties at their home. He'd have students over to debate philosophy and current events among his fancy antiques. But my friend at Yale said that a year or two ago, he stopped having them. I guess around the time his wife died. Ovarian cancer." Kim tsked. "A shame. She had one of the best antique shops on the East Coast. I got that mahogany grandfather clock for your fortieth birthday from her shop."

"Are you telling me I contributed to the financial well-being of the Kilpatrick family?" Carrie asked with a shudder.

"No, I did." Kim smirked. "And you're welcome, because I'm pretty sure their Connecticut mansion speaks to the fact that they don't need the money. Anyway, with respect to these dinner parties . . ."

"He stopped having them when his wife died," Carrie surmised.

"Mm. That, and the university told him he needed to start inviting women and people of color because the old boys' club was starting to look bad. Instead, he just . . . canceled them. It's unfortunate his wife died, but it's also unfortunate that he'd rather sit alone in his house than let a minority student eat his filet mignon."

Carrie huffed. "You see what I'm dealing with?"

"A man clinging to the social climate and legal theories of two centuries ago?"

Carrie shook her head. *Stubbornness.* "I can handle the law. What I can't handle is Adam irritating and undermining me every chance he gets."

"Yes, you can. Forget him. You're made of tougher stuff than he is."

"Yeah?"

"Yeah. Just tell him that back in college you literally blackmailed the head of the basketball team so he would get more people to take the survey for your thesis on campus political attitudes. That'll shut him up."

Carrie laughed. "If Adam tries me, I might consider blackmail again." She bit her lip. "I'm worried that other than Adam and Owen, we don't have enough voices in the room."

Kim sipped her water. "Weren't you thinking of hiring a research assistant? Maybe you hire a few to get all the work done and get some different perspectives."

"That could work. Goodness knows I need the help." She'd been considering three of her top students, Lori,

Parker, and Evie, for the job. If she hired all three, they could accomplish significantly more of her research goals.

Kim's expression softened. "I'll try to visit soon. In the meantime, when you go home, pour yourself a stiff drink. Pour two. And in a few days, get cracking again."

She flagged down a waiter as though to kick off the week of drinking, and within seconds had ordered them a bottle of wine so overpriced it made Carrie wince.

Kim was right. Though it was something Carrie had never told her about, she knew exactly what she would do to relax when she got home.

CARRIE'S EYES burned the next weekend as she sat on her couch, like she'd plunged wide eyed into a chlorine pool. She surveyed the mess of papers scattered on the chenille cushions, the mountain of books threatening to tumble from her oak coffee table, and the dozens of tabs open on her tablet. Six hours of work had made this mess, and six hours of staring at incomprehensible text had made a similar mess of her brain. The four hundred pages she'd read that day felt physically jammed in her head. The tiniest wisp of a tension headache was blossoming between her eyebrows. The grandfather clock in the hallway read seven o'clock. She thought about what Kim had said: Take a break and get a drink. *Relax*.

Before she could think much more about it, Carrie shoved her hair into hot curlers and fished around her bathroom drawers for an old eyeliner pencil to run along her lids. Within an hour she found herself in the parking lot of Birdie's Tavern. Carrie flipped open the visor mirror of her Audi coupe and swore. She tugged at the ends of her brownish-black hair, loosening the tight curls that bumped against her shoulders. She didn't know how Kim could manage her sleek, straight press every day. The hair situation was one thing, but only advanced makeup skills that she didn't have could fix the deep bags under her eyes that screamed overwork. She pushed her square-framed glasses further up onto her wide nose, wondering whether they might make her look edgy rather than professorial tonight, and smoothed deep-red lipstick over her full lips. Forget it. She had on her go-to red velvet wrap dress, tall boots, and her mother's gold earrings. It was a going-out look that had never let her down, and she didn't expect to be disappointed tonight, other aspects of her appearance aside. It would be fine.

Carrie stepped into the bar and squinted. On the far side of the room, women older than her sat at two rough-hewn wood tables, clutching beer bottles and watching a football game projected onto the back wall. At the U-shaped bar, a few women sat interspersed, and a group of younger women in matching bachelorette outfits clustered around a short butch bartender pouring rum and cokes. The bar didn't advertise itself as a gay bar, but it was women friendly and just run down enough to be unassuming. Carrie sat at the bar on a smooth wooden barstool and hooked her ankles around the stool legs. She ran her fingers along the lacquered bar top and waited for Hannah to come find her.

A minute later, Hannah slid a coaster across the bar.

"Haven't seen you here in a couple months."

"Been busy," Carrie said, pulling the coaster closer to her.

"Work?"

"Work," she agreed.

"Looks like it's beating the shit out of you," Hannah observed, her expression neutral. "Wine?"

"How about pinot noir?" Carrie said hopefully.

Hannah snorted. She extracted a bottle from behind the counter and poured a glass, then slid it across to Carrie. "How about a red blend I opened last night?"

"Forget work; where I've really been is at bars where they actually serve you the thing you want." Carrie glanced around the room, where the older women had started hollering at a video someone was projecting from their phone. "But it looks like things haven't changed much in here."

"The usual crowd. A few in town for a trade show in Petersville. But there's someone who started coming in last month I think you might . . . be interested in."

Hannah nodded toward the end of the bar, a slight smile playing on her lips. Carrie looked over. A petite woman with a thick mane of blond hair trailing down her back was in the midst of full on shouting at the football game, one hand wrapped around the neck of her beer bottle and the other jabbing a manicured finger toward the projection screen. Her full chest was pressed flush against the bar as she leaned closer to the screen in anticipation.

The woman, satisfied that she'd told off the referee, sat back on her barstool and glanced around. Catching Carrie's eye, she lifted her beer to her lips and took a deep swig. Carrie raised an eyebrow and, feigning disinterest, turned her attention to the screen and pretended to understand the intricacies of the game. It was a college game, as far as she could tell. The local team was apparently losing, by the slight frown that twisted the woman's features.

Carrie lost herself in pretending to understand what was going on, her body angled away from the woman she wanted nothing more than to approach, so much so that she nearly jumped when the barstool next to hers scraped back. The woman she'd been trying fixedly not to watch stood beside her, close enough for Carrie to guess at her height—she had to be five two, tops—before she clambered onto the stool and flagged down Hannah.

"I'll have another," she said. Her voice was low, husky, leaving Carrie full of anticipation. "You can put it on my friend's tab." She tilted her head toward Carrie.

"I'm buying you a drink, am I?" Carrie arched an eyebrow.

"Tell me, without looking, the score of the game on TV."

Carrie's mouth flew open. "What?"

"An impressive attempt to pretend you wouldn't rather be staring at my tits, but I've been around the block enough to catch on."

Carrie stared. The woman smelled like smoke and something sugary, like strawberries. A second later she popped her gum, and Carrie realized she was chewing old-fashioned bubble gum.

"I'm Carrie."

"Shauna." She flicked Carrie's hand away from the stem of her wineglass and slipped her hand into Carrie's. Her fingertips were rough, but the back of her hand was soft and smooth, almost girl-like, even though, from the creases around her eyes, she had to be in her mid-forties.

"I've never seen you here before," Carrie said.

"Just moved six months ago, and it's taken a while to find my bearings. But sounds like you're a regular."

Carrie shrugged, an embarrassed heat flooding her face. "No, once a month or so. To unwind."

"You live nearby?"

"No." That was one of the things Carrie liked about the

place. It was thirty minutes from her house. She'd had one embarrassing fiasco with an older graduate student asking for her number in a dimly lit bar, and that had been the last time she'd tried to go out anywhere within a twenty-mile radius of campus.

Shauna narrowed her eyes, glacial blue orbs cutting into Carrie like ice. "So, you're married," Shauna surmised.

Carrie barked out a short, surprised laugh. "No." She held up her hands. "All above board, I swear. Divorced."

Shauna looked her up and down. "Your ex couldn't handle an accomplished woman? Ego got in the way? What do you do for a living, anyway?"

Carrie looked down at her dress and the sleek black knee-high boots Kim had picked out and wondered what Shauna saw. She was off the mark, but not by much. Devon had found her brilliant and out of his league for about two years before he realized that the bookish professor persona was not an act covering up a horny thirtysomething with pent-up energy from years of study. Carrie genuinely liked books and was not bored by them the way Devon quickly grew bored with her. When they made love, he pawed at her with rough hands in a hasty attempt to get her wet when she was not. It wasn't until he started cheating on her with the girl at the Verizon store who had set up their family cell phone plan that she stumbled into Birdie's Tavern. An older woman flirted shamelessly with her, and Carrie nearly slid off her seat in a puddle of lust. She'd had a prior inkling she liked women, and boy was that intuition right.

"What do you do?" Carrie deflected.

Shauna glanced away. "A bit of odds and ends. Last gig was pet sitting, until I got a massive scratch down the length of my arm. Managed the movie theater for two months.

Right now, I'm at the Z Mart down on Pinehurst." She poked Carrie's arm, leaving Carrie tingling and anxious for Shauna to touch more of her. "I asked you first, though."

"I'm writing a constitution for planet Mars," she said dryly. She laughed as Shauna rolled her eyes.

"You could've just said you're an accountant. Something believable."

"I'm an accountant."

Shauna broke into a slow smile. "How impressive."

Carrie didn't worry about what tomorrow would hold. Hannah refilled her glass of wine, and within a half hour poured her another. She grew closer to Shauna as they watched the game. Shauna maintained a running commentary on her favorite players and who was carrying the team that season, her hopes to go to a game in the new year, and how to understand the ref's calls, all while their knees brushed under the bar top. Carrie liked the way Shauna gripped her arm every time there was a good play and a heavily clad player bolted toward whatever the hell the end line was called. Before long the game ended, and Shauna turned abruptly to her.

"What's the best apartment above a convenience store you've ever been to?"

"Can't say I've been to one."

"I guess it'll be mine, then." She hopped off the barstool and strode out the front door of the bar.

Carrie stared at her departing back, the curve of her tiny hourglass figure and the strip of smooth skin visible above the hem of her jeans. She glanced at Hannah, who waved her away.

"Go. I'm leaving myself a 30 percent tip for making this happen."

Carrie scrambled out the door and found Shauna leaning against her Audi.

"Lucky guess," Shauna said.

Her apartment, less than a five-minute drive away, was up a steep staircase on top of the Z Mart convenience store. The sparse studio featured a squat tan love seat with a green Eagles NFL throw blanket, a folding table tucked beside the neat kitchenette, and a queen bed pressed against the far window.

Shauna threw her keys onto the kitchen table, then sidled up to Carrie. She put her hands on Carrie's waist, and Carrie was struck again by the height difference—even if she stooped, she wasn't sure she could kiss her.

"I think we'll need to be horizontal," Carrie said breathily as Shauna stared at her with that same piercing blue gaze, seeming to size her up and mentally undress her at the same time.

"I think that can be arranged," Shauna said. She pulled her shirt over her head as she padded across the apartment to the bed. Carrie swallowed thickly and followed, drinking in the tight press of Shauna's full breasts against her ill-fitting bra and the butterfly tattoo on her back. She slid her hands down the other woman's body, and for a second, she couldn't even remember why she'd been stressed that day.

From her office on the corner of Williams Quad, Carrie could hear students thrashing in the leaves below her window as they chased down a stray football. She was sure on the next throw that the ball would shatter Perkins Hall's historic and paper-thin glass windowpanes. No doubt pregaming for the annual fall concert later that night had rendered the students even more inebriated than usual—at only two in the afternoon. Carrie pressed her fingertips into her temples, willing away the distraction and staring at the Supreme Court's latest opinion on her computer screen. Thank goodness she was still in good spirits from her weekend escapades.

"Knock, knock, boss!" Anna popped her head into Carrie's office, and Carrie waved her forward.

"Tell me you've brought something to brighten up this distracting Friday."

Anna bit her lip, her cheeks flushing a light pink. "So, about that." She brushed a long lock of jet-black hair out of her face and pressed it into the hold of a turquoise butterfly clip. Carrie couldn't help but think the brilliant, animated assistant looked like a dog caught in the middle of ripping homework to shreds.

"Lay it on me."

"Have you read the new issue of *Controversies?*" Anna sidled up, pulling from behind her back a thick academic journal.

"Oh, excellent, it arrived. I'm actually featured in this quarter's issue, believe it or not." The journal prided itself on addressing hot-button issues and pitching academics with varying viewpoints against each other for friendly debate. Carrie had always admired the scholarly rigor and unflinching willingness to thoughtfully consider tough topics. She'd spent six weeks crafting her own thoroughly researched article providing a historical and comparative overview of voting rights. "I see you've read it before me, as per usual," Carrie chided, though her lips twisted into a smile.

Anna frowned. "Professor Davenport . . . it's not good. I went to add the online version to your faculty web page and noticed a recent comment I think you should see."

Carrie matched her frown. "What?" She navigated to a new tab in her browser and pulled up her article on the *Controversies* website.

Her article looked just as she had written it. Balanced, nuanced, advocating for an expansion of voting rights. She'd provided a thorough history of the founding fathers' views on voting that she'd spent hours in the library researching. Sure, she'd mentioned that the history reflected an unfair and biased view of voting, but that was true: the Constitution had prevented women from voting; it had also been written by people who'd literally owned slaves. Perceptions of who should vote couldn't be taken from back then. And her comparison of American voting practices to other countries' was fair and steeped in research, too. The culture in many other nations was to encourage people to vote, like in Australia where election day was a national holiday. What was the problem? It was all true.

She scrolled down to the comments section. The most recent comment was only a day old.

LIBERTY_ADK_JUSTICE
(1 DAY AGO)

> Professor Davenport advocates for an unfettered regime where anyone, from the convicted felon to your neighbor's dog, can cast a ballot. Such a broad expansion of voting disrespects the Constitution and the upstanding people in this great nation. It's unclear whether the article shows any understanding of voting at all. To make election day a holiday? Sure; why not deprive every corporation of the labor needed to support our fragile economy all for the sake of uncultured rabble casting misinformed ballots? One has to wonder whether the letters 'PhD' after Dr. Davenport's name were indeed earned.

Carrie's face tingled as if she'd been physically slapped. Her cheeks flushed, and frustration pricked her eyes with tears she was embarrassed to shed. She'd read numerous prior issues of the journal and the comments section did often feature lively debate. People were always argumentative in an academic sense—passionate, but polite. But this was a body slam. The comment had been petty and condescending. There was deferential neutrality, and then there was this: a personal, combative attack. It wasn't a website for internet trolls; it was created specifically for academia. She scrolled desperately through the other articles, skimming the comments for any sort of insult or haughty tone. No. They'd maintained the respectful academic discourse.

Her heartbeat quickened until it thudded in her chest at a dangerous pace. It wasn't supposed to be like this. Her vision blurred until, instead of sitting in her university office, she was thirteen and staring down at her mother's hospital bed, holding her mother's hand and begging whatever higher power would listen to spare the person she loved most.

Two weeks before that day in the hospital, her mother had been fine. Carrie entered classroom 5 after school, slouched off her pink plaid JanSport backpack in the last row of desks, and slid open one of her mother's *National Geographic* magazines, which she propped up as a shield to hide her Walkman. Behind the thrumming beat of Destiny's Child, Carrie could hear her mom—no, Mrs. Davenport, she always had to say at school—tutoring two eighth graders after that day's biology lesson on mitosis. They were a year older than her, intimidating enough that she pretended they weren't there. Carrie snapped her Juicy Fruit, then winced. Her mother shot her such a sharp look that Carrie slipped off her headphones and trudged to the trash can to spit out her gum, hiding the roll of her eyes.

Carrie pretended not to listen as her mother answered their questions, even about topics beyond the lesson plan. She described how rain fell, and how the atmosphere bent rays of light to make the sky blue, and how snow was the same thing as rain, only colder. The sky outside the classroom darkened, and Carrie shivered at the thought of the December air. She could have walked home by herself, but then she'd have to face the cold half-mile walk alone instead of with her mother. And . . . she couldn't help but stay. Her mom knew the answer to every question and every secret of the universe, from the cells inside Carrie's body to how far away other planets were in the solar system. Carrie had always been driven by the act of *knowing* something, of turning it over in her mind. She wanted to know all the things her mother knew. The delight in her mother's voice when a student finally got hold of an idea was addictive, like candy. *To impart knowledge was to give someone the gift of knowing,* Carrie thought. *To leave a mark.*

That night, when they got to Long Ridge Road, her mother pressed a gloved hand to her cheek and split from her, headed in the opposite direction. Carrie turned her mother's bizarre departure over in her mind until she got home and found a note from her father that her parents would be home late. He'd taped the note to a newspaper article for her to read. An agricultural and chemical manufacturing conglomerate, FarmPro Industries, planned to build a factory four blocks away from Johnson Elementary School down the road. Her mother, who knew the effect the production of toxic insecticides would have on the poor Black kids in the neighborhood, wouldn't stand for it.

It wasn't unusual. Her parents, Ruth and Earl, had met at age eleven, brought by their own parents to a march for fair housing policies in Washington, DC, in 1966. Her mother's family had driven all the way from Tennessee to participate in the march and for her grandfather to give a guest sermon. The two families had hit it off. Her parents had been pen pals throughout their teenage years, talking on the phone when they grew older. They became so close that her mother decided to study teaching at South Carolina State University, close to where her father had started working as a mechanic. They spent weekends road tripping to Atlanta, Charleston, or Columbia for rallies and to mobilize the community. Their hunger for change hadn't let up. Her father spent most of her childhood writing Congress to pass an antilynching bill while her mother had advocated for more education funding. Together they'd successfully picketed their local hospital, which had an unspoken policy of not hiring Black nurses, until the board committed to fair hiring.

The toxic pollution facing their local elementary school was no different. Her mom had petitioned city hall and rallied the other parents for three months. When that didn't work, she started, that night, a picket line outside the proposed building site. The air crackled with frost and a fierce winter wind that time of year, especially by the time her mom finished her tutoring sessions each evening. Even as a cold spell descended over the neighborhood, for two weeks her mother stood in front of a chain-link fence at the construction site with a sign that read, YOUR BUG KILLERS WILL KILL OUR KIDS, sometimes alone, sometimes with Earl, and occasionally with a small crowd of other parents.

On the thirteenth day, a day her mother had gone alone, the cold overwhelmed her. She'd stamped the cold out of her feet and screamed herself hoarse, teetering on the brink of hypothermia, until she could not scream anymore. From pneumonia. Carrie's father carried her mother to the car in the middle of the night and drove straight to the hospital. Her mother never returned home.

The eulogy in the local paper declared Ruth Davenport a hero. But what she really was, was gone. Gone from Carrie's life a mere month before she got her braces off, before the summer when they'd agreed they would finally drive out to the Grand Canyon, three years before Eddie White would tell her that smart girls needed to loosen up—gone from the world.

Her mother had given her life to protect their community, but it wasn't worth it, couldn't have been worth it, because she had died right when Carrie needed her. Advocacy meant passion. But it also meant danger. Activism required putting oneself at risk with irrevocable—and, for her mother, deadly—consequences. As soon as she was old enough to choose, Carrie chose what was safest: become a professor, a field that was slow-moving and theoretical, removed from the messiness of life and any notion of desperate, passionate acts. Nothing was heated. Carrie focused on the doctrine, on knowing and understanding the law, and on teaching it to her students with the same patience and care that had made her mom shine. She was the master of the law and in control of her classroom. That was as far as she went, as far as she could go in her careful, controlled, and *neutral* world.

Until now. The needlessly negative comment had slashed through her carefully sculpted world, the one crafted around detached scholarship. It yanked off her safety blanket.

Carrie swallowed thickly. "Okay," she said, taking a deep breath. She wasn't thirteen. Her mother was long gone, and she was a grown woman who could handle a challenge. She fixed Anna with a level gaze. "Well, what did you think?"

"It was such a harsh comment. Totally unfounded. Are you . . ." Her hands twisted in her lap, her fingers tugging at a pink plastic beaded bracelet her daughter must have made for her. She cleared her throat. "Are you okay?"

"I'm fine, Anna," Carrie said automatically.

"I know you are," Anna jumped in. "I didn't know if maybe there was something personal at play."

Carrie stared at the comment, focusing on the username and pushing aside the desire to drive home and curl up in bed. She felt naked. "I don't even know who this could be."

"Why is the middle word misspelled?" Anna asked. "'Liberty adk' . . ."

"Wait," Carrie said, holding up a hand. She opened another tab and typed her least favorite name into the search bar. "I'm such an idiot," she whispered, shaking her head.

Anna stepped closer to the desk and bent over Carrie's shoulder.

"Adam David Kilpatrick?" Anna read from Professor Kilpatrick's faculty web page at Yale.

"A-D-K," Carrie spelled out slowly.

Anna whistled. "It certainly sounds like it could be him."

"I don't want to jump to conclusions, but I don't see who else it could be."

"So, Adam decided to basically attack you in front of all your peers, because of—"

"Jealousy?"

"Racism," Anna finished. She frowned. "You don't think the fact that a Black woman bested him has anything to do with it?"

Carrie shrugged. "There is no shortage of reasons for Adam to dislike me."

"I mean, I guess so." Anna shot Carrie a long, quizzical look, but didn't comment further. "Well. Since I assume you'll be taking the high road, let's at least drown our feelings. I'll bring back burgers from Freddie's. Nonnegotiable."

Carrie smiled, fondness for her assistant and friend spreading through her like a ray of sunlight on a cold day. "I'm very, very upset. I probably need a milkshake, too. For my health."

"Obviously." Anna grinned.

As she departed, Carrie stared at the screen. She thought about what Kim had told her, about the dinner parties. Sure, race could be a factor. But she had to think Adam's disdain was about something more important. Something meaningful and consequential, like academics. Her own race, her own identity, hadn't been a dominant aspect of her career. Yes, she taught a seminar called Race and the Law every three years. But that was mainly because there weren't enough faculty of color at Briar to teach the course, and so much of the country's racial history was tied up in constitutional law, her area of expertise.

As avidly as she followed current events, it was easy enough to ignore some of the country's pressing issues; if she ignored newspaper headlines, she could almost pretend 2032 was beyond race. There had been progress. President Elena Garcia was running for her second term, and all recent polling showed she would win. She was a conservative, but the half-Mexican former Arizona governor had at least been the country's first Latina president. Her efforts to protect abortion rights and raise the minimum wage had been admirable, especially as a Republican. She'd even appointed the country's first Asian Supreme Court justice—a Korean American moderate who thought people should actually have rights, no less. These things had been worthwhile, even if she'd also barred immigration at the southern border.

Problems remained—hell, the first colonist class for Project Mars, her own little baby, was 95 percent white, certainly not representative of the country at large. But she was one person. She couldn't convince an entire company, or an entire country, not to be racist. The enormity of the country's race problem both astounded and terrified her. It was a toxic, raging fire so hot and untamable that even just poking the idea with a fingertip would leave her singed. It called for advocacy. And if her response to Adam's comment was anything to go by, she was the last person emotionally equipped to handle any sort of racial attack. This wasn't her fight.

She closed her eyes, willing herself to forget the words that slashed at her in the *Controversies* article. If the milkshake didn't cut it, she'd have to resort to something else to weaken the tense knot in her shoulders, something she was loathe to do—let someone take her on a second date.

The milkshake wasn't enough. Two days later, on a sleepy Sunday with nothing to distract her from the nightmare that was the *Controversies* article, and Adam, and the lingering fear that she'd doom the colonists to a dysfunctional government, Carrie resigned herself to texting Shauna. *Just this once.* One sweet final moment of relaxation would be enough to get her through the maelstrom. In line with the straightforward and intimidatingly assertive woman she'd met in the bar, Shauna replied with an immediate invitation to the movies that night. Carrie slipped on comfortable stretchy jeans, a chunky burgundy turtleneck, and gold jewelry and drove to the Z Mart.

Inside the convenience store, under stark fluorescent lights that paid no kindness to the bags under her eyes, Carrie found Shauna seated on a stool behind the gray speckled counter, a wall of e-cigarettes behind her and towering shelves of gum and M&M'S crowding the counter and nearly shielding her from view. Her long hair was pulled into a casual bun, platinum-blond tendrils spilling forth to frame her face and the pink lip gloss on her lips. Her yellow-and-red oversized polo shirt, baggy on her slender frame, had a name tag that simply read "S."

Shauna whistled as she spotted Carrie.

"I must've been pretty good if fancy Ms. Accountant is back for seconds."

Heat crept up the back of Carrie's neck. She glanced

around the store. The convenience mart was empty, save for two teenagers pulling energy drinks out of the cooler at the back wall. She smiled.

"No, I just really like Z Mart. I had a desperate craving for some peach rings."

"Well, we've got plenty of things to eat here," Shauna teased. "Actually, though, let's stock up on snacks. I still get free popcorn at the theater, but grab anything else you might want. I'll close up."

Carrie snagged peach rings and two bottles of Coke as Shauna rang up the teenagers and flicked off the lights at the back of the store. Carrie dumped her goods on the counter, digging around in her purse for her card, but Shauna waved away her efforts.

"It's fine. Let's go."

Shauna pushed open the door and strode across the parking lot toward a slightly rusted champagne-colored sedan with a deep scratch down the driver's side door. It had a lumpy-looking back tire that gave Carrie pause.

"Meet Bertha. She's a 2008 but in great shape."

Carrie wondered when the word *great* had been redefined but opened the creaking passenger's side door despite her better judgment. She tried not to gawk as Shauna pulled the gaudy Z Mart shirt over her head, shoved it under her seat, and pulled on a baby blue top with a deep V-neck.

"Date night, here we come," Shauna said.

She careened out of the lot onto the winding country back road that connected the semirural suburbs to the mall twenty minutes away. The road was dark and unlit, the small houses set far back from the road, providing little light. Shauna set a breakneck pace of what felt like eighty miles an hour on the twisting road, her headlights flicking around each curve with barely enough time to see what lay ahead. Carrie dug her fingers into the door's sticky armrest as she fought to keep down her late lunch.

Shauna flicked on the radio to an oldies station—Carrie couldn't remember the last time she'd listened to the radio instead of streaming directly to her car—and sang along to Taylor Swift, loud and unabashed. Carrie didn't dare sing, lest she distract Shauna from the road ahead.

"So, will you tell me what you really do?" Shauna asked, adjusting the volume to something slightly lower than a full-on screech.

"In my time off from being an accountant?" Carrie joked. "I'm a law professor."

"A lawyer," Shauna said, turning huge eyes on Carrie. "No shit. I may need one of those someday."

Carrie frowned. What had happened in Shauna's past, and why did she always seem to be on the move, working a series of odd jobs? She didn't really know her companion that well, apart from the way one glance set her pulse racing.

"I hope not," said Carrie. "I'm absolutely awful in court. Apart from teaching, I hate public speaking. You'd kill me by the end of trial."

"Well, at least you'd look hot doing it. One last look at those legs would probably get me through a few years in the pen." She reached into the car's center console, pulled out a bag of Fritos, and extended it to Carrie.

Carrie quickly took a small handful, hoping Shauna would soon return her hand back to the wheel as the road continued to twist. She wondered what secret talent Shauna possessed that enabled her to hug every curve of the dark wooded road in leaf-riddled November.

As they dipped down a hill, glaring lights suddenly

pierced the darkness. Flashing red and white lights. Carrie whipped her head around and stared at the headache-inducing brightness squarely in view through the car's back window. Distant, but fast approaching. Seconds elapsed as the flashing lights inched closer, closing the distance between them as the driver struggled to keep pace with Shauna's speed. Carrie's heart plummeted into her Frito-riddled stomach as, second by second, the car approached. Before long, she spotted the unmistakable black-and-white sedan body of the county's police cars in the cracked rearview mirror.

"Shit," Shauna said under her breath. "Maybe I really will need that lawyer." She slowed, the car descending from upward of eighty to a manageable forty, only slightly above the thirty-five-mile-per-hour speed limit. Shauna peeked at her left mirror, as though expecting the police car to pass them. Carrie could not imagine on the deserted road who else Shauna could have thought the lights were possibly for. They sat in silence, chugging along at forty, the car behind them refusing to budge. Carrie's stomach clenched painfully around the Fritos.

The police car's siren flicked on with a long jarring wail.

Shauna's white teeth dug into her glossy bottom lip. She let out a sharp, tense breath. Before Carrie could blink, Shauna slammed her foot on the gas again. The car rocketed forward with a disgruntled puff of brown smoke from the engine. Carrie's head snapped against the headrest and she cried out, her hand once again finding the sticky armrest.

"What the fuck, Shauna. What are you doing? You don't mess with the police."

"Carrie . . ." Shauna started, her tone almost childlike. Her voice wavered, and her hands began to shake, the car coming dangerously close to leaving the road at the fast pace she'd resumed.

"Don't forget who you're with," Carrie urged. "You can't . . . it's not the same for . . ." She swallowed. For most of her adult life, she'd grown increasingly depressed by the headlines, helpless as time after time routine traffic stops went wrong. Thanks to Shauna, this situation looked anything but routine. Carrie placed a gentle hand on Shauna's on top of the wheel, ready to coax her to stop. Shauna flinched. With a spasm, her hand jerked the wheel hard to the right. Shauna slammed on the brakes, and the champagne sedan flew off the road onto a muddled dirt path.

5

THOUGH THEY'D SLAMMED to a stop, the car still shuddered, like a violin echoing the final notes of a concerto. Carrie's nails had dug so hard into the side armrest that she'd ripped a small hole. White fibers peeked out, brilliantly clean in contrast to the dingy faux-leather trim. Shauna's face was red, hot blotches staining her skin in patches. A low noise gathered in her throat, somewhere between a growl and a whimper, and she drove her palm hard into the edge of the steering wheel. A car door slammed. Carrie began to breathe through gritted teeth, fighting to keep her lungs pushing air in and out to stave off the breathlessness of a panic attack.

A sharp rap tapped the glass of the driver's side door. Carrie squinted as a flashlight suddenly pierced through the dark safety of the car. Shauna jumped and jammed one finger onto the button that controlled the windows. The window slowly lowered, letting in a gust of cool air.

"Put your hands on the wheel right now!" shouted a gruff voice. The officer's hips were visible through the window.

He had young, taut, burly thighs pulling at the seams of his pants. The dark metal of a gun flashed at his waist.

Shauna put her hands on the wheel and glared up at the officer. "You don't have to fucking shout at me."

The officer's thighs jerked. He bent so that his face suddenly became visible to Carrie. Dark hair spiked with gel straight out of the nineties, thick brows, and hostile eyes. "Excuse me? You better watch your mouth." His lips twisted into a sneer.

"Why should I?" Shauna snapped. "It's not like you've treated me with any respect."

Carrie was going to vomit. Everything she'd eaten that day—the leftover crab dip and crackers for lunch, the lemon cake she'd indulged in afterward, the Fritos on top—danced a tango in her stomach, hot and fresh as if dredged up from the depths by a boat's propellers.

A second officer, this one significantly older than the first, approached the car. Unlike the first officer, his skin sagged—a deep pocket of skin hung from his neck, and a slumping middle hung limp over his loose belt. He clapped a hand on the shoulder of the younger officer, then pulled out his gun. The gun hung in his right hand, pointed to the ground, low by his hip. Carrie could barely take her eyes off the barrel. What in the hell was happening.

"Where you coming from?" the older officer asked in a measured tone.

"Why?" Shauna retorted.

"Don't fucking ask why," the younger voice snapped. "We saw you leave the convenience store. We know you fucking robbed the place."

Some survival instinct seemed to kick in within Shauna.

Her hostility suddenly shifted, her narrowed eyes blossoming into a painfully obvious wide-eyed stare. "Oh my," Shauna said. She angled her body toward the officers, pressing her chest into the door in a way that squeezed her breasts flush against the low cut of her V-neck. "Do you think two girls like us could do something like that?"

The flashlight beamed toward Carrie.

"Hoo hoo!" the younger officer screeched, slapping his hand against his thigh. "We got 'er now!"

"Easy now, son. Not like last time. Let's think this through." Low voices reverberated outside the car as the two officers conferred.

"Come on. That passenger lady looks like the sketch from last week. And she certainly came into money. How'd she get to be so well dressed in a car like that? We got ourselves the ringleader."

Their words just barely reached Carrie's ears, but they set her stomach churning even fiercer. There was nothing she could do; it was throw up all over herself or exit the car. She flung off her seat belt and opened the car door to vomit. In her haste, she stumbled onto the dirt path, taking three fumbling strides toward the tree line as she lost her balance.

"She's running!"

Boots tore after her, first crunching against gravel and then squelching, with three rapid paces, into the mud before softening on the dirt path. Before Carrie could even retch, a blunt object pounded into the back of her head. Her body jolted at the surprise, any urge to vomit knocked out of her. She tumbled to the ground in a hard crumple.

"Hey!" shrieked a voice behind her.

Carrie's face pressed into the dirt. The ground was damp and crumbly, smelling of pine. A discarded scrunched-up

Taco Bell wrapper, tossed out the window by a careless driver, no doubt, tumbled in the wind inches from her face. She got a strong whiff of tangy, acidic hot sauce. A sharp knee pressed into her back, painfully jutting against her spine.

"You're gonna get locked up, and then we'll get it all out of you. This whole network you've been running, all your little minions and all these robberies, we're gonna figure out all of it." Hot breath washed over the back of her neck, moist and pungent in the cool autumn air.

Desperation welled up in Carrie with such swiftness that she physically convulsed, her muscles straining against the tight hold. This couldn't be happening; this wasn't meant to happen. Her turtleneck felt hot. It had twisted and bunched under the officer's knee so that it was choking her.

"It's not me," she finally managed to eke out, panting. "You don't know anything about me." She choked on a puff of dust and dirt. "I'm a professor." *I'm different,* she wanted to say. *I have three degrees and a Briar faculty web page. My published research is cited worldwide. I don't know how to rob anything. I teach the law; I am the law.*

She tried to twist around, to tell him, to set the record straight. As she thrashed beneath his knee, trying to rotate and get her words out, her elbow hit his side, hard.

"Fuck!" He jumped up, and from her peripheral vision she saw him spit. "She fucking hit me." A second later, the blunt force of a boot hit her side, pummeling her ribs. She screamed, red spots coloring her vision. Vaguely, she could hear a cry of dismay that was not her own. Again the boot rammed her side, this time lower, into the soft curve of her stomach. She curled up, self-preservation and bodily instinct driving her to wrap her arms around her knees, protecting her core. "Piece of shit," he spat.

"Enough," the gruff voice intoned from somewhere above her. "We saw them flee the crime scene, we've got enough to take her in. Get this done."

Rough hands pawed at her shoulders and back as she was smushed unceremoniously back into the ground, like a bug flattened under a boot. Her face ground against a twig, scratching the tender flesh of her cheek, as she was made to spread flat onto her sore stomach. Impatient hands yanked her arms behind her back, and she groaned low in her throat as a muscle pulled and tore. The cold of metal cuffs clanked around her wrists.

Carrie registered her body being maneuvered upward, her limbs somehow locking into the right place as she was pushed and pulled into the back of the police sedan. She slumped against the window, resting her head against the coolness of the glass.

"Turn that off!" a voice shouted from outside the car.

"Too late, you dumb fucks. It's already up." There was a shriek, and a click. Carrie heard the car door open, but she couldn't bring herself to lift her head. She sat, slumped, as the car began to rock and sway with motion.

Carrie, in spite of everything, fell asleep. The car was hot and stuffy, with only a light breeze trickling back from the open front passenger's window. She'd pressed her forehead firmly against the glass of the car door, as if she could physically push herself through the thin pane and disappear out into the night, pretending she was anywhere else.

Her eyes had closed, and moments later she was sitting on the floor of her childhood living room on the royal blue carpet her parents had been proud to install when they'd first moved in, before she was born. Her mother always sat on the beige Raymour & Flanigan love seat, and Carrie would crawl across the carpet to sit on the floor between her legs. Her mother would extract a giant tub of yellow grease and slide the end of a plastic rattail comb in a straight line from Carrie's forehead to the nape of her neck to part down the middle. Once the important work of the center part was done, her mother would flick on the television, and there Jessica Fletcher would be, solving the latest mystery on *Murder, She Wrote*. Her mother, fiercely competitive, always bet her father, Earl, that she could nail the killer before she finished Carrie's second braid. She normally did. In her dream, Carrie stared at the TV set as a middle-aged Black woman pleaded with Jessica to find out who had murdered her university department's dean. Carrie glanced upward, but her mother's face was twisted in confusion, her face devoid of that knowing certainty, the confidence she always wore.

The car slammed to a stop, and Carrie jolted awake. Dusk had descended into night, and in the dim light she could make out the West Lafayette police station in front of them, one town over and a good twenty miles from the university. Shauna sat on the opposite end of the back seat, her eyes so narrowed they were practically closed.

Carrie's heart began hammering, and she wished she really had thrown up her lunch. She'd never known much about criminal law. She'd been relieved to receive a B minus in the subject in law school, uninterested in the advocacy and emotional pain that came with representing underrepresented clients. While her classmates completed pro bono legal defense clinics or interned at the Innocence Project, Carrie did research on constitutional history with her favorite professor. And not on the Fourth Amendment. After *Murder, She Wrote*, her next closest brush with the world of criminal investigations was in college. She'd trudge home after a long evening studying at the library, and she and Kim would crawl into their respective beds and watch *Law & Order* until one or both of them fell asleep. She'd awake to the familiar "dun dun" of the opening credits for the next episode and would stumble bleary eyed to run a toothbrush over her teeth and switch off the television.

Law & Order was not going to save her now.

The car door opened, and the officer pulled Carrie out of the squad car by the chain connecting her handcuffs. She followed Shauna, uncuffed and for once silent, up the stairs to the station. Inside the deserted lobby, reminiscent of a 1990s McDonald's with rust-colored tile flooring and off-white stucco walls, the older officer pointed at a wooden bench against the wall. Shauna stalked over to the bench and slammed herself down on its hard surface. Carrie sank onto it, feeling like she'd aged ten years in the last hour. The two officers conferred with a young woman in uniform staffing the front desk.

"God, I hate cops," Shauna spat. "They're going to pay when everyone finds out what they did to you."

"What do you mean?" Carrie said. The one saving grace was that the whole ordeal was occurring outside Briar city limits where no one knew her. She'd show the officers her university ID as soon as they returned, and she'd be safe in her bed with no one the wiser by morning. "No one is going to know about this."

"Why? This shit has been happening for decades; they just get worse if you don't expose them."

"Shauna . . ."

"Are you okay?"

Carrie swallowed. "I guess so." She ran a hand over the back of her neck and winced as her fingers traced a bruise.

The two officers reappeared, looking bored now that they'd returned to the station.

"We'll hold you overnight," the older officer said. "Our lead detective won't be free until morning. Separate cells, no talking." He nudged Carrie's foot with his boot and cocked his head toward a door at the far end of the lobby. Shauna rose and glared at him.

"Wait!" Carrie exclaimed. "Don't you need to check my ID? I'm a Briar professor; surely you need to know my identity first."

"We'll take care of it," he said. He looked as though he was ready to ease off the restrictive waistband of his pants and climb into bed.

Carrie and Shauna followed him through the door into a small chamber. Two metal cells separated by a thick concrete wall faced the door. Another officer sat behind a desk, playing solitaire on his phone.

"Roberts, I'll leave these two women with you. Hartridge will be here in the morning."

The new officer—Roberts, apparently—directed Shauna to sit on a nearby chair, then gestured at Carrie to join him at the desk.

"You have ID on you?" he asked.

Crap. Her purse must still be in Shauna's car.

"No. But I can tell you who I am. I'm Carrie Davenport, I'm a Briar professor, and this is all—"

"A terrible mistake," he finished for her. "Yeah, I've heard that before. I'm gonna take your prints now." He uncuffed Carrie and gently placed each of her fingers on the scanner pad.

Her fingerprints uploaded into the system, and the officer scanned a result page on a screen that was angled too far away for her to see.

"You been fingerprinted before?"

"Yes. I had an FBI background check for . . . for a project I'm working on." She narrowed her eyes. "And cleared it, I might add."

He surveyed his computer screen. "Checks out."

"So, I'm free to go?" Carrie said, relief flooding through her that someone finally recognized how out of place she was in a police station on a Sunday night. She could get an officer to drive her back to Shauna's car, grab her purse, and finally make her way home.

"Oh, absolutely not," he said, his tone light. "We still have to hold you overnight for questioning."

Carrie gaped. While she spluttered and fumed, he directed her to sit down, and he repeated the fingerprinting process for Shauna.

"Shauna Taylor," he said. "Quite a history."

"I'm trying to rack up enough frequent-flyer miles to go somewhere nice," she said.

Shauna had a record? Sure, there was her recent unexplained move into town, the string of jobs gained and lost, and her reckless disregard for speed limits and, it seemed, the law generally. But Carrie hadn't realized the extent that Shauna . . . She wanted to mentally kick herself for not making the obvious logical conclusion.

"I recommend Hawaii," the officer said, cracking a smile. "One call for each of you, then off to bed."

Carrie glanced at Shauna, who shook her head. Carrie approached the old-school landline phone on the desk, lifted the receiver off the hook, and dialed one of only two numbers she knew by heart.

"Kim," she said. "I need your help."

6

FROM A SWIRLING SEA of incomprehensible nightmares, Carrie awoke the next morning to the out-of-place smell of delicate perfume. She probably wouldn't have blinked at the scent had she been at home, had she rolled over in her 1842 Victorian-era four-poster bed that she'd fitted with thousand-thread-count Egyptian cotton sheets and a heavy embroidered floral duvet. But she wasn't at home. Instead, she'd survived a surprisingly chilly one-night stay in literal hell.

She shifted into a sitting position on the so-called cot inside the cell and glanced up to identify the hundred-dollars-a-bottle scent. She found her own personal angel standing on the other side of heavy iron bars, outfitted in a pale-pink Armani blazer and slim-cut jeans.

"Forgive me, but did I miss the chapter where George Washington was held in jail overnight for organized crime? We may need to come up with a better nickname for you."

"The founding fathers had no swag. Real historymakers are gangsters."

Kim snorted and averted her eyes as Carrie stretched her sore back with an entirely un-gangster-like groan. Kim's manicured mauve-colored nails flashed as she wrapped slender fingers around one of the cell bars. Carrie stood and mirrored her pose.

"I'm so glad to see you," Carrie said under her breath.

"I don't even know what to say," Kim said. She bit her lip. "I called a lawyer. He's waiting in the lobby."

"Not a big fancy DC lawyer?"

"No, no. Someone local, who knows the system. And who will keep the whole thing under wraps."

Carrie sighed, letting out all the air within her. "I love you."

Kim's eyes flashed to the left, toward the second cell in the little police station. Carrie couldn't see Shauna through the concrete wall that separated them, but she could read the rampant curiosity on Kim's face. Carrie shook her head.

The jangle of keys punctuated the general silence. The two officers who had handcuffed her the night before appeared and nudged Kim aside as they opened Carrie's cell door.

"Detective is here. You wait in the lobby." The older officer pointed at Kim. Carrie followed the two men out of the cell and down a long hallway until they reached a sparse conference room. Two men sat on either side of a rectangular wooden table, nursing Styrofoam cups of coffee.

"Professor Davenport," said a young lean man with glasses fogged from the steaming coffee and a slight gap between his two front teeth. He jumped up to shake her hand. "I'm your attorney, Bill Randolph. A pleasure to meet you, and I'm sorry it's under such unfortunate and unjust circumstances."

Carrie shook his hand firmly. "Thank you for your help."

The detective tugged his fingers through long gray hair and pulled a pen from behind his ear. "Take a seat, Ms. Davenport."

Carrie sat and folded her hands on the table. Her lawyer leaned forward, anticipating the first question.

"You don't have to look so eager, Mr. Randolph," the detective said. "I don't have much for her. We got the security camera footage from the Z Mart early this morning and know she herself didn't take anything."

Carrie felt like someone had unstopped the sink drain, and the sludge of fear and outrage churning inside her flooded out in a rush. "Great. I can go?"

"How do you know Shauna Taylor?" he asked, ignoring her question.

Carrie blinked. "I . . . I mean, I don't. I met her a week ago at a bar."

"And that's when you plotted to cash in on the robbery if you provided an alibi?"

"Don't answer that," her lawyer jumped in.

"Any reason you didn't say anything when Shauna failed to lock the front door to the Z Mart on your way out? No signs of a break-in at the crime scene. Five hundred in cash missing from the register, all the lotto tickets and over-the-counter drugs taken, some of the more expensive products missing but no broken glass and no broken lock." He raised an eyebrow, leaning back in his seat.

"Don't answer that," Randolph repeated.

"Look," Carrie said. Something snapped in her, like bone shattering under pressure. Everything she had worked toward for over twenty years, all the hopes her parents had harbored that she'd exceed every expectation for a young

Black girl from Darlington, seemed pointless if an officer could reduce her to a common criminal because of one mistaken night in a bar and a second date gone horribly wrong. "I'm a professor. I have a large and very public side project that has put me in the limelight. There's absolutely no reason why I would—"

"Dr. Davenport!" her lawyer interjected.

Carrie abandoned the rest of her tirade and crossed her arms across her chest. She could see now why most lawyers didn't represent themselves. She couldn't imagine having to keep her cool in a courtroom knowing justice wasn't being served.

"Let's face facts. You have no reason to hold my client. She didn't take anything, and you have quite literally no evidence that she conspired with Ms. Taylor or anyone else to bring about the robbery of the Z Mart. Let her go, and come back with a warrant if you ever have more than a mere feeling that she might be involved. Carrie, let's go."

He stood, and the detective waved a hand as he let Randolph pass. Carrie stared at his departing back, but a second later scrambled to her feet and bounded through the open conference room door.

"Here's my card." Randolph jammed a business card into her hand before Carrie could even drink in the sweet taste of freedom. "I'll make sure you're not implicated in the investigation. But if you ever want to do more . . . you've got a case against the department, and it would be worth it to sue these officers. In any event, the officers searched Shauna's car, so they've got your purse and stuff at the desk."

"Thank you," Carrie mumbled, her eyes adjusting to the bright morning light flooding the outdated lobby. She squinted as he swung open the glass door to the station.

Despite his offer of help, she had no intention of ever seeing him again. She needed the nightmare to end.

Kim joined Carrie at the front desk and watched as an officer removed Carrie's things from a locker.

"That's yours?" Kim whispered, pointing to a black cross-body purse with a frayed leather trim. "You might as well let them keep it."

"Sorry, I didn't read up on this month's issue of *Jailhouse Fashion*."

"Jailhouse fashion? You left the house like that yesterday." Kim shook her head. "Can we go shopping this afternoon? I liked what you wore to the Project Mars press conference, the shoes aside, but winter is basically here, and I don't even know what's in your closet."

The thought of Project Mars made Carrie's heart sink. There was so much work left to do. She'd skip shopping with Kim and get back into Francis Fukuyama's book on political decay. She could spend the afternoon figuring out what made modern democracies break down.

The officer handed over Carrie's purse and jacket. The bag vibrated with an insistent buzz as she took the bundle into her hands. She unzipped her purse and rooted around until she found her cell phone, lit up with an incoming call. She didn't recognize the caller, but the familiar area code and first three digits of Briar's extension made her heart sink.

Carrie left the lobby and stepped out into the cold morning.

"Hello?"

"Professor Davenport, hi. This is Talia, President Farrington's assistant. She'd like to set up a meeting with you for this afternoon to discuss the events that transpired last night."

"What?" Carrie nearly yelped. She swallowed a thick current of bile that had crept up her throat. How had Briar learned of last night's events? And what could the university president possibly have to say about it? "How does she . . . ?"

"President Farrington has a close relationship with the police departments of the surrounding three counties. To make sure we're taking care of and following up with any students with DUIs, minor drug issues, the like."

"Oh . . . kay," Carrie said, her mind reeling. She was on par with drunk twentysomethings? Except no, worse. She was accused of organized crime.

"We'll see you in her office at 4 p.m."

"Okay." Carrie sighed. "Wait, no. I have my upper-level Comparative Constitutional Law seminar at that time."

"You needn't worry about that," Talia said.

You needn't worry about that. The words echoed in Carrie's head, like her punishment for the weekend's events was a broken record of those five words doomed to play in her mind for eternity.

"I will be there at four," she confirmed, her voice steady and professional despite the distracting chorus of panicked words in her head. She hung up the phone.

"What's happening at four?" Kim asked. "And do they know we were supposed to go shopping?"

They arrived at Carrie's house as the late-morning sun flooded through the front-facing stained glass windows, bathing the entryway and living room with colored light. A serenity warmed the house, as if at any moment a Victorian family would descend from a restful night's sleep to tea and fresh scones in the salon. Carrie felt dirty, like she didn't belong in her own home, as if overnight something had changed her.

"You go shower," Kim suggested. "I'll stir up an early lunch."

Carrie squeezed Kim's arm and disappeared upstairs. She slumped against the deep-blue tiles of her shower, letting the water cascade over her shoulders and down her back. She felt as tired and solid as stone, only shifting when the water hit her shower cap and threatened to get her hair wet. She had been using a vanilla-and-sandalwood gel gifted by a colleague last Christmas, but she reached instead for a plain bar of Dial soap, the same kind her mother would use to scrub her when she was little. And she scrubbed.

Carrie returned downstairs in a sweater and stretchy pants. She found Kim at the kitchen counter, her hands splayed on the butcher-block countertop, a frown visible from her reflection against the shiny forest green tile back-splash. Kim was reading the directions on a box of linguine as a pot of water boiled on the stove.

"You don't have any prepared food," Kim accused, as though Carrie had regressed to a hunter-gatherer foraging the neighborhood for fresh game. She pointed an incriminating finger at Carrie's fridge.

"I live alone, so I cook in small batches."

"Doesn't that take forever? Where are the pre-prepared salads and little charcuterie boards?"

"What is my godchild eating?" Carrie teased, taking the box from Kim and breaking two handfuls of pasta over the boiling water. "In your eight years of motherhood, I'd have thought you'd have learned to cook."

"You have to be better than me at something," Kim joked.

"Marguerite knows how to cook. And Brian cooks on weekends. Besides, I have this. Put the pasta in the water, microwave some sauce, whatever. You do have a jar of sauce, right?" She bit her lip.

Carrie rolled her eyes and pointed at the pantry. "You're not missing class, too, right?"

"Just an upper-level seminar. They'll get over themselves; they're busy applying to jobs and graduate school anyway. I'll have to head home this evening, though, because the freshmen in my Intro to Political Science course are not so generous."

Carrie stepped up to Kim as she examined the pantry offerings and wrapped her arms around Kim's thin middle. Kim squeezed Carrie close, then twisted in her arms and rested heavy, warm eyes on Carrie.

"Are you okay?" she asked, her voice tender, like when Naomi had lost Mr. Snuffles.

"I don't think so," Carrie said. She swiped her eyes as tears gathered and turned toward the cabinet beside the stove where she kept her saucepans.

"Carrie." That one word, full of understanding and reproach for hiding her tears, was the key that unlocked the door to Carrie's emotions. Tears cascaded down her cheeks, and she abandoned her efforts to find a saucepan and let her sobs overcome her body. Kim pulled her by the hand toward the living room and pushed Carrie onto the sofa. Carrie curled into a ball, shoving her socked feet under the cushions, and Kim draped a blanket over her.

"Rest for a minute."

"Kim," Carrie said before her friend left the room. "You have to season the sauce. Oregano, garlic powder, red pepper flakes, salt, pepper. At the very least."

"Okay," Kim said quietly.

Carrie closed her eyes and pulled the blanket over her head until nothing existed, until she didn't exist. She pretended the darkness around her was permanent, like she could sink into an indefinite void, as if her body were suspended and floating in the vast blackness of space. She yearned for that weightlessness, that nothingness, but her body felt weighted down by more than gravity here on Earth, each limb sore and saturated with shame.

After what felt like mere seconds, Kim's footsteps pattered back toward the couch. She pulled the blanket off Carrie's head. Carrie blinked at the light and uncurled her body until she sat cross-legged, and Kim pressed a warm bowl of pasta into her hands. Steam rose from the fragrant bowl of linguine. It even had a sprinkling of Parmesan on top.

Carrie sighed as she took a bite of warm pasta, which filled her empty belly, and she turned to Kim, who sat cross-legged opposite her with her own smaller bowl of pasta.

"Tell me what happened," Kim said.

Carrie explained. How she had, not for the first time, gone home with a stranger from a bar, how she had sought release when academia wound her up. She explained how she'd needed a break from Project Mars, and Shauna had been there, but then, did she know anything about Shauna at all? And she recounted, detached, as though it had happened to someone else, the feel of the officer's boot driving into her side, the helplessness, the notion that *this did not happen to people like them.*

She wanted to describe the way her heart clenched, tight and sore like when her calves tensed up after too many hours exploring a museum, a strained muscle that sat like a heavy, convulsed knot in her chest. She wished she could hold her heart in her hands, work her fingers over the tendons, release the tension that cut through her hot and untamed. Pain and shame and disillusionment had tainted her, and she did not know what would make her heart beat freely and easily again. But she couldn't get those last words out, so she sat, the true depths of her pain locked inside, left unsaid.

"Are you going to do anything about what happened?" Kim asked.

"Like what?"

"I don't know. Sue the officers. Hold a press conference. Take a sabbatical, a few days off. Anything."

Carrie hit Kim with the same facial expression she gave Naomi when she begged for ice cream right after they'd eaten chocolate fudge. It screamed, *What do you think?*

"No," Carrie said out loud after a pause. "What I want more than anything is to go back to my projects and pretend this never happened." She wouldn't dwell on what had happened or fight back against the officers for what they'd done. What they deserved the universe would hand to them, and she certainly was not going to be the face of any movement.

Kim nodded, twirling a long curl of pasta onto her fork, her expression neutral.

"Business as usual then, I guess."

"Yeah," Carrie said heavily. She would put one foot in front of the other, and somehow she'd move forward.

"What about this meeting with the president?"

"You don't think they'll fire me, do you? God, I don't even know how . . ." Her insides twisted as if her intestines were a washcloth wrung out over the sink.

"Carrie. You're a tenured professor. They can't fire you."

"I guess not." She sighed. "They'll just take me off the bicentennial planning committee and tell me I can't teach my upper-level seminar next year."

Kim's expression softened. "You didn't do anything wrong."

Carrie exhaled a deep breath. "I hope they see that."

She slurped the last of her pasta from the bowl and set it on the coffee table. She would explain what happened. Remind them of her recent research and the positive press Project Mars had garnered for the university. Make them see she posed no threat.

When she finally retreated upstairs to dress for the dreaded meeting, she found that Kim had laid out a conservative black suit, beige blouse, stockings, and gold earrings on Carrie's bed; she had also plugged in her hot curlers. Carrie went through the motions of fixing her hair and getting dressed, zombielike, thanks to her best friend's organization. Then they took Kim's rental car to the Z Mart to retrieve Carrie's Audi. It sat untouched three parking spaces from the door to the Z Mart. She could barely look at the squat brick building and the apartment on top. From the few glances she did take, it looked the same; no broken glass, no swarm of police cars outside. Just the same tower of dusty postcards in a rack shoved against the window, the only change the dimmed lights with the store's temporary closure. A humble, outdated, homely building that had wreaked havoc on her over the last two days. The only work that remained was to explain her situation to President Farrington, and she'd be cleared of this mess.

"How dumb do they think I am?" Carrie grumbled, turning her gaze away from the cursed building and back toward Kim. "Why would I leave my car at a crime scene?"

"It's probably good that you did. One more sign that you're not wrapped up in this."

"Mm," Carrie agreed. She did not want to exit the safety of Kim's car.

"You'll call and tell me how everything went?"

Carrie smiled. She felt like Kim was dropping her off at summer camp for the first time.

"Yes. Safe travels back." She hugged Kim, closing her eyes as she leaned into the embrace. "Thank you for coming."

"Always. And in ten years, let's hope we're in a different place and I can gossip about your criminal history to all my new friends while you're off floating around on Mars."

"I won't be going to space, but if I did, I'd be flipping you off in my space suit."

Carrie exited the elevator on the top floor of the university's administration building and waited in the small lobby. Carrie toyed with her gold earrings until the backs nearly fell off and resigned herself to merely twisting her hands in her lap. She just barely fought the urge to tap her foot as she watched the administrative assistant, Talia, meticulously apply printed labels to a stack of file folders. It reminded her of the way she'd been gripped with nerves a little over a month ago when preparing to enter the Project Mars press conference. This most certainly couldn't be as bad as all that.

"President Farrington will see you now," Talia said, glancing up from her work.

"Brilliant."

Carrie entered the president's office. She had been awed by the rich wood-paneled decor the first time she'd visited during her first year of teaching. Dark wood coated every surface, and a cabinet housed delicate porcelain figurines. It was the kind of office she aspired to, one she'd settle into after she had scratched the itch of pursuing her academic research. A job of that scale meant the opportunity to shape a generation of students. The same way her mother had.

"Professor Davenport." Miriam Farrington stood from behind her mahogany desk and approached Carrie with an outstretched hand. She was a mid-height, sturdily built woman with a sensible brown bob and with a neck scarf straight out of a 1980s Ralph Lauren catalog tied around her neck.

"You know you can call me Carrie."

She smiled. "Likewise. I hate all that 'President Farrington' nonsense. Just call me Miriam."

Miriam eased into a cream wingback armchair and crossed her ankles. Carrie sat on an identical love seat across from her.

"So, you've been to jail."

"What?" Carrie squawked. She brushed down the lapel of her black suit and crossed her legs at the ankle just as Miriam had done, if only to quell the urge to collapse onto her knees and beg Miriam to forget the whole thing had happened. "I mean, excuse me?"

Miriam's eyes twinkled. "I'm kidding," she said. She reached into a small porcelain dish on the side table next to her and extracted a jelly bean. She held the dish out to Carrie.

Carrie shook her head. "Oh. Um, no thank you."

"I heard from our daily police report that you'd been arrested on suspicion of robbery. But it seems like that all got cleared up very quickly."

"Yes. I can assure you, I most certainly did not commit a robbery."

"I have no doubt." Miriam leaned in closer, resting an elbow on her knee. "But I mean . . . are you okay?"

Carrie took a deep breath. "I'm fine."

"Do you want to tell me what happened?"

Carrie looked out the window, where a landscaping crew raked leaves that had been shed from the campus's historic red maple trees. How could she explain in the middle of Miriam's pristine old-money decor that she'd fucked a stranger from a bar who lived a life in proximity to organized crime?

"There's not much to report," Carrie said. "I visited the Z Mart convenience store last night shortly before it was robbed. I don't know who did it, and it wasn't me. The police arrested me along with a friend who was at the scene. I was released this morning."

"And there was a physical altercation?"

"What? No." Carrie's heart thumped in her chest. She could feel Miriam's eyes on her, slightly off-center, near her chin. She touched her face and suddenly remembered the slight cut she'd received on her cheek when her face had been pressed into the dirt. She'd been too despondent earlier in the day to let Kim mask over it with foundation. Her fingers pressed into the tender spot there and quickly drew away.

"Not an altercation," Carrie amended. "I wasn't trying to resist arrest or anything. But the arrest did involve . . . some physical maneuvering by the officer."

Miriam stared at her for several seconds, head cocked and words on the tip of her tongue, hesitant like she had been tasked with telling someone they had gum on their shoe. Carrie could almost see the other woman's mouth moving as she tried to find the right thing to say aloud.

"The reason I wanted to talk with you in particular, Carrie, apart from making sure that you're okay, is that I wouldn't want there to be any action taken because of a potential . . . negative interaction with the police."

Carrie frowned. "I'm not sure I follow."

Miriam winced. "I just . . . want to make sure you're not planning to . . ."

The other woman's hesitance clicked in her mind. "Oh. You don't want this to become a Black Lives Matter issue," Carrie said. Miriam was trying to keep her in line.

"It's not that I don't support Black Lives Matter," Miriam jumped in. "I do—of course I do. But as you know from many a fundraising dinner, Briar's donors tend to lean conservative. With our bicentennial capital campaign fund-raiser well underway, I wouldn't want there to be negative press related to any of our Briar professors."

Carrie's shoulders sagged, her body finally relaxing now that she knew President Farrington's real concern. No one was trying to peg her as a criminal. They wouldn't be taking away her committee memberships or relegating her to some metaphorical purgatory for disfavored tenured professors. They understood who she was and all the many ways she contributed to Briar. Everything was going to be fine.

"Of course not. There won't be any issues. I'm not . . . that kind of advocacy is not for me. My goal is to carry on as if nothing ever happened and to focus on my scholarship. I wouldn't do anything to impact the capital campaign."

Miriam's face brightened, the tight pinch of her mouth broadening into an easy smile. "Excellent! I think you're making the right choice, Carrie. Project Mars has garnered such good press for you and for Briar. We wouldn't want to do anything to tarnish that."

"Right."

Miriam popped another jelly bean into her mouth. "I looked online and found a local Black church group that has an anti-crime ministry. From the website, it looks very promising. Why don't I make a donation?"

She wished the other woman hadn't said anything. She could picture Talia sitting at her desk earlier this morning researching "safe" nonprofits that lacked the "political" connotation of Black Lives Matter. Twenty years of advocacy, and still the very idea of Black lives mattering had donors ready to stow their wallets.

"How kind," Carrie said. A sour taste pricked her tongue, and she ground her teeth to keep from saying anything more.

"Good. It's settled. Thank you, Carrie, for keeping quiet on this. And do keep me posted on your Project Mars initial report. I can't wait to read it."

"Absolutely." She stood and exited the office, ducking her head to keep her expression from view. She'd dodged a bullet. She wasn't in trouble with the university. Yet her retreat from the president's office felt more like waving a white flag of defeat than a win.

7

THE SUN HAD YET to rise over Briar's campus the next
morning, but Carrie's office already smelled like a coffee
shop. She was on her third brew of the day, her oversized
bistro mug parked on a blue coaster with UVA's seal on it,
underneath her desk lamp, the only light glowing on the
otherwise dim and deserted floor of faculty offices. Classical
piano music played from her portable speaker, and she'd
draped her trusty cream chenille blanket over her lap. The
space heater she kept under her desk warmed her toes, and
she drank in all the comfort she could from it.

On her computer screen, Carrie scrolled through, for the
umpteenth time, the preamble to the South African
Constitution. She liked the commitment to equality.

We, the people of South Africa, Recognise the injustices of our past; Honour those who suffered for
justice and freedom in our land; Respect those who
have worked to build and develop our country; and

Believe that South Africa belongs to all who live in it, united in our diversity.

She especially liked the stated purpose of the document: to "heal the divisions of the past and establish a society based on democratic values, social justice and fundamental human rights," where "every citizen is equally protected by law."

A constitution was a foundation upon which the strong house of society could be built. It was a promise to future generations: This house will be a safe place to live. She reread the words until the sun rose and her third cup of coffee ran cold. Reflective ruminations transitioned into checking email, and, with a glance at the clock and a yelp, Carrie realized that in all the commotion of the last forty-eight hours, she had yet to finalize her lecture notes for the day.

A knock on the door an hour later startled Carrie out of her last-minute frenetic preparation.

"My favorite professor," Anna said, peeking her head into Carrie's office. "In the flesh."

"My favorite assistant," Carrie said. She offered Anna a small smile.

"Ready for class? I made the revisions to the slides you requested; they're all ready to go."

"Great, just finished my notes." Barely.

Carrie stood and, with a wince at the soreness in her side, left her desk. She and Anna exited the faculty suite of offices and traipsed downstairs and outside toward Butler Hall. The campus was bright and cold in the wintry late morning, and her feet easily followed the same comfortable route along the brick path she'd walked for years. After the prior two days, it was a welcome return to her routine.

"We missed you for yesterday's seminar. I got a call from President Farrington's office to prepare class for a substitute." Anna scrutinized Carrie, curiosity on her face.

"And who did they advise teach class?"

"Her office asked me to call Professor Simms."

She tried to hide her smile. "I'm sure the students loved that." Professor Simms had gotten her law degree at age fifty . . . forty years ago. She was old enough to be the students' great-grandparent. Every word that slipped from the tip of her tongue was feather light, as if it would be her last.

"They survived it. But I'm sure they'll be glad when you're back tomorrow."

"Yes. Yesterday was a bit of a hiccup. But that's resolved."

Anna's eyebrows raised, but she said nothing more.

The two entered the large lecture hall. Students chatted among themselves as they pried open backpacks and extracted laptops for the day's lecture. Carrie settled behind the lectern while Anna prepared to take attendance from her seating chart.

She addressed the class. "Good morning." She could feel her power return to her, as if, by assuming her familiar place at the front of the classroom, she'd been instilled again with the knowledge of her many years of study, her confidence in her ability to share that knowledge with others, and her sense of place. She was a professor. That mattered, and the way a room full of students looked up to her mattered. "Welcome to another exciting day of first-year US Constitutional Law. Today, we'll wrap up our conversation on federal power before we start in on the equal protection clause of the Constitution."

Carrie, like she had for years, swiped up on her tablet to project her slides onto the screen behind her.

"As you know, the Constitution gives Congress a handful of powers to regulate individual citizens. Who can recap for us?"

She scanned the room. Apart from a few students who looked distracted—online shopping or skimming social media, she figured—everyone's eyes were on her. No one raised their hand, but like most law professors fond of the Socratic method, she wasn't too squeamish about cold-calling on students at random. She selected a student who didn't look either too eager or mid-purchase.

"James."

A young man near the front cleared his throat. "Right, so. Last week we talked about the commerce clause. How the federal government has the power to regulate interstate commerce. And then we also covered the necessary and proper clause, which gives Congress broad powers to enact new laws. And the taxing and spending clause—the way the Constitution gives the government the power to tax individual citizens."

"Thank you," Carrie said. "And that's a helpful background, because today we'll talk about how the Constitution also gives Congress the power to regulate states, but how and why that power is limited—the federal government can't just do what it wants to states willy nilly."

Carrie launched into the substance of her lecture for the day, working her way through her slides and all the limitations on government power. She got through two more slides before the ping of a text message alert distracted her. She glanced away from her slides toward the lecture hall.

"Alright, I'm all good with using laptops, but I draw the

line at texting in the middle of class. Please silence your phones."

Carrie stared at her students in an attempt to be formidable, but she noticed that rather than stow their phones, three more students had extracted their phones from their pockets. A girl two rows from the back pressed her phone into her neighbor's hand. Their heads bowed together to watch whatever was on the screen. Carrie started to speak, but another notification alert pinged. For the second time in recent months, Carrie had no idea what was going on in her classroom.

"I'm going to continue this slide, and when I turn back around, I expect that every single one of you will have put your phone away."

Carrie turned swiftly to the board and clicked to the next slide.

"Okay, plenary power. Now, we're talking about the fact that any power that the Constitution does not expressly give to the federal government rests with the state. If the Constitution doesn't say 'no,' absent a few exceptions which we'll talk about in a second, the state of North Carolina can do it."

Carrie turned around, ready and expecting to see her normal class of slightly bored but generally attentive students. But rather than order, the attention of her class had further eroded. More phones were out. One man in the middle of the room was watching a video with the sound on low. Two students had stood to watch over his shoulder. She realized with a sinking feeling in her gut that something was wrong; news of some natural disaster or tragedy must have broken. A shooting, a terrorist attack, *something*.

"Does someone want to tell me what's going on?" she said

quietly. Even though the students had been shuffling in their seats in the commotion, the room went dead silent at her words. All eyes flicked to her face. The room warmed, as if the thermostat had been set to ninety degrees, as the silence stretched on.

"Um, Professor Davenport?" James, whom she had called on at the start of class, had spoken up. "There's a video that started circulating this morning. Have you seen it?"

"What video?"

"You know . . ."

Carrie raised an eyebrow. "I don't think I do."

James cleared his throat. "The, um, the one of you."

"What?" Carrie yelped. "From Project Mars, you mean? The press conference?"

A student in the back choked out a sound somewhere between a cough and a sob, and Carrie's gaze snapped toward her. The young woman had tears in her eyes. Carrie slowly ascended the stairs, climbing up six rows until she reached the girl's row.

"Show me," Carrie murmured.

The girl handed over her phone. The screen showed a caption: *What the Fuck is happening in north Carolina?*

Under the caption was a video. Before she could think, Carrie's thumb brushed the thumbnail. All of a sudden, the back of a dark figure moved across the screen. Then the video frame cleared, and there was an officer against a dark forest background. He stood above a woman—tall, a little plump, well dressed in a burgundy turtleneck, lying haplessly on the ground. A second later, the officer's foot pulled back and drove into the woman's side. The woman in the video cried out and rolled over just enough that her face was visible. The camera shook.

Carrie immediately clicked away from the video.

"Where did you get this?" she demanded of the girl. A fresh set of tears burst from the student's eyes and trailed down her face.

"Professor," James called from the front of the room. "It's on Lune. It was posted by some random woman, and it gained traction over the last two days. A friend from mock trial sent it to me this morning, so it has made its way around campus. And a friend from undergrad in Georgia texted it to me just now, so I think maybe it's spreading online."

Carrie felt as though everything were too small. The walls had crept in until they threatened to suffocate her; the silky fabric of her work blouse constricted until it was a body bag choking her, squeezing her, trapping her. She stumbled down the last few steps back to the front of the classroom and stared at the board so that none of the students would have to watch her unwind, watch her crumble. They could still see her, she knew, from her trembling back to the slight buckle of her knees.

She spun around. "We made good headway today on state power, so we'll adjourn for the day." Her voice shook, but she pressed on. "We'll have to do a few more minutes next class, but then we need to move on to the Fourteenth Amendment. It's an iconic, enigmatic amendment that will be relevant to all of your careers. 'No person shall be denied the equal protection of . . . the laws.'" Her voice cracked on the last phrase, and she ducked her head. "I'm sorry you all had to see the video. Thank you for bringing it to my attention."

She snatched her tablet and clicker and fled the room.

Carrie's office harbored her in safety, like a spaceship in the midst of the cold, lifeless void of space. She stumbled into her wood-paneled refuge and closed the door. Slumping into her desk chair, she kicked off her loafers under the desk and reached into her bottom desk drawer. She pulled out her chenille blanket, discarded her blazer on the back of her chair, and swapped it for the softness of the warm blanket around her shoulders. Then she reached into her middle drawer, where she kept her emergency stash of mini Twix bars, and unwrapped the first of what she anticipated would be many. She rested a heavy head in the palm of her hand and let the chocolate melt in her mouth.

She would have vastly preferred, for the second time that week, to curl up in a ball of blankets on her couch at home and cry. But she had office hours that afternoon, and she wouldn't let . . . extracurricular issues come between her and serving her students. *Just a few more hours.*

Still, she hoped no one would show up.

For the first hour, she sat blissfully alone, staring at her blank computer screen, unable to convince herself to do anything other than gaze into the black void as she awaited potential students. In the second and final hour, Anna knocked on the door to inform her that a student needed her signature as the faculty sponsor for his independent research project. She took a long look at Carrie's appearance.

"I'll tell him to leave the form and pick it up in the morning," she said. "And, well, I saw the video . . ." She trailed off as Carrie shot her a look. "Got it, never mind. I'll be right outside." She pulled the door shut softly behind her.

Bless her. She would have to up the ante on the fruit basket she usually sent Anna during the holidays. Double the fruit, chocolate, the works.

She wished she could hibernate and reawaken once the world felt less intimidating. How had she let this happen? Last week, she'd faced enormous concerns—figuring out how to draft a document that would govern the behavior and enshrine the rights of explorers thousands of miles away from home, on an unfamiliar planet. A document that would potentially be the governing constitution on Mars for years to come. Which, despite being difficult, represented the most exciting challenge and potentially the greatest achievement of her lifetime. She still had that monumental task before her, but somehow something even more terrifying had struck her—physically, bodily, pulling her out of the abstract thoughts in her mind and slamming into her with brute force.

Now everyone knew what had happened. Not just the university, but her students, the very people she hoped to inspire. Her trauma, her pain, reflected on tiny screens for others to observe. Thank goodness, her father wasn't on social media. She wasn't ready for that conversation, for his long, probing stare and convictions about all she should be doing to address what had happened.

She needed to prepare her lesson plan for Thursday's class on the Fourteenth Amendment. Year after year, Carrie instructed her students on how, out of the legacy of slavery and the Civil War, the Fourteenth Amendment had been born, intended to protect the liberties of formerly enslaved people and guarantee equal civil and legal rights. She had taught on it so many times that the words were ingrained in her brain: no state could "deprive any person of life, liberty, or property, without due process of law; nor deny to any person within its jurisdiction the equal protection of the laws." But how could her usual lesson plan to introduce the amendment ever suffice? There Carrie had been—well dressed, at the forefront of her field, innocent by all accounts —pushed into the ground before she'd even had a chance to defend herself. It was 150 years later, and Carrie had still been treated worse than Shauna, who had all but verbally attacked the officers. Her usual glowing, resounding lecture on the monumental feat that was the passage of the amendment rang hollow as she imagined speaking the words in Thursday's class.

A knock on her door startled her out of lingering, maudlin thoughts. She glanced at the clock—office hours had ended a half hour ago.

"Professor Davenport?" Anna peeked her head in again, and Carrie nodded to her. Anna stepped fully in and closed the door.

"It's after four. A late office hours straggler?"

Anna shook her head quickly. "No, no. President Farrington and another important-looking woman are here," she said in a stage whisper, pointing behind her toward the door.

"What? Here? To see me?"

Anna nodded. "Her office called a while ago to see if you were in, and I didn't think anything of it." Her wide eyes landed on Carrie's pile of Twix wrappers. "I . . . thought they were planning to call you."

Carrie followed her gaze down to the mountain of gold wrappers on her desk. Fuck.

"Give me thirty seconds," she said.

She shoved her feet back into her loafers, swept the Twix wrappers into the wastebasket beneath her desk, crammed the blanket back into her drawer, and pulled her blazer over her shoulders. She jabbed the computer monitor on to look like she'd actually been working and ran her tongue in a frantic path over the sticky toffee coating her teeth. And, with a knock, her door suddenly opened.

"Carrie," President Farrington said warmly, as though they were long-lost friends. It had barely been twenty-four hours since they'd last seen each other. She stepped into the room, followed by a younger white woman with a sleek brunette bob.

"A pleasure to meet you, Carrie," said the new woman, reaching out to shake Carrie's hand. "I'm Cameron Oliver, the university's director of communications."

"A pleasure," Carrie said, looking from Miriam back to Cameron. She had a sinking feeling this was about to be another painful meeting about what had happened. "Please sit anywhere."

Miriam chose one of the two green wingback chairs while Cameron settled onto the two-seater. Carrie sat in the other chair and raised her eyebrows at the two women.

"I'll cut to the chase," Miriam said. "While yesterday it seemed like we'd gotten the situation under control, today a video has spread across campus like wildfire of the incident that occurred. It was certainly more of a confrontation than you depicted, Carrie." Miriam's gaze softened. "It was very physical."

"It was so upsetting," Cameron said, her green eyes watery. "I can't believe something awful like that could have happened to you. All these years hearing about police mistreatment on the news, and here it up and happened to one of Briar's own."

"Yes, all so unfortunate," Miriam continued. "While I hate to be indelicate, I think we need to get ahead of things now. Get this under control."

"Under control how?" Carrie asked.

"Cameron will lay out the plan for you," Miriam said.

"Right," Cameron said, her expression brightening in relief, like an animal adoption commercial had finished its final plaintive refrain and finally transitioned back to her favorite reality show. "In my role as Briar's communications director, it's my job to make sure the university speaks with a unified voice and that we're always putting our best foot forward. First, we'll try to get the video taken down any way we can. There have been about ten thousand views so far, primarily on the East Coast. We'll go to the posts that have gotten the most likes and demand that users delete their repost of the video—and if that doesn't work, we can offer a limited amount of financial compensation to do so."

"Oh, excellent." Carrie heaved a sigh of relief. "I'd really appreciate that."

"Great." Cameron smiled. "And next, I've drafted a statement for you. With your sign-off, we'll post this to the website and to social media sites like Lune, which should dispel any negative aftershocks."

Cameron patted the spot next to her on the love seat. Carrie rose and squeezed in on the cushion next to her, pressed uncomfortably tight against the other woman, and looked down at the tablet Cameron had extracted from her bag.

There were two paragraphs on a blank slide, with Carrie's name centered beneath them.

A recent video posted online has circulated throughout the Briar community and beyond, depicting a misunderstanding that occurred this weekend with law enforcement. The incident involved a case of mistaken identity that has since been resolved. As I always have, I maintain a commitment to adhering to the fine laws of this country, and as a lawyer and citizen, I denounce any and all forms of illegal activity.

The video, I'm sure, may be upsetting to watch. However, I am in good health and appreciate and respect the officers for fulfilling their duty to keep our community safe. Laws are the constraints that keep our society free, and our officers are the front line in the fight for freedom. I hope you will join me in striving to build a peaceful and free community grounded in mutual respect.

— Dr. Carrie Davenport, JD, PhD,

Carrie finished reading the slide and sat back so sharply that the wooden frame of the love seat creaked as she hit the thinly padded backrest. A cop could not have crafted a better message.

"You drafted it?" she asked Cameron.

"I did," Cameron confirmed. "I think it strikes just the right balance to hit that thoughtful academic tone." She looked to Miriam as if gauging how soon her next raise would be coming.

Miriam's expression was calculating, sizing up Carrie and her reaction.

"Thoughts?"

Carrie turned the statement over in her mind, but something else prickled at the edge of her consciousness as much as she tried to focus on the words before her.

"What did you mean earlier, Cameron, that this would dispel any negative aftershocks?"

"I'm sure when you watched the video, you noticed that it . . ." She trailed off at Carrie's grimace. "You have watched the video, correct?"

Carrie looked down at her hands. "I don't see a reason for me to do so."

Miriam cleared her throat. "I think you need to, Carrie, to understand the full impact and why we're trying to manage it."

"Don't worry, we can watch it now," Cameron said. "That way you'll know."

"Oh good." Carrie could think of nothing less appealing than watching the video. She would sacrifice her home, her car, even the entire contents of her bank account, if it could spare her from having to relive what had happened. But that clearly wasn't an option, and perhaps Miriam was right. Her students, her colleagues, the internet at large—all knew what the video held, knew how Carrie had looked on the ground. And she didn't know what they had seen.

"Alrighty, here we are." Cameron clicked on a post containing the video and maximized the image so that it filled the tablet screen.

Just like the few seconds she'd seen in her classroom, the video started off dark with the back of a man crossing in front of the camera. Then the scene revealed two figures in front of a forest, one a man partly hidden in shadow, the other a woman lying face down on a strip of dirt that resembled the side of a road. The woman had on a well-fitting burgundy turtleneck and a gold necklace that had ridden up around her neck.

The officer pressed Carrie into the ground under his

knee. He bent down to reach for Carrie's arms. She twisted in response, bumping into him. The officer recoiled as if he'd been bitten by a snake, instant and shocked. After a beat, he shouted, "She fucking hit me!" His voice was cold, mocking, and punctuated a second later by the slam of his boot into the soft flesh of Carrie's side and stomach. In the video, she cried out in pain, and a second shriek pierced the darkness even louder, like it had come from closer to the camera—Shauna's voice from behind her phone camera. With a hot, angry twist of her stomach, Carrie stared at the officer's height over her prone body in the video, the sharp toe of his boot, and the barely discernable disgust written on his face, faintly visible through the darkness. His boot slammed into Carrie again and again—innocent, defenseless Carrie—causing her body to flop and shudder. She could feel it now, the sharp stab of pain with each blow that radiated from her flesh to rattle her bones, blood coursing hot with adrenaline and fear. She had been too stunned in the moment for the pain to have hit her then, but pain smacked into her now, fresh and searing in her side. In the video, her face angled slightly upward, turning to stare above her at her attacker, with a slight sheen of blood on her cheek. And then the video version of her started babbling helpless, desperate words, her face vulnerable to his blows. Until two words, spoken with perfect clarity.

"Have mercy."

Like a slave asking for absolution, she thought with disgust. In 2032.

She abruptly stood and distanced herself as far from the screen as she could, pacing to the window to stare out over campus. Her whole body shook, tremors rolling through her like thunder. She wished she could be anywhere else but in her office, scrutinized by her boss and the woman who wanted to erase what had happened. She felt as vulnerable and on display as she had been in the video, as she had been in class that morning. If she had been home, she would have thrown up, would have punched the wall, would have fallen to her knees with the heaviest weight of the universe on her shoulders and cried out, curling into herself for protection the same way she had done in the video. She would have broken down. But instead, she was in a tight-fitting dress under a blazer that pulled at her shoulders, her toes crunched in leather loafers, watching the evening's final rays of sun withdraw from Briar's campus.

Miriam stood and approached the second window in Carrie's office so that they were parallel figures gazing out over campus. She didn't look at Carrie, merely stared ahead.

"You see, Carrie, why we need to shut the video down. It's emotional, and hard to watch. It's the kind of thing that will incite the students to protest. It could cause national outrage. We don't need that kind of attention."

Carrie didn't want to be the face of a national movement. She didn't want to be reduced to a body on the ground or another voiceless protester begging for change. Her normal approach was to reinvest in her students so that *they* could go on to be civil rights lawyers and public defenders who would change the world for the better.

I'm not an advocate.

But this. She couldn't move on from this. Maybe she wouldn't be protesting in the streets, but what had happened was wrong.

Cameron popped off the love seat, her expression bright. "I really think this statement will nip all these problems in the bud. If people know you stand with justice, Carrie, they won't want to be out in the streets causing any ruckus."

She started to approach Carrie, but Carrie cut off her movement with a raised hand. She gestured for the tablet and stared at the statement again.

I respect the officers for fulfilling their duty to keep our community safe. She couldn't say that. How were they keeping people safe? *Those fuckers,* she wanted to say, *pounced on my back, ground me into the dirt, and eschewed the very nature of due process I spend so long teaching in my classes.*

She turned to Miriam, tablet in hand. "I can't sign off on this." She waved the tablet in the air, the slim device quivering as her hand shook. "I won't."

"Carrie," Miriam said, her tone patient and chiding, as if trying to convince a toddler to finish her vegetables. "I understand the discomfort that comes after watching the video. I wouldn't wish that treatment on anyone. But I want you to be known for your brilliant mind and not anything else."

"What happened is wrong," she said through gritted teeth.

"Yes. I know. And maybe Cameron can soften the language."

"I think it's already quite balanced—" Cameron started.

"If we don't want to say you 'respect' the officers, perhaps we could say you 'understand' them?" Miriam interjected. "Or you 'acknowledge their duty to the community'? Cameron and I will workshop it."

Her shoulders ached like she was physically being torn apart, like her identity and her academic position were two ends of a rope that was fraying at the middle. Everything in her being screamed not to sign off. She thought of her mother and father, whose relationship had blossomed as they journeyed to protests on weekends, a bond forged through the courage to stand up to injustice.

"Fine," she said. The single word burned her tongue. "With edits."

"You're making the right choice, Carrie."

"Hmm," Carrie said noncommittally, stopping herself before she said anything more. Every limb was bound to the university's will, her freedom of thought as trapped as her body had been in the video.

"Excellent," Cameron echoed. "And are you ready to sign this nondisclosure agreement saying that you won't comment publicly on the events of that night?"

Carrie blinked slowly, her eyebrows shooting up with an incredulous look. That look of exhaustion she'd seen from no shortage of fed-up women, from her mother to Kim. *Are you fucking kidding me right now?*

Miriam held up a hand. "Ah—I think we can stop there. We've accomplished enough for today."

Carrie stared back and forth between Cameron and Miriam. Then she set the tablet down and reached under her desk for her purse. Even though it was her office and her visitors could kindly show themselves the hell out, she made her own wordless exit, leaving the two women standing open mouthed beside each other. Her shoes squeaked down the hall in a rapid staccato as she escaped to the faculty parking lot.

8

AFTER THE DAY she'd had, Carrie needed a drink more than she needed blood in her veins. The clock, improbably, only registered the time as early evening, when Carrie had most certainly lived at least three days in the last twelve hours.

She shifted the car into gear and pulled onto the two-lane road out of town, her instincts dragging her to an all-too-familiar spot. It was a bad idea; no doubt it was a bad idea. There were other places nearby to drink. But there also . . . weren't. The bars closest to campus teemed with undergraduates, eighteen-year-olds with fake IDs, stumbling to the bar to order vodka Red Bulls. The nicest restaurant in town was a faculty hot spot, the dark carved wood of the bar filled with men in tweed jackets jockeying to out-order their colleagues. The thought of stepping one foot into a room where most of the professors had probably already heard or seen what had happened to her made her want to hide under her bed and never emerge.

And so, that left Birdie's Tavern, a safe twenty-odd miles from campus and her security blanket after the divorce. The tavern had gotten her into this mess in the first place. But she couldn't drink alone at home with her mood as dark as it was. She might not wake up in the morning.

When she entered the squat, rustic building, she was greeted with the weekday crowd—quiet conversation at booths, low country music, people eating the scant healthy items on the limited food menu rather than fistfuls of French fries.

Only one other patron sat at the bar, so she easily caught Hannah's attention.

"You're in luck, I actually have a good red this time."

"Save it," Carrie said. "Whiskey. Neat."

Hannah frowned. "Bad?"

"Catastrophic."

Hannah nodded and poured a top-shelf whiskey into a glass. "Something happen with that woman from last time?"

Carrie had been watching Hannah make her drink. Her gaze shot up. "What do you mean?"

Hannah cocked her head toward a booth at the back wall. Carrie turned.

Shauna sat alone with a beer bottle, three other bottles forming a triangle on the table beside her.

"If something did happen, duck, because she's here."

Carrie let out a long, shaky breath. Her hand trembled as she reached for the drink Hannah had placed in front of her. She knocked it back in one gulp.

"We had a good time, the first time I met her." She coughed.

"And then?"

"And then we had a bad time."

Hannah's watchful eyes poured over her, and Carrie

wondered what she saw—if Hannah could see the shame and regret like a tangible mark on Carrie's skin.

"One more. I promise I'm okay," she added as Hannah sized her up. "Thanks, Hannah."

Carrie took her second whiskey, stood, and crossed the deserted bar to Shauna's booth. Shauna's eyes widened as Carrie approached.

"A whole booth to yourself?" Carrie asked. "You waiting on someone?"

At Shauna's shake of her head, Carrie slid into the booth opposite her.

"No. Just wanted to be alone. Been feeling out of sorts." Shauna's eyes were dark and red rimmed, heavy with badly drawn eyeliner. Her blond hair was scattered and unbrushed over her shoulders, and she wore a tattered green sweatshirt.

"Why? You been beat up by the police?"

Shauna glared at her, her hand tightening around the neck of her beer. Then she glanced away, her teeth pulling at her bottom lip. When she looked back, her eyes glistened.

"Carrie, I . . . I'm sorry for what happened. I owe you an explanation."

Carrie sighed. It was, in truth, the missing puzzle piece. She had worried about her job, her reputation, her Project Mars work, her students. She had nursed her bruises, both physical and emotional. But she had stuffed the actual details about the encounter into a box and put it on a mental shelf in her brain, not willing to examine how she'd gotten into the mess in the first place, unwilling to engage enough with the reality of what had happened to her. Anger at Shauna, and a tiny wisp of guilt for not even checking if she'd been released from police custody, surfaced in her mind, emerging from behind the wall of denial her brain had erected to protect her.

"You mean how I met you and suddenly ended up subject to police investigation?"

"Yes." Shauna swallowed. "I never expected all this to happen. I like you, Carrie. I didn't want something bad to happen to you." Shauna pulled at the label on her beer, rubbing the damp paper pulp between her fingers. "I knew something might happen at the Z Mart, but not when. My brother—he's been in a bad way for a while."

"What do you mean?" Carrie prompted after Shauna had gone silent for several moments.

"He . . . well, we both had a tough time of it. My dad was a bit of a mixed bag. He taught us both to play football, and every year he would take us to a big game. But he also drank, and was always disappearing, until finally he died in a bar fight when I was eleven. My mom tried to keep us afloat through her hair salon, but we were falling short, so I had to take what we needed when I could. My younger brother, Tommy, saw some of that. My mom died of cancer two years later, and when we went into foster care, he started stealing. It was easy to justify because we needed the extra cash, but it changed him. I finished high school and moved away, but Tom . . . he didn't clean up his act."

"Oh," Carrie murmured. "There's a bit of a history, then."

Shauna rubbed her hands over her face. "I feel like I failed him. He got worse and worse. Five years after I moved away, Tom went to prison, and since he got out, work has been tough. He and his girlfriend have targeted stores in the past; they hit the car wash where my cousin works earlier this year. I don't support it, but I don't want to see him suffer. So, sometimes I'd leave the door unlatched, just in case."

"Your brother robbed the Z Mart."

"I don't know," Shauna said, forlorn and confused enough that Carrie couldn't help but believe her. Shauna met her eyes. "I really don't know. No one at the station told me anything."

"But you suspect."

"Yeah."

Carrie nodded. "The police think you did it?"

"I'm still part of their investigation. Because of leaving the door unlocked, and the driving, and . . . my past." Shauna pulled at the drawstring to the hood of her sweatshirt until the fabric pulled in close around her neck. "But they haven't locked me up for it or anything."

Carrie thought of Shauna's string of odd jobs and her recent move to town. Why was she always running?

"So, you really haven't . . . anything recently?" Her mouth skipped over the word *stolen* as if it could save her from making the accusation, from probing into her companion's morality.

"What? No. I'm done with that life. I mean . . ." Shauna shrugged one shoulder. "I want to be. Something happened in my last job. I was a nanny for a wealthy family. And the dad, he was a state senator. He kept hitting on me, you know? Touching me casually. Until it got worse. I was only a year or two younger than his wife, but I was something different, I guess. I got out of there and took three grand from their petty cash stash with me. It's not all that much money compared to what they have, but I keep looking over my shoulder, wondering if they reported me, if he wants to punish me in case I speak out. That's what had me speeding that night."

Shauna had probably risked their lives for nothing, since

the police hadn't even commented on the petty cash when they fingerprinted her. Carrie shook her head. "So you did take something."

"Other than that, not since my early twenties. I keep working these dumb jobs so I don't have to. I sold makeup out of my car for six years because I wanted to visit as many states as I could. I had a roadie gig for a country band and saw even more places. I've done that. And I'm tired now." She offered a tentative smile to Carrie. "It's lonely moving around."

Carrie said nothing. Her family hadn't been rich growing up, and like Shauna, her own mother had died much too early. But mostly, her life had been nothing like the other woman's—especially not after she'd gone to college and law school, entering an elite academic world. Doors had been opened for her that had been closed for Shauna. Still, it would have taken every ounce of empathy and grace within her to express comforting words, when all she wanted was to scream in Shauna's face. She couldn't forget what had happened to her over the last few days. They had both been stopped by the police, but it was always going to be riskier for her. It had been a catastrophic meteor to her life.

Shauna broke the silence. "You're okay, right? They let you go with no issues?"

Carrie thought back to Monday morning. They'd let her go. She hadn't been at the scene of the crime and didn't work at the Z Mart, and she imagined the university had intervened on her behalf.

"Shauna, they let me go, but it has wreaked havoc on my life. The embarrassment of being chewed out by the university president aside, a video of what happened got out and circulated all around campus. Want to tell me how that happened?"

Shauna's eyes blazed. "The world needs to see what they did to you. How they treated you."

Carrie slammed her hand down on the table, rattling the empty beer bottles. "Damn it!" Her anger shocked her and Shauna alike. Shauna blinked. "You can't go around deciding for people—deciding for me—how to handle this. I'm a lawyer. I'm supposed to be teaching my students the value of the rule of law."

"What about the Constitution?" Shauna shot back. "Equal protection of the laws?"

Carrie could not believe Shauna was going to lecture her on the Fourteenth Amendment. She wanted to laugh at the absurdity of the situation. Her, a Black woman, raised by compassionate community leaders who had fought injustice at every turn, and an esteemed law professor no less, lectured by a white woman with an apparent criminal history. On police brutality.

"Shauna," Carrie tried again. "What happened was wrong. And it does make me sick to my stomach. I cannot even describe to you how saddened and angry and disgusted I am. But I've just gotten the biggest career opportunity of my lifetime, and I don't want to throw away my shot. I want to be known for one of the biggest things mankind has ever done, not for what a white man did to me. Okay?"

Shauna said nothing.

"Have you heard of Project Mars?" Carrie tried.

"You mean the thing that billionaire B-Ball is doing?"

"Yes. The experimental colony on Mars."

"Sure, everybody's heard of it."

"Well, I've been chosen to design the system of government for the colony."

Shauna's eyes widened. "No shit."

"Yeah. And that work matters. Can you see that? I've spent my whole career studying and comparing constitutions, all leading up to this moment." Carrie took a deep breath. "I'm asking . . . begging. Please don't mess it up for me."

"I would never," Shauna said.

"Then will you take down the videos?"

"Well, fuck," Shauna said. "I don't think I can—"

"There are a lot of ways to change this world," Carrie interrupted. "Changing the way cops treat people like me is important. For years I've followed the news headlines, anguished at how we've been treated. Being a role model, a beacon of success for future generations, is another way to help the community. Let me be the one to decide how to make an impact. Please."

Shauna paused for a long moment. "Fine," she finally said, her tone heavy. She raised her beer to her lips but found it empty. Carrie caught Hannah's attention, raising her own empty glass, and sat silently, not meeting Shauna's gaze, as Hannah brought over another round of drinks.

Shauna took a long swig of her beer. She cracked a smile.

"Truth be told, I didn't like looking at the video of you. Didn't match the image of a sexy accountant I had in my head. And now I know you're like a dominatrix space commander."

"Oh lord." Carrie groaned. "You know I don't actually get to go to space, right? Or even lead anything. I'm just thinking through how the Project Mars participants will be governed."

"What I'm hearing is that it's not too late for you to be their dominatrix dictator."

"It's a shame you're not turned on by a frustrated professor banging her head against a book written in 1638."

"I never said that."

Carrie wondered what she was doing. She was mad at Shauna. Livid. Shauna was the source of all her problems of late. She and Shauna were nothing alike. But still she felt, overwhelmingly, relief at her grudging willingness to take down the video. The loneliness of her vulnerability and public display still felt like sores on her arms, like she'd been burned and the flesh was still tender and raw. She begged for a salve to soothe her wounds, to let her forget. Even if the source of her relief was the fire that had burned her in the first place.

"Oh lord," Carrie said again. She willed herself to say no, to look anywhere else but at Shauna's playful smirk, or the way her fingers traced the trails of condensation along the beer bottle, or *that look* in Shauna's eyes daring Carrie to rise to the challenge, even after what they'd been through. This would be the last time.

A week later, Carrie could breathe again, even if just the tiniest bit; like when her ex-in-laws finally left after a week-long stay and she could strip the guest bed and reorganize her spice cabinet back the way she liked it. Shauna had taken down the original video, causing all the other reposted videos to disappear. The students had quieted, absorbed with the crush of reading and studying leading up to winter exams. They treated her as nothing more than the font of knowledge standing between them and their A's, content to understand the Supreme Court's dormant commerce clause and strict scrutiny doctrines more than probe into what had happened to her. The professors remained ambivalent and distracted. There had been one reporter who'd called after the university released her public statement, asking whether she'd do an interview for WNTV, the local TV station. But the reporter had been scared away after Carrie told her emphatically that she would not be doing any interviews, and Cameron had nipped in the bud any other media interest. She no longer felt quite like an overstuffed suitcase threatening to burst.

It was good that everyone left her alone, because pressing otherworldly concerns clamored for her attention. In only a week, her little Project Mars constitutional design team —Owen and Adam, the man quickly growing to be her arch-nemesis—would be on her very own campus for their next team meeting.

Five days before their arrival, Carrie convened her research assistants for an informal evening prep session and celebration of the end of final exams. The students kicked cold crusted dirt off their boots on her front porch and entered her living room in winter socks and knit sweaters. Carrie directed everyone to a sideboard she'd loaded with an afternoon's worth of cooking: fresh crumbly gingerbread, savory meat-filled hand pies, and mulled red wine that had simmered for hours with cinnamon sticks and star anise. She settled on a plush armchair and smoothed down her own oversized red sweater. Her three best students gathered their notes and met her in the circle of chairs and love seats.

"Thank you all for coming this evening," she said once everyone had found a spot. "The three of you have been tremendously helpful in pulling together research for Project Mars, and your written memos have been exemplary. I sincerely hope you will all continue on as research assistants next semester."

Evie, Lori, and Parker met her words with general nods and smiles. "Good. Now, this first stage of research has been focused on *how much* direction the colonists will need. What level of control should the government have over the people? Is democracy best, even in the unique environment of space? Or will the colonists benefit from a stronger unifying leader?"

Her students' eyes shone with the same excitement as hers, knowing that they were confronting fundamental understandings of their world and building something unique for the future. Carrie reached for her mulled wine and let the fragrant liquid quell the eager bubble of her stomach.

"You've been working relatively independently, but all of your research interconnects. I'd love for you to get to know each other and see the bigger picture so we can probe into your findings and move forward. Would you mind starting for us, Evie?"

Carrie nodded at a young white woman with a floppy mass of curly reddish-brown hair.

"Sure." Evie set down her hand pie, a chunk of beef spilling out onto her plate, and brushed her hands just above the rip in her jeans. Her toes curled on the carpet in chunky red-and-white checkered knee-high socks as she reached for a tablet resting on the coffee table. "I'm Evie," she said, smiling slightly at the group. "Originally from Ohio. Professor Davenport roped me in because I majored in psychology and got a master's in sociology before I came to law school, so I'm the 'people person,' so to speak. I spent the last few weeks evaluating the unique environment and potential interpersonal dynamics the colonists will face."

Evie took a deep breath. "Long story short, Mars isn't Earth."

Lori let out a low snort. She brushed her waist-length box braids out of her face. "Good catch," she joked. "It's the big red one, I'm pretty sure."

Evie grinned. "The big dusty red one." She swiped on her tablet and pulled up an image of Mars. "Unlike anyplace humans have been before. More dangerous." She zoomed in, the planet coming into focus in more granular detail. "Picture this. You've spent your whole life thus far on Earth. You're crammed in with ninety-nine other astronauts on a spaceship for seven or eight months, traveling millions of miles away from home, impossibly far away. Alone with your thoughts and fears with no escape, your body facing radiation, and isolated from all comforts, including your friends and family. Even if there's a death in the family on Earth or tension among the crew becomes unbearable, you're stuck. Then, you get to Mars, and even more work kicks in. New planet, new home, less gravity, and little autonomy to do any of the things we enjoy on Earth, like . . ."

"Going outside or driving yourself to the store," Carrie supplied.

"Vacation. Having nonwork friends," Parker said.

"Dining out at a restaurant," Lori said.

"Right. Plus, there's the distance thing. A twenty-minute delay in communications with Earth means not being able to talk with the people you love in real time, or with headquarters. A medical emergency that requires knowledge outside the colonists' skill sets will be deadly. How would all that impact the way you relate to other colonists?"

Carrie thought of not being able to call her father, or Kim, if something went wrong. If some incident left her feeling alone and helpless. She stared down at Evie's patterned socks, distracting herself before her thoughts could trail back to that night.

Lori's shoulders slumped. "Guess I won't be going to Mars. I actually like talking to my family and breathing fresh air. How do we know they won't kill each other?"

"NASA has studied people in extreme, isolated situations for years. They've studied research groups at Antarctic stations, for example." Evie scrolled through a couple of pages on her tablet. "Starting back in 2013, NASA conducted missions at a remote location in Hawaii called HI-SEAS that tested things like social cohesion and stress for a group wholly cut off from the real world. Like our astronauts will be."

Evie turned her tablet around and showed an image of a remote outcropping of dark volcanic rock against a wide, undisturbed blue skyline. "This is what HI-SEAS looked like, where the test subjects lived in their little bubble. It taught us basically that . . . shit gets real. Team members in longer missions generally don't spend as much social time together as those in shorter missions. To me, sounds like they get sick of each other, which will particularly be the case for the first class of a hundred before there's a healthy colony of people up there. Conflicts arise. There will be drama, technical mishaps, and unknown risks. By 40 percent of mission completion, most teams report some interpersonal issue. There's this theory called the 'third-quarter phenomenon,' where after the midpoint of the mission, mood levels drop and conflicts blossom. Plus, the more time that passes from launch, the less likely teams are to communicate with mission control about the issue. They tend to fend for themselves and go offline."

"Conflict and isolation together can't be a good mix," Parker mused.

"Yeah. It's a death knell to productivity." Evie bit her lip. "It can be bad, but it's not *all* doom and gloom. A little tension—'creative friction,' they call it—is a good thing. People need to challenge each other, and members of the group need to feel productive."

"Interesting," Carrie said. "To me, that sounds like it's better to have a government that gives more citizens an active role, rather than a select few, to allow for that feeling of involvement and friction. And that tracks with what NASA found with its Artemis mission to the moon?"

Carrie thought a few years back to the Artemis launch and the general feeling of possibility it inspired—for her, and for millions of people around the world. She would've never guessed back then that she'd be involved in sending humans even farther from home.

"Generally, yes. Artemis doesn't tell us much about long-term space governance because the mission was shorter than ours. Mainly, we learned that we can house and feed people in space for a long time. But it tracks with decades of data from astronauts on the International Space Station and from organizational psychologists."

"Good. And I note, Project Mars concurs with all of NASA's data," Carrie explained. "Evie and I both reviewed the Project Mars astrosociologists' reports. The goal should be avoiding excessive fracturing to prevent infighting—in other words, not letting people get too divided; we've seen what a mess that is on Earth. We want to keep the colonists engaged, minimize conflicts, and maintain an ongoing dialogue with headquarters for as long as possible. We don't want them to be so independent that they never report back to Project Mars." Carrie turned and nodded in Parker's direction. "And this all ties in to the work you did, Parker."

"Yeah." Parker smoothed out the wrinkles of a comfortable striped sweater with an Exeter patch on the breastbone and glanced over at Evie's tablet. "It fits in perfectly."

Parker withdrew a slim Moleskine notebook from their satchel and gave a half wave to the group. "I'm Parker, *they/them* pronouns. I'm originally from Vietnam but grew up in Connecticut." They took a sip of mulled wine. "I studied the success of different forms of government, particularly during acute moments of stress for citizen populations —whether an authoritarian government versus a democracy does a better job at handling, say, a natural disaster or an uprising. In other words, a big conflict."

"My question for Parker was whether democracy is best, no matter the circumstances," said Carrie. "Globally, studies show that most people favor a representative democracy over other forms of government, including autocracy, military rule, or communism. I wanted to know whether the same would hold true in light of Evie's research on the conflicts that will arise."

"When it comes to conflict, I read studies showing huge citizen support for authoritarian regimes after a crisis. For example, after the 2010 forest fires in Russia destroyed many rural villages, the government promptly provided aid and in-person attention to those citizens, which actually really helped with their satisfaction and trust in government. Essentially, when an authoritarian government responds by actually being helpful, it's an effective form of government in times of crisis," Parker said.

"Somewhere far away, Professor Kilpatrick is getting chills at your Russia comparison," Lori joked.

Parker let out a short laugh. "Probably. But overall, most studies show major citizen grievances with leadership when things go wrong. People question the legitimacy of their leaders. As people get angrier and society gets more unstable, most authorities crack down with coercive violence to reassert control. That leads to repression by the government, for both democracies and authoritarian regimes. Now, a little bit of repression may be helpful"—Parker winced—"in outer space, where we may need to control the colonists and make sure they don't majorly disrupt the Project—as long as we can effectively address the issue. But only a little bit."

Carrie stood, fetched the gingerbread, and passed the platter around. "So, it sounds like the difference is how quickly and effectively the government reestablishes control during a crisis . . . and how much violence they use to do it." Her mind whirred with the implications. A space commander needed to regain order quickly, but not at the expense of treating people fairly. She chewed on a slice of gingerbread.

Parker tugged a hand through the dark waves of their mohawk, studying their notes. "Yeah," they said after a long moment of concentration. "Bottom line is democracies are more measured in their response. They use less violence and give people the option to vote their leaders out. It's a more stable choice in the long term, and we want that."

Carrie nodded. *Less violence.* "Right. Okay." She breathed out heavily. "A lot to think about. How about we take a fifteen-minute break before turning to Lori, and we can try to wrap up in the next half hour?"

Carrie stood and excused herself, then made her way to the kitchen to refill her mug of mulled wine. She took the mug of steaming liquid and quietly slid open the door to the back deck. Outside, the air was frigid and still, the bare trees stoic in the darkness. She leaned against the deck railing and stared up at the sky, where the first stars were just beginning to appear. Her free hand rubbed her opposite shoulder as she clung to the warmth from inside.

She'd pushed Parker to study other types of governments alongside democracies because she didn't want to leave any stone unturned. She hadn't been gunning for an authoritarian government for general oppression's sake, but she didn't want to assume, as Adam had, that democracy was the default when it came to space. From all she'd studied over the last few weeks, representative democracy indeed made the most sense. But that conclusion, even if legally correct, nagged at her. The real problem was that their current democracy, which many Americans held up as a gleaming beacon of governance, didn't seem to be working very well. The prior few days still haunted her, as had Parker's words moments earlier. Democracies weren't meant to inflict *violence* on law-abiding citizens. But what happened when the law failed those citizens, like it had her?

"Professor Davenport?"

Carrie jumped so quickly that a hot rush of wine sloshed out of the mug onto her hand. She brought her thumb to her lips. "Sorry, Lori, you scared the hell out of me."

Lori had approached the railing with her own mug of wine. She bore an apologetic smile.

"Sorry. I was just going to say, we don't have to go over

my research today. You have my memo already, so you know it's a ringing endorsement of how much happier citizens are in democracies. I can update Evie and Parker later."

Carrie's eyebrows raised, and she pivoted to face Lori more fully. She'd asked Lori to study citizen happiness in democracies around the world. Lori's memo had summarized her finding that most people supported democracy despite feeling that as a practical matter it functioned poorly in their country. "You know that I'm proud of your research, and I have nothing against—"

"Democracy. I know," Lori finished. "And I'm proud of your research, too."

"Me?" Carrie laughed. She wondered whether she should stop supplying her students with wine at their research meetings.

"Yeah. I just mean . . ." Lori bit her lip, smudging her brown lip gloss. "With everything that has happened, not just to you but in our country, year after year . . . I'm proud of you. And me. And this team. For doing our best to provide the colonists with an experience even better than ours."

Carrie studied Lori. Beyond the twist of her lip there was the wrinkle of a frown between her brows, a deep embedded line like she'd frowned this way many times before. Her eyes were glistening, but she wasn't crying. She was . . . remembering. "Is there something in particular you're thinking of?" Carrie asked, her voice low.

"I . . . my brother. Brothers, I should say. Liam and Ray."

"Are you worried something will happen to them?"

"It already did." Her fingers tightened around the mug of wine. "When my younger brother, Liam, was in high school, someone alerted the school that a student had brought a gun. We lived in rural Indiana at the time, and Liam was one of few Black students, so the campus officer immediately thought it was him. The police roughed him up, and while they were doing that, a white student shot five classmates."

Carrie's throat was so dry she could barely speak. "That's awful," she whispered.

"That was bad. But when my older brother, Ray, led a peaceful protest against how Liam had been treated . . . that was worse. A fight broke out, they arrested him, and he was expelled from his university. He was a chemical engineering student."

Carrie blinked so heavily she didn't know if her eyes would open again. She reached for Lori's hand and squeezed it. "I'm so sorry. I am so sorry your brothers and your family had to endure that." All the anger and shame and powerlessness Carrie had experienced must've rocked Lori tenfold over the last few years. And yet, here she was, a student at one of the country's most prestigious law schools, delving deep into groundbreaking research. Not only still standing but making an unshakeable mark on the world.

Lori squeezed Carrie's hand back. "Thank you. I didn't realize . . . I mean, when I accepted this position, it was the most incredible opportunity to see firsthand how government would work in space. But now it's more than that. It's . . . things have to be better."

Carrie raised her mug and clinked it to Lori's. "To a better future."

"Yeah." Lori smiled. "And I mean, I know it sounds stupid, but I had this line in my memo about how democracy permits a single individual to bring about change. I think maybe we can go further."

Carrie didn't respond. She didn't dare ask what "further" meant. She took a long gulp of wine, and in the quiet, she could hear through the open porch door the tick of the grandfather clock she kept in the hall. It was getting late. She beckoned Lori inside and found Evie and Parker slumped in a mild food coma on the living room couch. Carrie quickly suppressed a laugh.

"Ahem. As we're running out of time and you two are drunk off of hand pies, we'll call it here. Thank you, truly, for your contributions. You're going to improve the lives of hundreds of explorers. In the spring, we'll need to transition into building the democracy—what values matter most, and what ideals need to be translated into constitutional text. I'm already counting the days to the start of next semester."

"Thank you, Professor." Evie and Parker offered sleepy smiles, and Lori's smile in return was so genuine it made her heart ache. She sent each of her students home with a foil-wrapped package of gingerbread. The productivity of the evening lulled her into a sated satisfaction. They were building something real, something big, and they were going to get it right.

9

CARRIE PACED on the sidewalk outside Lexington Hall as two black cars wound up the snow-speckled hill, tracing the curved driveway leading to the historic central building. Their approach filled her with a deep sense of purpose. She'd spent the last week poring over her notes and her research assistants' memos to refamiliarize herself with all their research. Her constitutional design team was on the right track to create the best possible government for the space colonists. They would meet today, come to an agreement, and after Christmas they'd start the next phase of honing the government's democratic ideals, drawing on the fresh energy of the new year.

As long as she didn't kill Adam. Carrie couldn't help but hope that whichever black car carried Adam would suffer a setback. She wasn't asking for him to be pulled from the car and beaten by the police. That only happened to . . . her. But maybe the car doors would malfunction and fail to unlock. Maybe he'd spill coffee onto his lap and hide in the car in hot-coffee-stained shame. Maybe he'd suffer an asthma attack from the driver's cologne and . . .

"Carrie!" Adam Kilpatrick stepped from the first black car, unencumbered by coffee stains or anaphylaxis. His cheeks flushed red as his pale face met the winter's cold, but he grinned. Carrie blinked. She studied his face even closer as his grin broadened and twisted. Almost like . . . a smirk. His thin lips cracked in the cold as if they'd never been asked to contort themselves into such a smile. She nearly grumbled as Owen's arrival distracted her from dissecting Adam's relative glee.

"It may be winter, but I'm still trying to get some of that North Carolina barbecue!" Owen bellowed. "Glad to be here." He wrapped her in a one-armed hug as he stepped out of his car and up to the sidewalk. Carrie fumbled for a second but eventually leaned into his brief embrace.

"I'm glad we can make some progress. And I didn't forget about the barbecue, I promise. Let me show you to the room we'll be in today."

Carrie led the group up the storied front steps and into a large conference room in the central building, which offered a sweeping view of the main campus. An oval conference table faced floor-to-ceiling windows that let in a sweeping view.

Adam headed for the seat at the head of the oval table, and Carrie stepped closer to him.

"Ah, Professor Kilpatrick. I don't want you to miss this stunning view. Please, if you sit to the side here, you'll be able to appreciate the full effect."

Carrie slid into the head seat before Adam could protest. "If I could introduce you to my faculty assistant, Anna

Nguyen. She'll be sitting at the table with us and taking notes."

Carrie did not look up at Adam, instead scrolling through her notes as he and Owen settled at the table. Once everyone had seated themselves, she looked up again.

"As you'll recall," she jumped in, "last meeting we discussed a timeline for our report, certain sources we'd all read, and this first stage of the project, which involved determining what form of government, including democracy, is the right starting point. Each of us has thought hard about that question, and it will be good to discuss it today."

"A short discussion, I presume," Adam murmured in his low baritone. "For there never really has been a doubt that democracy is the best course."

Carrie gritted her teeth. "Yes, well. Why don't you go first, Adam?"

"Happy to. Now, it was our esteemed leader Jefferson who once said in a letter to Madison that 'we should have such an empire for liberty' as has never been seen since the creation. He was 'persuaded no constitution was ever before so well calculated as ours for extensive empire and self-government.' And our Constitution, as you know, is founded on democracy." He rolled his hand with a flourish. "Those who believe in the theory of a human right to democracy go so far as to say that all human individuals, everyone everywhere, have a positive moral right to live in a democratic state that maintains the rule of law, regardless of history, culture, or geographic location. And, with that in mind, let's turn, then, to some of our foundational scholars."

"Great," Carrie said, she hoped unironically.

"Now, Carrie, I presume that you've read *The Federalist Papers* authored by our great founding fathers? I'd hope even a freshman political science major has done so. Many high schoolers now, even—"

"Yes," Carrie interrupted.

"Good. Well, in *The Federalist Papers* number ten, we learn that a well-constructed democracy does a key thing: it will 'break and control the violence of faction.' That is key in a society like ours with so many, ahem, *minority* viewpoints. The founders warn that 'the unsteadiness and injustice' of a factious spirit will taint our public administrations."

Carrie proceeded to, at that point and for her own sanity, tune out. Adam proceeded to, for his part and without pause, launch into a monologue that roused the passions of him and him alone about the sources he had read. He delivered an impassioned recitation of Montesquieu's idea that a state must have a separation of powers among the legislative, executive, and judicial authority. He retreated to eighteenth-century England and Blackstone's musings on the role of the king, to whom the law ascribes "not only large powers and emoluments which form his prerogative and revenue" but also "attributes of a great and transcendent nature; by which the people are led to consider him in the light of a superior being," to warn that modern government should not place one person on such a pedestal—either monarch or dictator. He concluded with a stream of dead white men who shared his ideals, from John Adams's "Thoughts on Government" to George Washington's private letters, and a scathing rebuke of the more recent work of John Rawls in *A Theory of Justice*. Finally, with a small bow and an hour of their time down the drain, he closed his leather padfolio and sat back. She could've sworn his glance around the room was a stunned and silent question as to why no one had applauded.

Owen had been picking at his cuticles for the last half

hour, but his gaze snapped up as silence settled over the room. "Excellent work," Owen said. "I have to agree. I think. While I wouldn't put it quite like that, I've got a lot of data from the Hill on citizen satisfaction with democracy."

Carrie glanced at the clock. "Okay, Owen, shoot."

"Let me pull up some charts on the screen."

She perked up at the opportunity to look at something other than Adam's face.

"Looky here. The last thirty years have seen some of the most dysfunctional politics I've ever witnessed. Congress doesn't deserve a damn penny we pay them. But, based on Pew Research, as of 2030 most Americans still say democracy is working in the United States. Not very well, but well enough." He flicked to a new chart done in blue and red. "There's a big partisan divide here. We've got 72 percent of Republicans saying that democracy is working at least somewhat well, while only 48 percent of Democrats say the same. By two to one, the Democrats say that significant changes are needed in the design and structure of government."

Owen flicked to another slide. "I don't think the fuss the Dems are raising is cause for us to change course. You've still got 40 percent of Americans saying the US political system is the best in the world or above average, and 70 percent of people think it's at least average or better. Average isn't the ringing endorsement we might want, but by this measure, we're also not trying to copy what anyone else is doing."

"What's the initial takeaway, Owen?" Carrie asked.

"Confidence in democracy has majorly eroded, but I don't think it's time to move on from it. People still think it's better than the alternative. So, let's not throw the baby out with the bathwater. We can keep democracy as a general matter but think critically about how to keep it from becoming as dysfunctional as it has been in the past. We need to design the government more carefully to avoid such an unshakeable two-party system and partisan divide."

"How do we set the colony up for success?" Carrie asked.

Owen heaved out a huge breath. "To be honest? After decades on the Hill, I've seen a million things die by committee. I think if the colonists get to Mars stressed and tired and start trying to negotiate over everything, it'll result in chaos and hurt feelings. We need a clear vision and strong hand to kick things off. Then they can debate the finer points later. I suggest we put a leader in place for the two-year experimental colony to set some initial rules, and let them try a representative democracy after that."

"Now, wait a minute," Adam chided. "Putting a leader in place is inherently undemocratic. I agree that the general citizenry can be misinformed and disengaged, but the founding fathers still thought that . . ."

"I haven't read all the sources you have, Adam, but I've seen how people work in practice," Owen said. "They retreat to their worst instincts, even under the system the founding fathers set up. That's too much pressure early on . . . and in space. I don't know if we can draw all our conclusions from two centuries ago."

"These principles aren't outdated. They're from trustworthy, historical sources. Good men and good leaders."

None of it sounded good anymore. They'd settled on a democracy of some fashion, but the very democracy she lived in had allowed a toxic culture to surface, such that law enforcement designed to keep her safe had not only criminalized her without basis but harmed her. Putting a strong leader in place might keep society from going off the rails, from allowing a leader to rise to power who would undermine the colony's success. But on the other hand, that person could doom the colonists more than any representative democracy could. Who could be trusted to fill such a role?

Carrie took a deep breath. "My research confirmed the conclusions you both reached, that democracy is likely the best approach." She briefly summarized the results of her own weeks of reading and the discussion with her research assistants, her voice hollow as she listed her sources. At least she'd had women and people of color on her reading list.

"As for anything else, why don't we take our lunch break now, and after lunch we can talk about next steps?" she offered.

They proceeded downstairs to the faculty dining room, empty now that the semester had ended, where Carrie had brought in a full smorgasbord of barbecue. Although both men had trudged into the room a bit disgruntled by their disagreement, they perked up at the sight of the feast. They fixed plates of hickory-smoked beef brisket, seasoned pulled pork, fall-off-the-bone ribs, and potato salad, and sat at one of the four-top tables.

"I'm glad you're on board with democracy, Carrie," Adam said as he cut a tiny sliver of brisket for himself and carefully chewed. He ate his meat dry, and she wondered if he'd choke on the meat. Across the table, Owen slathered on a thorough helping of gold sauce.

"Our government is strong and principled. Smart, worthy leaders have done the right thing time after time. Our institutions are foolproof. We have our laws and our police force to keep us safe and to apprehend the worst of society. I stand fully with the police."

Carrie had liberally buttered a roll, but she set it down. What was he getting at?

"Law enforcement has to face the tough reality that certain types of people are more likely to commit crimes, and act accordingly. Some suspects just take more manhandling than others. Some women."

Carrie stared past Adam at a fixed point over his left ear, feeling her world fall apart like someone had pulled out the one Jenga block that was her undoing. Adam had seen the video—and he felt no remorse at taunting her about it.

She took a sip of sweet tea and cleared her throat, willing away the lump that was forming. "To what specifically are you referring?"

"Professor Davenport. I saw the video," he said, his voice sweet and smug, condescending like he'd caught a child midway through stealing a cookie from the jar. "And I would not want it to cause you to question any of our institutions. These structures have been successful and must be written into whatever world order we establish."

"I don't believe I have ever expressed disagreement with that point."

Oh, but had she. Even if she hadn't expressed it to him, her thoughts had run wild. How could they enshrine institutions that were clearly failing into the pristine new world order that Project Mars represented? Traveling to a new planet meant a fresh start. They could learn from the last millennia and avoid the prejudice, bigotry, and shortsightedness espoused by so many former societies. And yet, her country had clearly learned nothing at all. Because nearly two hundred years after her ancestors had been freed from slavery, after the country had waxed poetic again and again after the Civil Rights Movement that *all men were created equal (and we really mean it this time)*, her government still treated her as less than. If Adam had his way, the same thing would happen in space. The only barrier to his line of thinking was her.

And what could she even do about it?

"Nevertheless, the concern remains," Adam said. "The success of this project is vital. The colonists need someone who can think objectively about the law. We owe them a government that will keep them safe and in order. What happened in the video compromises your judgment on the success of American democracy. I would not object if you needed me to take over leadership of the committee."

"For the love of god—" she started to snap.

"This barbecue sauce is heavenly," Owen interrupted loudly. He had finished his brisket and the mound of pulled pork formerly on his plate and held a rib in his hand. "The thing about North Carolina is the sauce here is so vinegary. You don't find it in Texas barbecue. Not that I'd ever speak ill of Texas barbecue." He held up his non-rib hand in defense.

It was a hard pivot, but Carrie grabbed hold of it like a life preserver before she lost her cool. "You've really got three camps of sauce," she explained, retreating to the comfort of her professor role. "North Carolina gold, which has got a great mustard-and-brown-sugar base; a vinegar camp in the eastern part of the state; and then a more tomato-based version in the west. You're getting a good sampling of all three." Carrie dunked her roll into the gold sauce pooled on her plate. If she concentrated on the fluffy roll soaking up the sweet sauce, she could turn off the complete panic racking her brain that, absent Owen's intervention, she'd been seconds away from losing the thing that mattered most to her. It was unsurprising that Adam, as someone who'd been unable to publish a halfway decent article in years, would gleefully leap at the opportunity to usurp control over a highly publicized endeavor and enshrine his values in space. If she lost her cool again, he'd probably succeed.

"Some of these sauces have a kick!" Owen raised a conspiratorial eyebrow.

"Just because they're sweet doesn't mean they won't bite," she said. *And some of us better not forget it.*

"I hear ya," Owen said with a chuckle. "I come from a big Texas football family, and four out of us six siblings played. If any of us won on a Friday night, my mother would host a huge barbecue at our house for Saturday lunch. Burgers, hot dogs, and brisket. Pound cake, too. My brother and I would fight like cats and dogs all day. He was a senior in high school, and I made it on the team as a freshman. He'd always try to beat up on me for outshining him on the field. But my mom, she was a peacekeeper. There's no messing with a strong woman. Especially not a Texas woman with a voice louder than hell."

Carrie reached for the tongs and placed the last rib on Owen's plate with an appreciative smile. *Amen.*

"Taught me how to keep the peace, too. It came in handy when I played college ball, since we were all idiots on the team. But really, it came in handy after I got hurt and had to quit the Cowboys. Got my first job on a political campaign. An election is just a fight between two people who think they know best how the other side should live. And once you get to the Hill, it's a game of who likes who, and who would drop dead before supporting a political opponent's bill. I've heard more catfights behind closed doors than I care to recount."

"Our country's fearless leaders," she said under her breath.

Owen let out a huff of air. "Hey, now. If they were more

competent, they wouldn't need overpaid political consultants like me. And I like my paycheck, thank you very much. From Project Mars, too. I may not understand all the history and legal jargon like the two of you, but I'm glad to be a part of this team. We should be proud we've been working so well together. Keeping things civil. For the benefit of the colonists."

There was a long pause, in which Carrie fixed her eyes on her plate to avoid looking at Adam. She wasn't sure *civil* described his behavior, or the string of curse words ricocheting in her head.

Finally, after the pause stretched on long enough that Carrie started to wonder whether Adam really had choked on his brisket, there was a small cough.

"The food was good," Adam ground out begrudgingly. "But unnecessarily messy. I'm going to wash my hands."

She tracked his departure as he exited the faculty dining room. There was a tight set to his shoulders as he walked away. She felt as stiff as a board herself. In their world of democracy, she was staving off her own coup.

She didn't say anything for a long moment, and Owen didn't either.

"Did you see the video?" She asked finally.

Owen opened his mouth, then closed it. He nodded. "I saw it before it got taken down."

She didn't meet his gaze.

"Hey, I'm sorry that happened to you. I wanted to send you an email, but I thought it might sound disingenuous based on some of the senators I've worked with. I mean it, though. My dad was a cop, and I'd like to think he wouldn't hurt anybody like that."

Owen was different than she'd imagined when she first

met him at the press conference. He was a politically minded moderate, blowing whichever way the paycheck took him, but he wasn't cold hearted or stubborn like Adam.

"Thank you. Your idea about an initial installed leader . . . Adam may disagree, but I'm willing to keep it in mind. I'll see what I can do."

"Spectacular," Owen said. "The right person could lay a strong foundation for a stable colony."

Maybe. If anyone was trustworthy enough.

"In any event, this barbecue alone was worth the trip out here," Owen said, easing back into his chair. "I'll be sleepy this afternoon. Not too sleepy, though, to discuss next steps." He laughed easily, wiping his hands on a moist towelette, then took a deep swig of Coke. "Especially with this caffeine. I'm looking forward to whatever plan you lay out for us, Carrie. I'm at your mercy."

If only Adam were so easy.

With the semester's exams and her Project Mars meeting complete, mid-December rolled into the holidays. It was a time of year that often left her feeling unsettled. After Carrie's mother had died, she and her father spent that first Christmas alone. They sat in the living room ignoring the third couch cushion, where Carrie's mother used to sit, pretending the store-bought glazed ham and potato salad were better than the creamy, tangy potato salad her mother used to make with a dusting of paprika on top or the marshmallow gooeyness of her sweet potato casserole. After that first depressing Christmas, they made a pact to never spend the holidays alone. For the next few years, they celebrated

Christmas with her mother's sister, Viola, and, when Viola eventually died, Carrie's crotchety Uncle Steve. It was easy when Carrie was married for her father to join her and Devon at the North Carolina house. Until her marriage failed. With Devon gone and her father's lung cancer diagnosis, she clung to their holidays together even more fiercely.

Kim had saved the day this year, as she had last year, too. It was a relief for Carrie and her father to make the road trip to Washington, DC, to Kim's Potomac McMansion. They arrived late the day before Christmas Eve, and Carrie collapsed on the pull-out sofa in the den while her father eased into the comfortable guest bedroom upstairs.

The next morning, after a Christmas Eve breakfast of waffles and bacon that, mercifully, Kim's husband, Brian, had made before heading to the hospital, Carrie and her father settled into the deep-cushioned couch in the living room. Kim's daughters Gabby, Naomi, and Imani plopped on the floor in front of them and clicked a series of remotes until a Disney movie came to life on the impossibly large flat-screen TV.

"Auntie Carrie," Naomi said as she sidled up to the couch's armrest. She extracted a red-polka-dot-wrapped present from behind her back, her mischievous eyes sparkling. "What did you get me for Christmas?" She gave the box a little shake.

Carrie tugged the end of one of Naomi's four braids, her fingers wrapped around the tiny pink barrette at the end. "I don't know if there's anything inside. It's awfully naughty to steal presents from under the Christmas tree. Maybe it's coal," she teased.

Naomi shook her head vehemently. "It's not naughty if the present is for you."

"Hmm. That's some good reasoning, I suppose. Well, I'll say this. When you unwrap it tomorrow, I think it'll be just as fun to shake." Carrie had searched for hours to find someone who could handcraft a snow globe with her goddaughter inside, a tiny little Black figure inside a dome, with star-shaped snow and a dark background meant to represent space.

Naomi's eyes widened even more, darting around the room as her mind turned over the puzzle.

Carrie laughed and pulled Naomi onto her lap. She wrapped the little girl in a hug from behind and breathed in deep—her goddaughter smelled of bar soap, leave-in conditioner run through her tight curls, and maple-syrup sweetness from the waffles. She threw a blanket over them as the opening credits of *Encanto* began to play on the enormous screen, Carrie's father nodding along to the opening song.

By the time Mirabel had saved her family's home, Carrie's eyes were drooping. She barely noticed as the girls scampered away to choreograph a holiday dance to perform that night. She had been pushing herself hard with work, and battling the frustrations with Adam, and . . . everything. Her body sagged like a stone into the cushions.

"Carrie, baby," her father said softly. She slowly opened her eyes. The room had dimmed as the wash of morning sun faded into fainter afternoon light. Her father still sat on the couch next to her, but now he held a mug of tea in each hand. He nudged her awake, the back of one hand pressing into the soft flesh of her shoulder. "I don't mean to wake you. But I was hoping you would tell me something."

She rubbed her eyes and sat up, readjusting the blanket over her and accepting the mug of spiced tea. She surveyed her father. He had started shaving his head ten years ago after he'd had enough of the gray, and the top of his head was taut compared to the wrinkles creasing the skin at the corners of his eyes and under his chin. His breathing, slightly raspy, a little breathless, had become a constant in the background for her, though his hands were steady around his mug.

"What is it, Daddy?"

"Kim and I were in the kitchen earlier, and she told me that you've had a bit of trouble recently."

"Oh." She should've known better than to leave her father and Kim alone in the same room.

"Why didn't you tell me?" His voice reminded her of her teenage years, of walking in past midnight to find him sitting at the kitchen table waiting for her.

"I didn't want you to worry."

"You let me worry about what I want to worry about."

She sighed. "Okay." She took a long sip of spiced tea and closed her eyes. She let the liquid give her strength, wondering whether Kim had stashed away anything stronger that she could use to spike her tea. Then she steeled herself and told her father in sparse terms about what had happened with the police and with Adam.

"The way they treated you isn't right," he said, practically cutting her off as she finished recounting the near coup at the latest Project Mars meeting. His voice rumbled with anger, not at all feeble now. "It's not right."

"I know."

"No, you don't know. I grew up watching my father struggle to get work because no one wanted to hire a Black man with a limp, even if he only got his disability fighting for a country that never loved him back. I risked my life in my twenties alongside your mother, marching on the front lines just so we could have equal education and housing and all the basic things we deserve. Safety. Freedom. There's a long legacy of white folks beating us down, and of your very family shedding blood, sweat, and tears trying to fight back. I thought we had made some progress for your generation. And yet, all these years later, my own adult daughter is pushed into the ground by the damn police." He coughed, and his shoulders shook. "I have half a mind to stay a few months in North Carolina with you to set those cops back in their place."

"Dad," she said heavily. "It's fine."

"It's not fine!" he exclaimed. "Nobody lays a finger on my child. I could kill them for that."

"I'm okay now." The bruises had thankfully healed before she'd had to face her father. The physical ones, at least.

"Carrie, what are you going to do about this?"

"Nothing!" she said. Her voice rose more than she intended. "I want life to continue like normal."

"Normal? Carrie, baby, those cops ripped apart any sense of what's normal and good. We can't retreat to the status quo."

Her face flooded with heat. "Well, then, I don't know! I don't know what I want to do, or what I can do. I've got a job, I've got a big project, and . . . I don't know! I'm angry, too, but I just don't see . . ." She grabbed fistfuls of blanket and clenched, squeezing the fabric tightly in both hands and begging her tear ducts not to let her down.

Carrie's father pushed himself to his feet and slowly paced the room, eventually stopping so that he stood over her. He leveled a long pointer finger in her direction. "Now, I'm sorry for what happened to you. Believe me, I am heart-broken. But your mother did not die fighting for our community for you to cower in the princess tower of your white institution and ignore what you need to do."

"Dad, please," she begged. "What could I possibly do? I'm not allowed to speak out."

"When has that ever stopped anyone?" His own voice grew stronger, louder, as they argued. Both their heads whipped around at approaching footsteps.

"Holiday cookies?" Kim asked cheerily, bearing a red lacquered platter towering with sugar cookies. "Not made by me, I swear, but from a fancy bakery that charges a million dollars a cookie and—" She trailed off as she grew aware of the tension cutting hot and thick in the room.

"You told my dad?" Carrie glowered.

Kim gaped. "Er. Did I just hear Santa on the rooftop? Let me run him these cookies or I won't be getting the Louboutins I asked for." She took a slow step away from her living room.

"It's alright, Kim. Here, bring one of those cookies over. You did the right thing by letting me know." He chose a Rudolph cookie and pried off the red gumdrop nose, then popped it into his mouth.

"I've thought about it," Carrie said quietly to the room at large. "What I can do to make a difference."

Kim sat on the couch next to Carrie and handed her a cookie. "How you want to respond to what happened?"

"Yeah. I know that I should speak out about the incident. But every time I think about stepping into the limelight, I panic."

"You don't want the national attention."

"Not for this. I don't want to be a victim," Carrie said. "I don't want to be a Black Lives Matter figure. I'm so much more than what happened to me. I want to do something that fits who I am and the resources I bring to the table."

"You're no victim," her father said. "I'm not asking you to be one. But there's value in using your platform."

"My platform?"

Her father cocked his head. "You're a professor. A scholar. A key player in a multi-billion-dollar space endeavor. Just to name a few things."

"I do want my students to understand some of these broader issues."

"So, your course syllabus is gonna read 'Anyone who enters this classroom supporting the police will get a one-way ticket to Mars, sans space suit,'" Kim joked.

"Yes, exactly. Maybe I'd change the wording." Carrie cracked a small smile. "I could devote a class or two to teaching them the history and law of police violence."

Carrie's father took another cookie and sank back down on the couch by Carrie's side. He patted her knee. "You don't have to march in the streets. That's not what I'm saying. But if you raise your voice, baby, I know you can change the world. And I think you need to."

Kim leaned in close to Carrie and pressed her lips to Carrie's ear. "Not to ruin the father-daughter moment but . . . yeah. Fuck the racists."

10

Two days into the new year, Carrie sat at her kitchen island back at home with a tub of leftover chocolate chip cookies that she, Kim, and the girls had made over the holidays. The treetops this morning glistened with a white dusting of snow, and Carrie watched thin flurries fall over her backyard as she dipped a cookie into her morning coffee—the breakfast of champions.

Her father's words had plagued her for over a week now, slipping into her thoughts during the day and running rampant in her dreams at night, which were angry and red, as if the ancestors had descended in their full shame and anger to condemn her for not doing enough. For not rising to the occasion, to the unique challenge they had given her. She *had* to do something. Even if only to save her sheets from the nightly soaking of sweat.

She was ready.

Since the Incident, Carrie had shuffled any and all emails inquiring about what had happened—from the local TV station, the regional newspapers, and every non-Briar email address—to a folder she'd labeled "Do Not Open." It was a Pandora's box—open it, and she'd be burned. She had been adamantly ignoring the folder for weeks, even though she had received nearly ninety emails.

Now, with a foreboding feeling, Carrie clicked on the folder. She scrolled through the first twenty or so emails, scanning the subject lines.

WNTV Wants To Interview You About Your Police Encounter
The North Carolina Sun is interested in your experience
Time for coffee with the African American Studies department?
Video Interview with Students for Police Abolition USA
Top Civil Rights Lawyer -- Call Me For Representation
Blue Lives Matter Coalition Mid-Atlantic—Any Chance You'd Speak on the Record?

Carrie didn't even know what she wanted, exactly, by contacting a reporter. To become a nationwide sensation would give her nightmares worse than the ones she already had. The only thing that really made sense was to temper the message the university had sent out. Even that made her skin itch when she thought of Miriam's wrath.

Carrie stopped scrolling when she spotted an email from Kandace Pinkney. *Would you be willing to chat with me for an episode of The Black Box?*

Kandace Pinkney. She'd started a podcast six years ago, after the police killing of a pregnant woman on the subway had shaken the nation. The Black Box broke down news stories and tough issues to understand how an incident was shaped by larger history and politics—inspired by prying into a plane's black box after a crash to discover what went wrong. Kandace was thoughtful, funny, and a little academic, backing up her stories with well-researched facts and data from peer-reviewed studies. The students liked her, professors respected her, and her friends and former classmates tuned in solemnly. Most important, a podcast would mean Carrie wouldn't be staring into the harsh, hot lights of the local television studio and wouldn't be subject to a reporter's spin.

This could work, she thought. She typed out an email to Kandace and pressed Send. *Take that, Dad.*

Low lighting bathed the Briar lecture hall in a muted glow as Carrie entered ten days later. Tucked in the basement of Eads Hall, the forty-person lecture hall had a few rows of auditorium-style chairs that framed the intimate space. As she approached, Carrie spotted a petite Black woman standing in the first row with a few students who'd arrived early. She had dark skin and long caramel-colored locs pooled on top of her head, and she was wearing a pale-pink blazer and jeans. Her expression was earnest and engaged as she chatted with the students. Her face lacked the same wrinkles Carrie was just starting to sport between her brows and at the corners of her eyes; it didn't surprise Carrie to see her smooth, youthful skin since Kandace spoke with that Gen Z spitfire energy. Carrie had been certain when she'd reached out to Kandace that they'd do a remote video interview—Kandace in her Brooklyn studio, Carrie in the safety of her home office. But Kandace routinely recorded podcast episodes on college campuses, in bookstores, or at rallies, and this episode had, according to Kandace, been prime for an on-campus taping at Briar.

Boo.

At least the university had signed off: she'd explained to them that she only wanted to set the record straight and highlight her academic work. And at least it would be quick: The audience had already seen what had happened that night. Carrie planned to explain her solution to address the issue going forward, and she'd be done with the whole affair. Carrie reached into her pocket and reapplied brown lipstick before she stepped up to Kandace. Two young women holding canvas *Black Box* tote bags and markers in hand parted to make space for Carrie, their eyes never leaving Kandace as she finished an energetic story about a spiritual healer she'd sat next to on the plane ride to Briar.

"Excuse me, ladies," Kandace said as she spotted Carrie out of the corner of her eye. "We've got an important guest here." Kandace smiled warmly at Carrie and, rather than a handshake, squeezed her upper arm, a gesture that felt intimate and knowing.

"Welcome to Briar. It's an honor to meet you."

Carrie had been prepared to usher Kandace to the stage, but Kandace beat her to it, stepping up onto the low wooden platform and settling herself in a low armchair. Carrie perched on the armchair opposite her while someone from Kandace's team pinned microphones to their lapels. She said nothing as crowds of students poured into the space as if floodgates had been opened. Within moments, the room grew stuffy. She recognized some students from her classes, but otherwise it was a sea of unfamiliar, mostly brown faces, first packing into the rows of auditorium seats and then pressing themselves against the back wall.

Kandace's assistant handed Carrie a water bottle. "Thirty seconds, and then we're on."

Kandace studied her notes in a small leather notebook, and after a beat looked up and nodded at Carrie.

"The plane has crashed, and we're here to bear witness to the stories of the survivors. This is *The Black Box*, and I'm your host, Kandace Pinkney." She paused, and Carrie could almost hear the intro music that accompanied every episode, the blend of hip-hop, jazz, and the *Law & Order* theme song listeners had come to know. In the room, though, there was a beat of silence, and Carrie's stomach knotted in anticipation.

"I'm here with Professor Carrie Davenport. In November, Dr. Davenport was pulled over by the police and subjected to police violence. A video circulated online in the days that followed. We've seen this story countless times, Black bodies summarily judged and made victim to bias, hatred, physical assault, and, all too often, death. It is a refrain so old we have come to expect nothing less. But Dr. Davenport's story has got a twist."

I didn't die. Carrie mentally added the *Law & Order* signature "dun dun" after Kandace's words, the melodramatic introduction to her tragedy.

"Dr. Davenport grew up to working class parents in South Carolina. Her mother was a beloved schoolteacher and ardent champion of the Black community who faced an untimely death launching an important protest against a company called FarmPro Industries. Her father was an auto mechanic. She received a full-tuition scholarship to Duke University, where she graduated summa cum laude with a bachelor's degree in political science alongside her best friend, Kim Taylor, whose father you all probably know from the hit 1980s television sitcom *Ain't She Pretty*."

Kandace offered a small smile to the audience and turned the page of her notebook. "After Duke, Dr. Davenport pursued her JD and PhD from the University of Virginia—again, unsurprisingly, summa cum laude. Next, she set out to complete a postgraduate fellowship. Although I think our community would have greatly benefitted from her incredible mind and insights, she turned down the prestigious Shirley Chisholm Fellowship for the Study of Race in America at Howard University. Dr. Davenport instead completed a Climenko Fellowship, teaching legal writing at Harvard Law School. For ten years and counting, she has excelled here at the illustrious PWI Briar University and just celebrated seven years as a tenured professor. She is the leading expert on constitutional conventions."

That's me, Carrie thought. It was the bio on her faculty web page, and then some.

"Carrie," Kandace said directly to her now, "we're honored to be here with you. Tell us what happened that night."

Carrie flinched. It was the easiest question, the obvious one, and yet it was the one question she did not have it in her to answer.

"On that night," she began, and wetted her lips, "I was a passenger in a vehicle that had been pulled over by the police. I grew nervous as the police questioned us, and I had this immediate and visceral need to exit the car to . . ." She paused. "Um, be sick. And when I lost my footing stepping out of the car, a young officer chased me, and pinned me to the ground, and hurt me."

"What provoked the violence you experienced, Carrie? Did you say anything to either of the officers to precipitate their chase?"

"No."

"Did you attack the officers?"

"No."

"Had you done anything to make the police think you would be a suspect for any sort of crime?" Kandace's eyes were searching.

"No. I mean, right before getting pulled over, we had left a convenience store that was later robbed. But the robbery happened after we left. We didn't know about it."

Kandace pursed her lips. "And I'm sure the officers carefully questioned you to make sure you were appropriate targets before they manhandled you?"

"I wouldn't say that."

She nodded. "As I thought. You were judged before they had any proof."

"I guess. Yes."

"And your name has been cleared, correct? The police have determined you are not a suspect, and you were incorrectly the subject of their scrutiny?"

"Yes."

Kandace leaned forward in her seat, clasping her hands together. "What apology or restitution have you received from the West Lafayette Police Department?"

Carrie blinked. It had not even occurred to her that this could be the case. That, after all that had happened, someone might take accountability for treating her the way they had. "I have not been in contact with them since the incident," she said.

"I see," Kandace said. "It's a shame, because I think for those of us who saw the video before it was taken down, there was a real cruelty there, in a way that was hard to watch. I urge the police and the town to take responsibility for their heinous actions," she added, her tone growing fierce. "And I hope our listeners will support you in holding the police accountable. They should not be let off the hook."

"Thank you." Carrie nodded.

Kandace cleared her throat. "One question or point of clarification I have for you though, Carrie, is that many of your supporters grew frustrated with you after the university released a statement on your behalf. You said, 'The video, I'm sure, may be upsetting to watch. However, I am in good health and acknowledge that the officers have a duty to keep our community safe. Laws are the constraints that keep our society free, and our officers are the front line in the fight for freedom.' Why the statement? Why absolve the officers of their responsibility to do their job correctly and to protect Black lives?"

"I don't think the statement does or is intended to absolve the officers," she replied. "For me, the statement is a means to close that public and violent chapter of my life. And to redirect attention to my other work. Right now, after having had the time to process everything, I'm excited and committed to moving forward."

"Okay," Kandace said slowly, stretching out the word. Carrie could almost hear the words *the statement begs to differ* behind her long pause. "What does moving forward look like to you? How do you plan to support and honor Black lives—recognizing where we have been and the work yet to do?"

Carrie took a deep breath. "That's actually one of the reasons I was looking forward to this interview, to share with your listeners and with the students here a positive outcome of this experience. I'm a teacher. I have strived my entire career as a professor to inspire my students and give them the tools to bring about change. They are the next generation that will make this nation a better place for all of us. And so, starting this semester, I am going to design and implement an entire unit on police brutality for my constitutional law class. We'll dedicate two entire class periods to the history of these issues, including a deep dive into the Fourth Amendment and a practical discussion among students about how these systems can be changed. To my knowledge, it will be the first formal program at a top-fourteen law school."

Kandace nodded slowly, stealing a glance out at the audience. "Okay," she breathed. "Interesting. I'm glad your students will benefit from an enhanced discussion of these issues in class." She glanced down at the notes in her leather notebook, cocking her head. "I'm curious though, Carrie, whether you think that solves the issue. Whether that goes far enough."

Carrie frowned. Good lord. What the hell did people want from her? She was a professor. She was doing everything she could, using her specific skill set and expertise to inspire change based on an event that had happened *to her*. She'd already spent hours—numerous hours, despite how little time she already had—researching and developing an appropriate curriculum on the topic, one that would hit hard and give students practical tools without signaling alarm bells in the minds of the university's conservative board. This wasn't a challenge she'd asked for.

"Would you care to explain?" Carrie asked neutrally.

"I'm just reflecting on your words. Students are our future—I don't think anyone would disagree." Kandace glanced at the audience again and winked. "But I also deeply believe each of us has a personal responsibility to act. And

I'm wondering whether you think you've risen to that occasion."

Carrie did not say anything. She had poured everything—every ounce of bravery and determination—into arranging this interview and brainstorming ways to make change. There was an answer Kandace probably wanted to hear, but she couldn't give it. *Yes, I've risen to the occasion!* she screamed in her mind.

"I believe I have," she said aloud. She left it at that.

There was a pause. "We haven't talked about Project Mars yet," Kandace said, after she realized Carrie was not going to elaborate. "I first learned about the work that you're doing through Owen Hughes. I worked opposite him nearly five years ago when he was helping some Republican senators undermine our efforts to improve SNAP food stamp bene-fits. I've been keeping tabs on him ever since, and earlier this fall, I was incredibly excited to see an article published on your Project Mars constitutional design team. To see a Black woman at the helm had my heart beating fast." She pressed a hand to her chest. "You are quite literally sculpting our future."

Carrie smiled. "It's an honor to be in this role. And it's important to me to get it right, to build a better society in space than the one we have here."

"I'm glad to hear you say that. Because many of us know that this colony Beau Ball is creating is basically a space playground for white people. Sure, the initial colonists will be researchers, scientists, astronauts, and the like. But he's running a for-profit enterprise, am I right? Mars isn't immune from capitalism. The tickets won't be cheap, which makes one thing clear: Rich white people have already planned their escape from the problems they've created on Earth. They ruined the planet with smog and oceans full of garbage, created the worst wealth inequality in the history of humankind, sowed widespread fear of Black and brown people, and zapped valuable natural resources from indigenous and Global South communities. Rich people made this mess, and now they're condemning the rest of us to live with the consequences. And so, again, I'm wondering what's being done about that, in your eyes."

"I can't talk on the record about Project Mars," Carrie cautioned.

"Well, someone has to," Kandace said with a shake of her head. "And I can't think of anyone better situated to ensure the society built there is fair and good to people like us. Because, right now, it's looking like a segregationist escape."

There were snaps from the audience. Carrie dared a glance toward the crowd. Heads nodded along to Kandace's words. A girl near the front called out, "It ain't right!" while another called out, "Preach!" Beads of sweat formed at her temples. What could she even say about that? What did they want her to do? Did they expect her to solve society's problems on an interplanetary level?

"Right . . ." Carrie said out loud, although her internal fight-or-flight instincts had been activated, and her brain screamed that fleeing provided the surest path to self-preservation. Her hand fumbled around on her chest until her fingers closed over the microphone on her lapel, ready to snatch it off and make her exit. She had turned her gaze back toward Kandace, but she could feel the stares of the students on her skin, the collective weight of their disappointed gaze, heavy like a blanket. *She wasn't woke enough. She wasn't Black enough. She wasn't doing enough.*

I'm just . . . not enough.

Kandace held up a hand like she was calming a wayward animal, attuned to Carrie's efforts to flee. She clutched the lapel of her blazer to bring her own microphone closer to her mouth.

"We've had the pleasure of speaking with Dr. Carrie Davenport, one of the brightest minds in the legal world in generations and a renowned constitutional law scholar. Dr. Davenport's name is one we all should know, not for what happened to her on a single day in November, but for the lasting legacy she will have for what may be hundreds of years as Mars colonists live under a system of government she helped design. The Black community is proud of the work Dr. Davenport is doing, and we trust her," Kandace said, putting more emphasis and warmth and hope in the word than Carrie had ever heard before. "We *trust* her to have our backs in that process. This is *The Black Box*, and we hope you'll stay tuned for our next episode in two weeks."

Carrie's muscles ached two days later as she stormed past Perkins Hall. Though the morning air was frigid and damp with cold rain that had fallen the night before, her thighs and calves radiated heat from her efforts. She'd pulled on thick wool socks and crammed her stiff ankles into oversized black boots shortly after waking up and had made the quick drive to Briar in a fury. She exited the car, left the faculty parking lot, and clomped across campus, no destination in sight but anger driving her away—away from home, from her office, from her thoughts.

She crossed the undergraduate campus, passed the football stadium, and sloshed her way through icy puddles onto a dirt path leading to the biology program's herb garden. Her breath puffed out in thick clouds that were satisfyingly snatched away by the wind. A thick cropping of trees loomed ahead, and she entered the Briar-owned forest that ringed campus, scrambling to catch her footing on the tree roots jutting up through the wood-chipped trail.

If what had happened to Carrie before had broken her—despondence and disappointment causing tears to well up in her eyes, embarrassment so overwhelming she could only hang her head—Kandace Pinkney had ushered in a new reaction, a new stage of grief: anger. A fury that she could not take sitting down because it zapped at her skin from the inside like tiny electric pulses. It was all so . . . stupid.

Like, it was enough for the Incident to have happened to her. But now, it seemed not only was she unable to escape what had happened, but everyone—from the university, to Kim, to her father, and to Kandace—had expectations of her, of what she should do. And when she had finally landed on a neat solution, Kandace had taken that solution and blown it up, like dynamite to a straw hut. Even though Kandace's critique had been professional, it stung like a personal blow.

Because Project Mars was her baby. The constitution was hers to build, her project to shepherd to completion. Carrie had turned an objective, academic gaze toward the project, studied her subject as if an experiment in a petri dish. But, annoyingly, Kandace was right that this was no petri dish. This was a project of universe-level proportions that could not be divorced from the social ills plaguing their society. Obviously. But she had, whether consciously or not, spent weeks divorcing her work from the world around them, because there was no other way to get the job done. Because, if she looked too close, she would have to confront the issue tugging at the back of her mind.

This can't be the kind of society we carry forward into space.

Project Mars isn't going to fix anything. It's just going to make life for people like me worse.

"Ugh!" Carrie snarled out loud, emitting another steamy cloud of hot air into the cold morning. She rounded a corner on the forest trail. Briar's campus was faintly discernible through a thin line of trees. She huffed and kicked the nearest tree stump before she could come into view for anyone to see her. Her toes ached as she made contact with the wood. It felt good. She kicked it again.

She clipped along at a brisk pace as she returned to campus, hoping the exertion would keep her thoughts at bay. She didn't want to retreat into the darkness again. The thought of questioning, as she had for weeks, whether she even liked the country she had grown up loving exhausted her. All the experiences and core values that made up her identity were puzzle pieces—her understanding of the country's history; the way she valued equality, peace, and intellectual pursuits; her sense of self. She'd spent several decades putting together each puzzle piece and adjusting them to make up *her*. She'd felt complete, accomplished, having slotted each piece together. But the last few weeks felt as though someone had taken the finished puzzle and ripped it apart. Torn away shreds of her identity and shoved them back in the box, until nothing made sense anymore.

"Professor Davenport!" A voice called to her at a distance. She stopped so abruptly she nearly slipped on the slick pavement. She glanced around. She'd reached the faculty parking lot again, nearly two miles from Briar's forest.

She spotted her assistant hunched behind a silver Toyota, a stack of binders in her arms.

"Anna," Carrie greeted. She coughed, hoping it would mask her attempts to rapidly regain her breath.

"Could you not hear me?" Anna asked. "I called your name a couple times, and by then you'd already done two or three laps around the parking lot."

"Sorry. I had one too many cookies over the holidays. Trying to burn some of this off," Carrie said. "And I'm on campus because . . ." She trailed off. She'd driven to campus in a huff, needing to blow off steam, but in truth she hadn't even looked at her schedule for the day.

"We were going to go over the syllabus for this semester," Anna reminded her.

"Right." Carrie smiled. "That. Of course. Let's go upstairs."

Once in her office, Carrie peeled off her winter coat and sweaty fleece headband, then dabbed at her forehead with a tissue. She eased into her desk chair and swiveled to face the window, looking out over the winter landscape she'd just traversed.

"Hot tea for you," Anna said as she entered a few minutes later. Carrie accepted the tea, wrapping her hands around the steaming mug.

"Thank you." She watched Anna settle into the wingback chair opposite the desk, setting her own mug of tea on a side table.

"I hear we're going to stuff a new unit into this spring's jam-packed syllabus," Anna said with a raised eyebrow.

"Yes, that," Carrie said with a slow nod. "It's important to me, and I think we can pull it off if we shorten the commerce clause discussion. But I think we may have bigger fish to fry."

"Bigger than being the first professor at a top law school

to create a constitutional law curriculum centered on police brutality and the Fourth Amendment?"

"Somehow, yes." Carrie groaned. "The interview I did with Kandace was a wake-up call. What happened to me reflects broader problems in society. Part of me knew that already, of course, but I've been turning a blind eye to an issue directly in front of me—Project Mars. I'm in a position to bring about change on that front, too. And that starts with understanding the organization's key players. How much do you know about Beauregard Ball?"

"The same as anyone, I guess."

"I think we need to know more."

"Ooh, a reconnaissance mission," Anna said with a conspiratorial waggle of her eyebrows. She grinned. "Call me double-oh-seven." She flicked up on her tablet, and the screen projected onto the side wall of Carrie's office.

"We know he's the CEO of Perpetua," Carrie started.

Anna gave her a "well, duh" look. "Let me take it from here," she said. She pulled up Beau's Wikipedia page. "Beauregard Ball, originally from Alabama. His father's brother was the governor for two terms, deep pockets of family money. Beau and his own brother both moved to California for college; Beau studied business, and his brother, Silas, was a genius software engineer at Caltech. And . . . hmm," Anna hummed and scrolled up and down on the page as if confirming. "Curious. Beau is two years younger but graduated four years after Silas. Don't know what the delay was. In any case, they started Perpetua in Silas's garage in 2002, and it's now worth $728 billion. The two fought bitterly when Beau redirected their focus to space, and now Beau is the egomaniac that calls most of the shots while Silas spends time with his family."

"Interesting," Carrie said, skimming the information projected onto the wall. A news article showed a picture of two white men in polo shirts, arm in arm: Beau, shorter with an impish grin, and Silas, taller with dark, heavy eyes. "And so, Beau himself is worth how much?"

"About $150 billion," Anna said breezily. "And he's single, so if you could find a way to marry him and have his babies, then in that case . . . I expect a raise."

Carrie laughed. "If that happens, I will happily buy you a mansion and give you a full billion."

"I'm holding you to that."

Carrie smiled. "And his politics?"

"The Ball family is a conservative mainstay. Beau's uncle did some pretty gross stuff as governor, with policies that uniformly harmed people of color and the LGBT community. Like that whole anti-trans policy he had. But people don't know about Beau. He doesn't comment publicly, and Perpetua is highly secretive about its political contributions."

Carrie let out a huff of air. "I see. We have no clue how Beau might react to any discussion on race, apart from the fact that he is likely a conservative Southern billionaire."

Anna took a large slurp of tea, her dark eyes shining at Carrie over the top of the mug, one thin eyebrow raised.

"Anna?"

She set her mug down with a dramatic flourish. "There are rumors . . . let me do some digging." She swiped through a series of pages on her tablet while Carrie watched her in awe. When had Carrie gotten old and become a technological dinosaur?

"Right, okay, that's the tea I thought I'd read." Her gaze snapped up to Carrie. "Beau may or may not be overtly hostile if race issues are brought up. But, in high school, he had a pretty adorable relationship with a Black girl named Mikayla: photos at football games, an elaborate promposal, the works. They allegedly broke it off after high school, but there are rumors from an old Reddit thread that Mikayla got pregnant sometime thereafter and they have a son together whom Beau still supports. His family shut that down pretty quickly and there's very little on the internet about it, but the rumors are still there."

"Fascinating," Carrie said. "So, Beau had a deep love for a Black woman that his family forbade."

"Something like that." Anna nodded. "Allegedly. Which could be helpful if you're trying to . . . well, I don't know. What are you trying to do?"

"I don't know either, really. He's a major billionaire, but I thought maybe if I could meet with him or get his attention or *something* . . . I could at least give him a whole speech about Project Mars being too white and needing to diversify the participants." Carrie sighed. "But it'll probably be futile. That's not what he hired me for. My words aren't going to make a difference."

"It's good that you want to try, though. And you never know. He may have a soft spot for the issue. Apart from, like, hiding his love and his half-Black child."

"Apart from that," Carrie quipped. "We may have a one-in-a-million shot."

Anna's eyes softened as she gazed at Carrie. "There may be an answer. Maybe it's not with this first Mars class, but maybe in the second, or third . . . there could be a solution."

"Thanks, Anna. You're right. We've got a few years before the second Project Mars class launches. All hope is not lost."

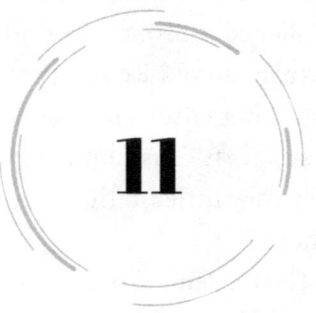

11

THE THIRD WEEK of January found Carrie at war. She marveled as she dug a tissue out of her purse and dabbed at the stray droplets of coffee dotting the sleeve of her second-favorite blazer. The day had started not, as it had the last three weeks, with a crushing sense of desperation as to how she would solve the impending space-versus-racial-identity issue. Instead, she had gone to battle with the Keurig in the fourth-floor conference room. She'd already wasted two pods of Coffeehouse Blend that had exploded in hot watery defiance the moment she'd pressed the Brew button. The third time seemed unlikely to be the charm.

At least it was her second-favorite blazer. Not the traditional tweed blazer her father had gifted her when she started her first job, and that Kim had—because of course Kim had—gotten relined with a hot-pink silk lining. Instead, she wore the burgundy power suit she started most semesters with. Today, the first research assistant meeting of the semester, was as auspicious to her as the semester's first day of classes. Because ... democracy!

She asked herself whether she dared to lick the offending coffee drops off her blazer sleeve for the iota of caffeine they might hold but was mercifully interrupted and spared the embarrassment by her research assistants entering the conference room.

"Professor Davenport," Evie greeted heartily. Amid a sea of red curls pushed forward by chunky knitted earmuffs, her green eyes shone. She had on only one glove, which she pulled off with her teeth, her other bare hand wrapped around a to-go cup of coffee.

Must be nice, Carrie thought as she stared at Evie's coffee.

Parker and Lori entered on Evie's heels, arm in arm, and Carrie wondered when they had grown so close. Lori gazed up at Parker from beneath thick dark lashes, a small smile playing on her lips as Parker pulled out a chair for her, and Carrie wanted to groan. Students. Always falling in love at inopportune moments. Like when Mars needed a government.

Carrie glanced down at her notes as the room bustled with the sounds of backpacks unzipping and laptops being slid out of sleeves and Lori pulling a muffin out of a crinkly wrapper. Then the sounds quieted, and Carrie glanced up at her students.

"Welcome. I'm so glad the three of you decided to stay on and continue our research. You will have a profound impact on this project and the future—"

"Professor Davenport? I'm sorry to interrupt," Lori said, her muffin pushed to the side for the time being.

"Yes?"

"Parker, Evie, and I have discussed this, and before we can continue with our research, we want to gain a better sense of what's being done to improve the diversity of the Project Mars endeavor."

"I see. And what prompted this?"

"We heard your interview with Kandace Pinkney," Evie jumped in. "We all happen to be avid fans of the podcast and were so stoked you were able to speak with her. But we thought her critiques were valid and echoed concerns we have with how the colony is developing and what implications that may have in the next twenty years."

"We met before this meeting and thought it imperative to discuss it with you," Parker said quietly. They opened their mouth to say more, but then closed it, sitting back slightly with a slight pinch between their eyebrows.

Carrie blinked. She hadn't had enough coffee for this . . . ambush. Intervention. She should have chosen conservative research assistants who wanted to further subjugate Black people in space, she thought wryly. Instead she had students with the fiery energy of Gen Z.

Carrie looked at Evie, at the Black Lives Matter pin on her canvas backpack, the green mood ring on her left pinky, and a dog-eared copy of a book called *Capitalism and Gay Identity* threatening to tumble out of her backpack. She loved her students, and their intervention was timely. Because she was ready now. Ready to change the curriculum in her courses, ready to take on Kandace's call to action, ready to stand up to Beau and Project Mars and all of it. Her prior reluctance aside, she was going to battle, with students who cared. About the racism-in-space thing, not her ever-present battle with the Keurig.

"I've been thinking about this a lot, and I care deeply about making sure the Project Mars explorers represent and reflect the population on Earth," Carrie said. "And from your work, you also know that Project Mars has a tight corporate structure that we don't have full rein to criticize."

Lori stared at her, her eyes earnest and full, and Carrie could feel her gaze burning into her skull.

"There's more we can do. We will figure out a way," Lori said.

Carrie offered her a smile. "I know. I want to do this. I'm going to find a way to get the PM team to focus on the issue of diversity in terms of the makeup of the colonists. Leave that to me; I promise I will work on it. But what we do here can be different. Here, we have the academic freedom and resources to enshrine the values we all hold dear into a document. Like diversity. Our work can extend into the text itself."

Lori chewed on her bottom lip, in thought. "I've heard about some of this. I read an article on feminist constitutions after taking your Comparative Constitutional Law class last year."

"Yes!" Carrie said. "On how constitutions can be used to protect the rights of women and minorities. We can do that in space."

"So, we're writing a feminist constitution?" Evie asked, her eyebrows shooting up.

"An inclusive constitution," Parker said. "With language geared toward protecting historically underrepresented groups. Right?"

"Sure." Carrie nodded.

The three students looked at each other, and Carrie could almost read on their faces the question: *Is this what we want? Does it go far enough?*

"Maybe this won't seem as radical as what you had in mind," Carrie said. "But it's the solution that will stick, that will outlive you. The same way the American founding fathers' words govern us now. Project Mars has never said we can't specifically protect the rights of certain groups in the constitution. We can do that research and write the draft we want to see. The draft we'd want to live under."

"Do you believe that kind of constitution would have changed what happened to you?" Parker asked. Their voice was gentle despite the probing words.

Carrie pursed her lips. Would it have? Was she hiding, again, under her academic blanket? Crafting a solution that wasn't really a solution?

"I don't know if it would have changed anything. But it wouldn't have hurt. That kind of constitution would have given the Supreme Court the framework to protect minorities decades earlier. It would have allowed for better, more progressive laws to be passed, for the country to embrace and value diversity earlier on." Carrie took a deep breath. "And even if I've lost faith in our local institutions, if . . ." Her breath caught, and she forced herself to continue. "Even if those institutions have become instruments of injustice, I think that maybe . . . maybe I still believe in the greater picture, that humans can organize themselves in a way that is fair and just. Things are messed up here, but they don't have to be. I'm not going to reject constitutional democracy itself just because our country has made a mockery of our constitution."

Heads slowly nodded.

"Okay," Lori said.

Two weeks later, Carrie camped out on the lumpy couch in her basement, where she kept the big TV. She'd ordered a feast of Chinese food that she'd crammed onto the narrow coffee table—kung pao chicken stacked on top of a container of dumplings and soy sauce packets squeezed in the space between. A carton of lo mein propped her phone upright; Kim's face on the video call was a little square half covered by a dangling saucy noodle.

On the TV screen, the images flashed and alternated between Libby, Project Mars's communications director, hosting a broadcast from PM headquarters; B-roll footage of a spacecraft flying through space; and video feed of a brunette interviewing the chief system engineer at the Florida-based command center. Giant white letters flashed across the bottom of the newscast: *FINAL PROJECT MARS SUPPLY TOUCHDOWN—WILL BALL PULL IT OFF?*

"Big rocket," Kim said on the video call as the TV showed footage from seven months prior, when the third and final supply probe had launched from Kennedy Space Center on an Atlas V rocket. Now scheduled to make its landing, the supply probe carried the final module of the Mars habitat, an additional year's worth of food, and scientific equipment for the colonists' initial studies of the red planet. "Do you think Beau is compensating for something?"

"A big ego requires a big rocket," Carrie said around a mouthful of chicken.

"We like things big in this family." Kim waggled her eyebrows and raised a glass of champagne. "Veryyy big."

Carrie rolled her eyes but raised her own glass of champagne as well. "Brian's lucky I have no inclination to publicly share the *many* things I have not wanted to know about your sex life. I have far too much insight into how Naomi was conceived."

"Are we talking about discretion?" Kim screeched. "I found you in a jail cell next to a hot blond, and I said nothing. Nothing! I didn't even ask how she compared to Devon's giant—"

"Anyway," Carrie said loudly, "I think the supply probe is about to land. T-minus seven minutes."

She turned up the TV volume over Kim's protests as a grainy image of the supply probe rocketing down toward the red planet suddenly filled the screen. "Viewers," Libby said in a reverent near whisper, "if you listen to my podcast, then you know that it takes about seven minutes to get from the Mars atmosphere to the surface. Entry, descent, and landing are considered the seven minutes of terror. The show begins now."

Her voice-over cut, and the audio flipped to a stream from mission control.

"Successful atmospheric entry."

"Current speed is 12,888 miles per hour," said a gruff voice. "The spacecraft is slowing."

"Supersonic parachute to be deployed in thirty seconds."

Carrie and Kim said nothing. Carrie's eyes pierced the screen as if one blink would disrupt the entire landing.

"Confirmed, parachute successfully deployed."

She let out a breath. One by one, command-center operators confirmed final landing details and metrics. In truth, Carrie was excited. The successful touchdown of the supply probe would mark the final milestone before it was safe, from a scientific standpoint, for the colonists to actually inhabit Mars. The third and final module contained the initial sleeping quarters for the colonists that they would inflate upon arriving. Once the sleeping quarters had been inflated, the colonists would spend their first day connecting that module to the recreation area, kitchen, and science labs, which they'd also inflate upon landing. They'd then have two weeks to use the 3D printing equipment from the first launch to build bigger and more permanent settlements using Martian soil. If the third supply probe failed, though, the timeline for her report would be meaningless. It would be another year at least before the colonists could safely launch. But if it worked . . . it was go time.

The screen split between the probe and Libby's gleaming smile. Now that the parachute had deployed, the landing vehicle had slowed even more. Orange filled the screen as the surface of Mars loomed.

"As many of you at home know," the brunette at the control center explained, cutting into the landing metrics, "our communications with Mars are up to twenty minutes delayed. In fact, the Mars probe has either successfully touched down or . . . not! We'll continue to show this footage transmitted to us directly from the probe itself of the landing. Right now, the parachute has slowed the velocity of the probe from thirteen thousand to four thousand miles per hour to assist the probe with a soft landing that won't disturb any of the equipment. In a second, we'll ditch the parachute so that rockets can help us steer safely to our landing site beside the other sections of the habitat."

The mission control live broadcast resumed. "Parachute has been jettisoned, rockets initiated."

"Yes!" Kim cheered. "We're almost there. Where's the giant supreme court from which you'll be lording over all your subjects? I wouldn't want that to get disturbed on impact."

"Oh, they had that in the first probe," Carrie joked. She held her breath.

"Twenty meters to the ground."

Carrie wiped the soy sauce from her mouth and grabbed her glass of champagne, butterflies in her stomach. Her eyes were fixed on the screen.

"We can confirm that the landing gear has successfully deployed," Libby said.

All communication from the command center and commentary from Libby and the brunette ceased. It was quiet on screen, and quiet in the basement of Carrie's home during those final seconds as the probe inched downward. And then, with a hard crunch and a puff of Martian dust, the probe thudded down onto the red planet. Carrie didn't dare regain her breath.

"It's a success!" Libby cheered with a breathy laugh. "We did it! Project Mars has successfully launched and safely transported to Mars everything needed for one hundred humans to inhabit the planet for two years, with reserves to last another year. You heard it first here!"

"Hellllll yeah!" Kim cheered on the phone. "Take that, aliens! Mars is ours, and my best friend is going to be its superlord, and all of y'all can suck it!"

Carrie felt as light as air itself as she stared at the screen. They were doing it. Project Mars, and multibillion-dollar company Perpetua, but also just . . . humankind. Humans were going to live on another planet for the first time, ever. Though her eyes were dry, they stung as if she'd been crying for hours. She stared in wonder at the probe parked firmly on the rocky ground.

"Carrie?" Kim asked quietly, her mood shifting with Carrie's. Carrie picked up her phone in one hand and took a sip of champagne with the other to hide the depth of emotion playing out on her face.

"Yes?" she said after she'd taken a long sip, her tight throat constricting around the swell of bubbles and sweet liquid.

"I'm really proud of you."

Her heart clenched. "It's nothing. I didn't land the probe."

"It's everything. You may not be going to Mars, but if this colony works, you will have had every bit of impact as that supply probe. Probably way more."

"And if it fails? Anarchy and all that?" The possibility that she'd doom the colonists to dysfunction and disorder loomed over her at all times.

"Oh, then it was for sure 100 percent Adam's fault."

"Excellent," Carrie laughed. She took another sip of champagne.

She was poised to let the postlanding commentary fade into the background, but Kim spoke over the television.

"Wait, am I hearing this right? Let me turn it up."

"What?" Carrie said, turning up the volume on her own TV.

"To our loyal fans and viewers, keep watching to catch an interview with our chief engineer about what made this launch and landing such a success. And for the incredibly talented team working on Project Mars, we'll of course see you in one week at FrontierScape for the party of the century."

"What the hell am I hearing? What party of the century?"

"Um," Carrie said.

"'Um' what?"

"There's a postlanding party. For everyone contributing to the Project Mars endeavor. The high-level employees and special-project teams. And, like, some minor celebrities or whatever. A big party."

Silence reigned over the line until Kim finally shouted, "There is an enormous A-list party at Beau's gazillion-dollar California mansion, and you're only telling me now?"

"I wasn't sure it was a big deal." She cringed. It was, in fact, a big deal to Carrie, but not the party itself. She needed to get a better sense of Project Mars and its key players. Maybe if she knew who the power brokers were and who had sway over major decisions, she could make good on her promise to her students to raise her voice when it came to the diversity of the colonists. She hadn't wanted to endure weeks of dissecting exactly what outfit she would wear to the event with Kim—she was nervous enough as it was. But a few days, she could surely handle.

"Oh boy. Don't even try to argue your way out of this one, Carrie Davenport. We've got to figure out what the hell you're going to wear. And what in the world is FrontierScape?"

"From what I can gather, it's Beau's thirty-six-million-dollar home and playground of sorts out in Riviera Ranch. It's like a shrine to frontiers of the past and exploration and stuff. He's got this big house with a view over—"

"I've got to craft an A-list outfit that transitions from indoors to outdoors?" Kim's incredulous tone of voice made it clear that, indeed, the weight of the world was on Kim Taylor's shoulders. "This may call for couture. Take me upstairs to your closet at once!"

Carrie tried to hide her groan as a cough as she grabbed her phone and resigned herself to an evening of outfit shopping.

12

SATIN WAS the answer to the age-old question of what to wear to a billionaire's ego-inflating celebration—an expensive purple dress stowed away in her trusty rolling garment bag that was now tucked against the glass wall of her temporary office in a buzzing beehive of glass-and-chrome offices.

That morning, Carrie had departed SFO for Perpetua's Silicon Valley headquarters. Riding in her Uber up the winding main driveway, they'd passed a three-story Mount-Rushmore-esque statue of Steve Jobs, Bill Gates, Nikola Tesla, and (because of freaking course) Beauregard Ball towering over a flowing fountain and one of the actual retired NASA space shuttles in its gleaming-white space-faring glory, before reaching two glass office towers. Inside, she'd navigated the maze of a bamboo forest and taken a footbridge across an indoor lazy river all to reach the elevator bank. Mercifully, the upper floors of the building were full of regular employee offices, conference rooms like the one she'd waited in before the press conference, and plenty of visitor offices. Unlike some other tech geniuses, who favored an open-concept approach with rows of desks out in the open, Beau operated under the "mad scientist approach"; he firmly believed every employee deserved their own office where they could close the door and innovate.

Carrie valued the privacy. The successful supply landing had created a new urgency for the completion of the team's report. She wanted to get to work, that night's fancy party aside. She had the plan for an inclusive constitution to think about, as well as her regular preparation for her first-year constitutional law class, and for some dumb reason she still sat on the university's bicentennial fundraising committee. Despite all that, she found herself navigating to a more fun memorandum she'd had sitting on her computer desktop. She deserved a bit of a mental break.

Her first class after the press conference, a young undergraduate student whose name she later learned was Meghan had asked insightful questions about the international law involved in the colony. Carrie liked her spirit. She'd recruited Meghan to study a topic that was tangential but not entirely unimportant: examples throughout science fiction of how settlers beyond Earth had organized their societies. Grounded in constitutional history? Not exactly. But she wouldn't turn down examples from authors who'd already given long and creative thought to what human space settlement could look like. She kicked back in the ergonomic chair and skimmed through Meghan's analysis of space, government, and colonization in *Star Trek*, *The Expanse*, and *Across the Space Frontier*. Meghan had spent a good thirty pages on those works before even getting to the bulk of the memo, analyzing books by Robert Heinlein and Isaac Asimov. The printed memo felt like a hefty five to ten pounds in her lap.

Her head snapped up as her phone buzzed with sudden urgency. Crap, her alarm. Already 5 p.m. She'd have to hustle now if she wanted to get dressed in time for the Perpetua-organized limo from campus to the party, her ticket to enter. She turned back to her computer and determined she would only read the last paragraph in that section of the memo, just to close things out. It was game time.

She glanced up again a second later. *What in the fresh hell.* Her phone read 6 p.m. So much for only one paragraph. She closed the shades in the office window and slipped into the purple calf-length satin wrap dress and slinky silver heels. She made a frantic but Kim-worthy attempt at foundation and a smoky eye and opted for bold lipstick. Then she booked it to the front of the building. The glass lobby was empty, and the street beyond certainly held no stretch limo. She stepped outside. A man holding a sign with FRONTIERSCAPE in bold print stood in front of a black car. At least she wouldn't be missing the party.

"The limo has left, but Perpetua has arranged several cars for later travelers. I will be driving you and one other passenger. Please feel free to get in if you're ready to leave."

She climbed into the back seat, where a deeply tanned man in his late thirties sat beside the window. His luscious head of dark wavy hair, thick eyebrows, and impeccably tailored beard struck Carrie as so familiar that she nearly stumbled over herself as she got into the car.

"Hi," the man said with a flash of white teeth.

"Hi," Carrie said breathlessly, pressing herself slowly into the car seat, desperately aware of the mere foot of space between them as the car took off.

"I'm Carlos—"

"Martinez," Carrie breathed. She didn't know everything

about space or pop culture, but him she knew. Carlos Martinez had been a teen heartthrob for his role in a trilogy of movies, *Zero Dollars Down,* about high school spies who took down greedy corporate CEOs. He'd since been in a string of television shows; she and Kim had binge-watched his prestige drama *Neptune,* where he'd played a dashingly attractive space commander trying to keep their off-course spaceship afloat. She'd spent most of the episodes trying to fend off Kim's comments about what she'd do if she could get Carlos alone without his space suit. It had only gone off air two years prior after duly winning multiple Emmy Awards.

"Yes," he laughed, in a way that wasn't at all impatient, as Carrie had thought he should be. "And you are?"

"Carrie Davenport."

"Hmm," he said. His brows knitted together. "I haven't seen any of your movies."

"Oh, I'm—" She started to explain before she realized he was teasing her. "Only a movie star in my dreams," she finished in a rush. "I'm one of the Project Mars consultants. I'm on the team designing the government for the Mars settlement."

"Well, that's pretty legit. I'm on campus because I wanted a free tour of the Project Mars and Perpetua campuses, but you're here because you're literally helping to make life on Mars a reality."

"Oh, I don't know about that. And I don't even normally work here. I live in North Carolina. I can confirm there are no lazy rivers in my office building."

He raised an eyebrow. "Interesting. You're only in town for the party?"

Carrie glanced outside—they were now on the highway

headed inland—then turned back to Carlos. She wondered what she seemed like—the awkwardly dressed law professor who had flown cross-country for a single day to go to some fancy party. Adam and Owen certainly weren't making the trek. "Yes?"

"I don't mean anything by it," he said hastily. "You have every right to go. And you look absolutely fantastic in a dress that will have everyone . . . well, anyway." He cleared his throat and tore his eyes from her chest.

God bless Kim.

"I won't know anyone there," he confessed.

"A movie star won't know everyone in the room?" She stared.

He shrugged. "It's a lot of actual smart people like you. Scientists, space geeks. Beau invited me because he wanted to lower the collective IQ with people who've only pretended to be astronauts."

Carrie smiled. "Because he wanted someone who has been an inspiration for space travel for all of us for years."

"Thank you." He took a breath. "So, what's there for you besides the free food and mansion?"

Carrie wasn't sure what to say. Should she tell him about her real plans for the night? Was that appropriate? She was running on adrenaline, but at some point her brain was going to catch up and realize that she was having a casual conversation with a *movie star*, right?

"I mean, I like free food as much as anyone who lives near a college campus, but . . ." She licked her lips and cursed inwardly as she realized she'd disturbed her lipstick. "I have a bit of an agenda. You remember how . . . Well, I mean, I'm sure you're well aware how impactful it was for you to be a Latino space commander."

"I think one magazine dubbed me 'America's Sexiest Latino Space Commander,' as if I had actually beat out anyone else for the title." He laughed and crossed one leg over the other in the narrow back seat. "But of course, I couldn't forget the long-winded *New York Times* interviews and hours posing for *The Hollywood Reporter*."

Carrie was silent as she tried to gather her courage to explain her mission, but Carlos filled in the gap in the conversation.

"I mean, it was more than that, obviously." His long fingers played with the window button as if any moment he might open the window and escape. "Not to sound like a total cliché, but when I was a teenager I didn't really understand the impact that me being on the big screen would have, until I went back to my old neighborhood. My mom busted her ass to pay for my acting classes, and the day I landed the lead role for *Zero Dollars Down*, there was this infectious joy in the neighborhood. My grandmother cooked for days so that we could have a block party when the movie came out. And at that party, I became someone other than just me. I wasn't just Carlos. I was this persona, this even greater version of me, who had proven that kids with my background could be on the big screen." His finger jabbed the window button too hard, and a rush of air flooded in through the opening gap. He quickly hit the button again, and the window zipped shut.

Carrie patted her head to return any windswept hairs back to place. "I remember when the third *Zero Dollars Down* movie came out. Your characters were all in their early twenties by then, and your character had finally gotten with Laney. There was all this press about needing to have more smart, desirable Latino men as action movie heroes. Then this girl threw her underwear at you at some awards show when you were on stage."

"Not the panty incident!" Carlos said, slumping in his seat. "I don't think I've ever had a more ego-boosting but horrifying life moment. I remember it was while I was reading a tribute to recently dead Marty Leonard, and the whole room, like five thousand people, went totally silent."

Carrie laughed. "Oh, I forgot about that part. Yeah, that's awful."

"Ten years is still too soon to laugh! I haven't been able to look at another pair of panties since."

Carrie cut him a side-eye, and he burst out laughing. "Er . . . except for those models I dated right after that."

"A minor detail," she agreed, hiding her smile and ignoring the heat that was creeping up her back and warming her face. "Thank god you recovered enough to do *Neptune*."

He nodded slowly, his expression turning pensive. "I did *Neptune* because it was the right step for my acting career. But it was only afterward during those interviews with the press that I guess I learned—and it's only really hitting me fully today—what that meant for my community. Particularly for anyone interested in going to space. When the show started filming eight years ago, people who look like me weren't actually going to space that often. And now look."

"Right. Well, TV hasn't quite become reality yet. The first round of colonists is going to be 95 percent white. Which kind of answers your question about why I'm going to the party." Carrie squared her shoulders. "I want to do something about that."

He cocked his head and surveyed her with a long look.

"You want the colonists to look more like us. To represent us."

"Instead of a rich person's playground."

"Hey, no attacking millionaires who buy their way into space." He wagged a finger at her. "I may want to go someday, who knows."

Carrie laughed. "A rich *white* playground."

He grinned. "Okay, now we're talking."

Ahead of them, a three-story wooden arch reminiscent of classic Western ranches spelled out "FrontierScape" in a futuristic font. A broad sweep of slightly brown grass stretched onward against a green mountain backdrop. They passed under the arch and drove uphill until they could see a spectacular burst of metal and light off in the distance at the foot of the mountain range. Closer to them, a small blue lake to the right glimmered in the dimming sunlight. As they approached, Carrie realized the glittering came not just from the reflection on the lake, but also from a glass-walled boat floating in the center.

"What's your game plan?" Carlos asked, gesturing around them.

She bit her lip. "I don't really know. I need to meet more people and learn more information. Get a conversation going, then try to convince them."

"Carrie," Carlos said softly as they continued their path up the long driveway. He grabbed her wrist, and her heart beat at the contact. "I want to help with this. Maybe we can stick together for a bit? I can't open every door, but I can open one or two."

"It would be an honor."

Beau's house was a glass-and-steel three-story marvel at the end of an impossibly long driveway lined with his guests' luxury convertibles and chauffeured black cars. Carrie followed Carlos through floor-to-ceiling glass doors to the rear veranda, an enormous open-air stone-paved patio overlooking the sharp rise of the mountains. Flat concrete platforms cut into the mountain at various intervals, each forming the base for its own marvel. Near the bottom of the mountain was a cutout with a pristine custom race car. Higher up and to one side was the Project Mars–rover prototype, a gangly conglomeration of metal and solar panels. To the right of that was an old plane that Carrie figured must've been an original prototype for one of the first flights. Standing on the veranda gave the effect of staring up at a towering semicircle of novelties, each lit with soft lighting so the mountain glowed. She was so transfixed that she barely registered the party around her.

"Oh my god, look!"

Carrie's head snapped to her left, where she spotted three women staring at her, stage-whispering in excitement. Great. Had she not been invited? Had her fancy couture dress ripped? Had . . . oh.

"I told you I could open a few doors." Carlos led the way over to the group of three women.

"Ladies," he said warmly. "How did I get so lucky as to meet three of the most stunning women at the party? What brings you here tonight?"

"We're all astronauts in the first colonist class," said a tall woman with a strong Boston accent and an orange "I'm with Beau!" pin on her pink sequined blazer. "Although you're clearly the coolest astronaut among us. I'm Hadley, and this is Winnie and Michelle." She gestured toward a short, curvy brunette and an Asian woman with space-themed glasses.

"Nice to meet you. Have you all met Carrie? She's designing the government for your colony."

"Wicked," Hadley said. "Can I get special powers? Everyone has to share their three favorite things about me in order to vote or hold office."

"Seems extremely reasonable," Carrie joked.

"Do you know what the structure of the government is going to be yet?" Winnie asked.

"I can't say much yet, but it will be some sort of democracy. Something where you can be involved and have a say in how to govern yourselves."

"That's good," Hadley said. "We've got such a diverse group. So many different specialties, and from so many parts of the country. I'm glad we can all have a say."

Carrie glanced at the other astronauts. Winnie's eye twitched, and she saw Michelle wince slightly. The two other women were holding back. A promising sign for her to begin her inquiries.

"Do you all get along fairly well?" Carrie asked.

"It's a very cohesive group," Hadley said. "We've been training together for two years now, and it feels like a family." She looked at her peers.

"I imagine we'll have our fair share of conflict, like every analog team has had. Respect for different opinions and backgrounds will be key," Michelle said with a pointed look at Carrie.

The group fell silent momentarily, and Carlos cleared his throat. "Hadley, I hear there's a specialty cocktail tonight? Something springing from a rock fountain with actual moon rocks? Would you like to accompany me for a drink?"

"Hell yeah, I want a drink with a movie star," she said with a grin. She wrapped a pink manicured hand around his bicep and pressed herself close to him.

The two departed, and Carrie sent a silent word of thanks to Carlos as she watched his departing back eventually meld into the crowd.

"Do you think," Carrie started tentatively, turning to the remaining duo, "if you had any impact over it, you would have composed your colonist class in a different way?"

A photographer brushed past, and Carrie stepped back so Winnie and Michelle could be in the frame together. Winnie's photograph-ready smile dissipated as soon as the photographer left, and she leaned in so close that Carrie could smell almost every ingredient of a fruity cocktail on the other woman's breath. Carrie resisted the urge to stoop to meet Winnie's height.

"Yes," she said breathily. "I'm one of only three queer astronauts. And they seem to have forgotten that people come in other colors than white."

Michelle stepped closer as well. "I . . . yeah. It's not about numbers, per se, but I'm one of three Asian astronauts. There's a single Black astronaut and one who is Puerto Rican. Against the total US population, that's not exactly the right ratio. Let alone the fact that we're meant to represent the future of humankind."

There. Exactly what Carrie needed to hear. Project Mars's inconvenient truth was out in the open. The colony was not representative, and people involved knew it.

Michelle held up her hands. "I get that there aren't as many Black or brown folks in science and tech or in leadership as there should be, so the selection pool isn't huge. Like, the diversity problem in STEM is well known."

"Well, yeah," Winnie interrupted. "But the PM numbers are still way, way off."

"And it impacts your experience?" Carrie asked.

Michelle nodded. "Living in space is already uncomfortable. You want everything else to feel as comfortable as possible. One astronaut asked me whether there'd been any Chinese food shipped up in the third supply probe. Needless to say, I'm not even Chinese."

"Oof, that was bad," Winnie agreed. "Let alone what happened in the locker room at the training center when those jerks broke Frank's clavicle . . ."

"They what?" Carrie exclaimed.

"Michelle! Winnie!" A young Black man bounded up to the group. "Come ride the roller coaster with me. It's a replica of an old mining cart, but it goes, like, fifty miles an hour."

"Sorry," Winnie laughed. "This is Kwame from the second class. He doesn't take no for an answer."

"I'm Carrie!" she jumped in to introduce herself before he could rush away.

"Kwame Mensah. Astronaut extraordinaire. It's good to meet you." His grip was firm as he shook her hand, but his eyes were soft and brown, and dimples on each round cheek bordered his grin.

"Same here. You've been training with Michelle and Winnie?"

"You mean, can I do three times more push-ups than them? Yes." He laughed. "I hate to interrupt, but this roller coaster is calling our names."

Winnie shrieked as he grabbed her hand and gave her a playful tug. They bounded off toward the lawn.

"Wait! I'd love to know how you would fix—" Carrie started.

"Take my card!" Michelle nearly flung a tiny cardstock rectangle at her as she rushed to catch them. "We're not the only ones," she said, her tone rather cryptic as she skipped off behind the departing pair.

Carrie stowed the card in her purse. She accepted a glass of champagne from a passing server and watched the group disappear down the veranda steps and toward a mass of brown metal at the foot of the mountain. Kwame. A Black astronaut. In the second colonist class. There was a solution there, but her mind couldn't quite wrap around it. It would have to wait until after this glass of champagne.

She made her way closer to the house and leaned against one of its columns. Ahead of her, a group of middle-aged scientist-looking types clustered around a rock fountain drinking milky-blue cocktails. To their right, a couple embraced as they stared upward, where stars were starting to appear. She chatted briefly with an engineer who'd helped with the living quarters and exchanged small talk with a journalist from *Science News Express* magazine who, thankfully, had no questions for her. It wasn't a surprise. She'd spotted the latest star of *The Bachelor* in attendance—a former Air Force pilot and space buff, which she supposed was enough of a connection to score an invite—downing mixed drinks. There were more interesting people for journalists to concentrate on. In light of it all, she remained pressed against her trusty column near a PM accountant who seemed intent on avoiding the crowd, too. She accepted another drink and kept her eyes peeled for her true targets: Beau, and if not him, then at least Libby.

Before she'd drained her second champagne, Carlos

appeared at her side and pressed another cocktail into her hand.

"This one will blow your mind, I promise you. Mint julep with mint grown on the International Space Station and some flavor I can't even identify."

"Thank you." She smiled at him. "Was it your reward for escaping Hadley?"

He made a face. "Not my favorite fan. Did you get what you wanted, though?"

Carrie nodded slowly. "Yeah. I think I did. I just don't know what I can do about it. There has to be someone more important than me who knows the diversity thing is a problem. And who has the power to solve it."

"It's not always the most important person in the room who has the biggest impact," Carlos said.

She stared at him in surprise.

"From the episode where the janitor fixes the leaking fuel system in season two," he said. "And also my own brilliance."

Carrie laughed. "You are a wise one indeed. Now all I need you to do is find Beau for me, and you'll be my personal hero."

"How hard could it be to find a billionaire who draws people to him like a magnet?"

Carlos took Carrie's arm and led her down onto the lawn, in the opposite direction of the metal masterpiece that was the roller coaster. There was a large catering tent blocking their view of the rest of the lawn, fresh with the scent of street tacos and roasted corn. But once they'd paced around the big obstacle in their path, suddenly—bingo. A short man in dark pants, an open white button-down, custom sneakers, and a grin brighter than the sun itself. Beau clutched a beer in one hand as he laughed in active and lively conversation with two men, though a crowd of around ten people hovered a few feet away, like his own personal moons in orbit.

"Well, I guess I have to call you my personal hero," Carrie whispered, although the shrieks from the roller coaster could have easily masked her words.

Carlos smirked. "I vote that be my official title from now on. It's no longer Carlos to you."

"Actors, such egos!" she pretended to lament. "Well, it's worth it. Now all I have to do is work myself into whatever conversation he's having. Let's go."

Carrie started to pace toward Beau, taking quick strides before her brain could panic and overanalyze the impending confrontation. Beau stood right there. *So close.* However reluctant she'd previously been to act, at this point there was no reason not to, if the very person she needed to convince was right within her reach. She could do it. She had to.

"What? No!" Carlos hissed, pulling her back. "No way!"

"What?"

"Do you know who that is? Look, next to Beau. Sky Halvorsen. He's beaten me for an Emmy two years in a row and mocked me with a crying emoji on Lune for not winning. I'm not talking to him."

Carrie squinted at the huddled group. Anna was always ragging her for being completely immune to the grip action movies and shows had on society. Carlos's beef with Sky only reinforced how clueless she was. At least she'd recognized Carlos. She stepped closer to him and peered at his expression. "Are you . . . jealous?"

Carlos rolled his eyes, but he had already angled away from Beau, the tiniest pout forming on his lips. "That's crazy. No. He's a jerk."

"Don't worry about it," Carrie said. "We don't need to go

over there right now. There are bound to be plenty of opportunities before the night ends. And I'm starving. How about a mini taco?"

She let Carlos lead her back toward the food tent, where a smaller crowd milled about. She snagged a small tray of shrimp tacos and plopped them onto the nearest cocktail table outside the tent. From her peripheral vision, she could see that Beau and his entourage had drifted away. *Damn.*

She shoved the tiny tacos in her mouth as Carlos picked at a basket of tortilla chips. The food helped dilute the three drinks she'd had so she could better focus. She needed to form a game plan. She looked up toward the house, where a mix of people continued to hang around the veranda and inside. She almost thought she could see a flash of red through the living room window.

"Hey," she said. "I need to use the restroom. I'll be back in a few minutes. I hope Hadley spares you her graces in the meantime."

Carlos's lips parted in surprise as she pulled away. She would welcome his efforts to escort her any other time, but she needed to break free from his comfort and finish what she'd come here to do. She climbed the steps to the veranda and slid open the glass door to the living room. Inside, a crowd of guests chatted loudly in front of a giant television replaying the successful launch that had brought them all together. She stood in the doorway for several moments, surveying the crowd of influencer types who stood by Beau's enormous fish tank on the opposite wall. Then she spotted a familiar flash of red hair near a glass-and-steel home bar.

As Carrie approached, she realized Libby was leaning so heavily against the bar that she could only be described as, well, slumped. Carrie brushed her arm, and Libby's eyes flashed to Carrie's.

"Oh, Carrie! Hi. Did you try the signature cocktail?" Libby attempted to stand straighter, and Carrie wrapped an arm around the other woman's waist.

"Hi. I tried one of them. I can assume you did, too?"

"Yes." She eyed Carrie and leaned into her embrace. "I'm not even going to apologize for my state right now. As you can imagine, this week was hell. Good hell, because everything went well, but insanity nonetheless."

"I know. I saw you on TV. I bet it was madness off camera."

"Indeed. I'm surprised you came tonight, Ms. Professor. I still remember coaching a very shy, nerdy professor on her acceptance speech for the lead role."

Carrie smiled. After she'd emailed back her acceptance, Libby had immediately flown to North Carolina to coach her on a quick live broadcast to Project Mars employees announcing her involvement. It had been a thirty-second spot, but Carrie had trembled like she were performing the Super Bowl halftime show. Libby's warm hand on her shoulder and the way she'd looked at Carrie had told her much about the other woman.

"Believe it or not, I was hoping to talk to Beau tonight."

"You came to a party with five hundred people to try to chat with Beau?"

"No one said it was the perfect plan," Carrie muttered.

"Why?" Libby shot. Her grip on Carrie tightened as she started to sway.

"I want to talk to him about the diversity issue in the colonist class. I think there's an interplay here between the type of government needed and the racial makeup of the colonists."

Libby pointed a wavering finger toward the opposite corner of the room. She vaguely recognized a tall white man with dark hair. That must be . . . Right. From the press conference. Grant something. He stood with his head bent low, talking to a dark-skinned Black woman with a perfect mane of long curly hair and a bright pantsuit that made Carrie's mouth water.

"If you can't find Beau, your next best bet is Grant, our head of strategy. Actually, both of them." She nodded to the pair. A second later, the Black woman shook his hand and disappeared into the crowd.

"Well, I guess now just Grant," Libby amended.

"Who was that woman?" Carrie asked. She had looked strikingly familiar.

A hand suddenly slipped across her ass, and a second later a body brushed up against her and Libby. She spun around, her eyes narrowed in anger.

"What the hell—" Carrie said. Her words trailed off as she realized she was staring into the one face she'd wanted to see all evening. "Oh. I'm sorry, um—"

"Whoops. Thought you were Libby's sexy model friend. But you're . . . whoever you are." He wrapped his arm around Libby and took on her body weight, Libby's head coming to rest against the top of his, covering his face with red curls. He pushed her hair away.

"Oof, Libbs. You're gonna suffocate me. This isn't last night."

"If it isn't Beauregard Ball." Libby smirked. "You remember Carrie? You're paying her to make rules, or something."

"She's a dom?"

"What? No! She's—"

"Oh, the constitution woman," Beau said. He reached behind them as a waiter passed with a tray of purple drinks and raised a glass to her. "Go, George Washington." He downed the glass in one go.

"Actually, Beau . . . Mr. Ball." Carrie straightened and steeled herself. "We need to talk about the colony. There are two major issues. First, the makeup of the colonist class is not representative. It's overwhelmingly white, and I don't think that represents—"

"Carrie." Beau propped Libby against the bar so that one arm was free and leaned in close, gripping her upper arm. "I hear you. I promise I've heard it before."

"You've heard it, but nothing has changed on the diversity front," she insisted. "This colony is meant to inspire a generation of explorers—"

Beau started to pull away. She took a step toward him. "Look, the second issue will be new to you. The constitutional design team has settled on a democracy, but we think that a carefully selected leader should be installed for the initial experimental colonist class to develop a strong foundation of leadership. I'm here to suggest . . . well, to implore you, really, to select an experienced, trustworthy leader committed to helping with the lack of racial diversity."

Beau's eyes turned to the ceiling, considering. "You want the first commander to be a minority?"

"I want them to be reliable and principled, first and foremost, but it would help if they could champion an inclusive community at the same time."

His grip tightened on Libby. "Did Kendra come tonight?" He asked the redhead.

"Yup," Libby said. "She was just talking to Grant."

"Alright, I think we're on the same page," he told Carrie. "I've got an idea with multiple layers of benefits. It's freaking insane how well it works out. So, don't worry about it. We'll update you on this in a few days."

Carrie faltered. Don't worry about it? That made her even more worried.

"You've come up with a solution for how white this class is going to be?" she asked, deadpan.

"Uh-huh," Beau said. He released her arm and pulled Libby close again. "Promise. I do like your fiery energy, though. Are you always like that? I thought you were a stuffy law professor."

Carrie ignored his remarks. "Your fix will benefit this astronaut class and all classes moving forward?"

"Hopefully. We're working on future classes. It'll be good. Me and you, we make a good team. I knew I liked you." He winked at her. Then, in a flurry of red hair, he parted the crowd to disappear who knows where with Libby.

Carrie stared ahead of her, uncomprehending, wondering whether she'd really talked to Beau and whether it'd really all been solved. As she blinked, the party guests continued to drink too much and shout in each other's ears and sway to the sound of distant alternative music. She followed in the empty wake behind Beau through the living room and to the open door to the veranda and peered up to the dark sky and its stars beyond, wondering what the world would, in fact, look like up there in the years to come.

13

THE FIRST DAY after Carrie returned from California, her head swam with the same turbulence as when she was little and would spin for too long in the lumpy desk chair they kept in front of the family computer. She would spin endlessly until she felt dizzy and nauseous, no longer able to tell left from right, up from down, until her mother placed a gentle hand on the chair. She was in a metaphorical spinning chair now, the world blurring around her, and her mother wasn't there to stop it.

By the second day, the blur had stopped, and reality dawned on her. She had met a celebrity. She had sipped moon cocktails and champagne so expensive she'd wanted to let it bubble on her tongue forever rather than swallow. She had eavesdropped on the conversations of the world's foremost scientists. And, more important, she had done what she had wanted to do. She had finally risen to the occasion and confronted Beau about the racial makeup of the colonists. And he had assured her that something would be done . . . if she could take him at his word.

She entered her office the third day after her trip with her arms full of flowers from the farmer's market. She cleared out her stash of discarded candy wrappers, restored books she'd finished reading to their rightful spots on her alphabetized bookshelf, and settled her new vase of hydrangeas front and center on her desk.

Anna knocked on her door shortly before ten. She stepped into the office with a wary expression.

"Good morning. I have a student here who is seeking a faculty sponsor for a rather long research paper he's hoping to write."

"Excellent! Send him in. I should have plenty of time to supervise this semester."

"Do you? With the report and everything?" Anna asked dubiously, the keeper of Carrie's calendar eyeing her with a suspicious frown. She bowed her head. "Er, I just think you should know about the topic of the paper. It's about dirt. Professors Wade and Lester have already declined."

"Political dirt?"

"No. Dirt dirt. Real dirt. Like, he wants to argue that Congress is violating the Constitution and treating different states unfairly by sourcing more dirt for federal construction projects from Republican- instead of Democratic-leaning states."

"He . . . what?" Carrie spluttered. She managed admirably to keep her mouth from falling open. But a second later she waved away Anna's concern. "It's fine! That sounds . . . fascinating. I will never stand in the way of someone's dream, Anna!" Carrie beamed. "Send him in."

Half an hour later, Carrie shuddered with only the slightest sense of regret. She had learned more about dirt from a squirrelly student who barely looked of high school age than she'd ever wanted to know. There were apparently at least three *types* of dirt. She wished she could erase the newfound knowledge from her head to leave more space for constitutions and Mars facts. Lord. At least she had hydrangeas in her office to maintain her mood.

Anna reentered her office as the student departed, smirking. "I hope you're not going to *soil* your good reputation by supervising that paper."

Carrie took a deep sniff of the flowers on her desk. "I'm not afraid of a dirty job, even if his paper is a disaster. Especially not today."

"What the hell happened on this trip to California?" Anna looked like she wanted to shake Carrie upside down to see what miracle elixir of satisfaction bubbled out of her.

Carrie smiled. "What's next on my calendar, Anna?"

"You have the faculty meeting. No lunch this time, just discussing procedural matters."

"Sounds absolutely awful. Let's go to lunch instead. Are you free?"

"You're going to skip a faculty meeting?"

"Yes. My treat."

Anna stared at her, lips parted, no sounds coming out. Then she grinned. "I have many questions, and I think you may have been abducted by aliens, but let me shut up before I cost myself a free lunch."

Carrie and Anna traipsed down the path from campus to the strip of restaurants at the start of town. They ordered grilled-chicken sandwiches and an enormous basket of truffle fries.

"You met a movie star," Anna summarized after Carrie had filled her in on the details of her trip. "I'm so jealous, I don't know if I should even be talking to you. You didn't get me Carlos's autograph!"

"I honestly was so overwhelmed by the whole ordeal that it didn't even cross my mind. I don't have his autograph myself." She hadn't managed to find Carlos again by the time an announcement was made that limos going back to the designated lower-budget hotel would be leaving in five minutes. She'd barely elbowed her way through the crowd to the front driveway to make it in time. She wished she'd been able to say goodbye.

"Well, other than that devastating fact, it's a good first step for Professor Carrie Davenport," Anna said as she crunched on a fry. "And, like, a generation of astronauts."

Carrie nodded. "Yeah. To be honest, it's a relief to finally start standing up for what's right."

"The only thing we don't know is what the solution they've come up with will actually be."

"No," Carrie agreed. "We don't. Libby said we'd find out this week."

"What's the worst it could be?" Anna raised her eyes to the ceiling and answered her own question. "Some thoughts-and-prayers bullshit about how they're going to reflect deeply on the issue?"

"Mm. A roundtable where they ponder whether diversity is in fact a worthwhile goal?"

"Yikes. But, on the other hand, I don't think Beau would've lied to your face," Anna said. She caught herself, waving a fry in the air to recant her statement. "Oh my god, scratch that. Not like a billionaire CEO has ever lied before."

"So, what can we even expect? They're going to make all the future colonists Black and brown now?" Carrie sighed. "I hope it's something good. I really, really hope." She sent up a silent prayer.

"Otherwise, your research assistants won't let you hear the end of it," Anna joked.

"I know. I've already placated them by incorporating equity clauses into the constitution—which is a good thing. But if Project Mars hasn't found a good solution to the colonist issue, I don't know what I'll do."

"Maybe your students will imprison you in your office until you demand PM puts some people of color on that spaceship."

"And where will you be while I'm locked in my office?"

"Sleeping in."

Carrie stole one of Anna's extra pickles off her plate. "You're fired. Preemptively."

Anna stuck out her tongue.

They returned to the office from lunch, walking more slowly this go-around, stuffed to the brim with ice cream.

"Can you email me a bibliography of Professor Vicki Jackson's work? Look up her Harvard faculty web page. I want to figure out how we can draft a feminist constitution. I'm ready to tackle something big today."

Anna bowed deeply before sitting behind her desk. "Professor Carrie Davenport, perpetually chasing big, big dreams."

On Wednesday afternoon, an email popped into her inbox with a red exclamation point and the subject line *MEETING SCHEDULED: PM Constitutional Design Team—Urgent*

Discussion. She opened the email, noting that it had been sent from Libby with the entire team and Grant copied.

> Project Mars has an exciting new development to share that has the potential to directly impact your team. Please see the attached calendar invitation. We look forward to discussing.

She double-clicked on the invitation. A meeting for the next day at midday via video call. Project Mars certainly hadn't concerned themselves with whether or not the team would be available. She hoped Adam had a pressing commitment that he'd have to miss . . . or better yet, he wouldn't make the call at all.

What could the meeting mean? Grant was a pretty high-up figure in the Project Mars hierarchy since he oversaw all the nontechnical operations for the endeavor. Perhaps Project Mars was doing the right thing. It was a corporation that often flouted the rules, sure, but maybe this time the company would choose to be unproblematic.

The next day, she sat at the computer in her office, sweating into her navy blazer as her mouse hovered over the Join Meeting button. She dabbed a tissue at her temples and finally clicked. Her video popped up, and she saw that her dabbing efforts had been successful. Her face was mirrored back to her beside only one other participant's video frame: Adam's. Oof. She clicked the Turn Video Off button so quickly her mouse nearly slid off the desktop.

"Professor Davenport, was that you?" said her least favorite deep, velvety voice. Curse her father for instilling into her the notion that to be on time was to be late. She

could've joined right as the meeting was starting, but no—
she'd instead invited strained small talk.

She clicked her camera back on. "Oh, hello Professor
Kilpatrick. There you are. A pleasure to see you."

"Ah. I have to ask. Do you know the source of this meeting? It was put on our calendars rather hastily, if you ask me,
with not even the slightest hint as to the reason. I assumed,
as our leader, you would know and could explain why I'm
missing a departmental meeting."

Have you heard of racism? she wanted to ask. *Hopefully
something to do with that.*

She bridled her instinctive response and took a long
pause, hoping she'd be interrupted.

"I'm hoping that soon—"

Her luck turned. Owen's image cropped up next to
Adam's; and a second later, Libby's.

"Excellent! I'm glad to see you're all here!" Libby shot
them an electric white-toothed smile. "Grant will be on in
just a moment."

Adam mercifully held off on his questioning, looking
disgruntled as he tapped a ballpoint pen against a yellow
legal pad. The persistent tapping was making her nervous.
She wished he'd put himself on mute.

The disgruntled tapping lasted for only a few staccato
beats longer until Grant joined, straightening the collar of
his white button-down and adjusting his screen so the team
could better view his face within the blue box of his office,
bright with morning light.

"Constitutional team, hello. Thanks for joining us on
such short notice. We wanted to loop you in on some developments we've been pursuing on our end that I hope will
benefit your work."

Grant had jumped in quickly, starting the meeting with no further ado. Carrie found herself sitting straighter in her chair at his stiff posture and direct approach.

Before he could continue, another person joined the video call. Carrie nearly jerked her head in surprise. A Black woman with perfectly unblemished brown skin framed by a voluminous mane of shiny loose curls blinked at the camera and then briefly glanced down to straighten the lapel of her emerald-green blazer. Glancing back up, she flashed a winning, slightly sheepish smile.

"I hope I'm not too late."

Carrie's mind reeled. She knew the woman. She had seen her talking to Grant at the party. But even more than that, she knew her from somewhere else. The woman's skin popped against the backdrop of a bright-yellow office in front of an American flag.

"Team," Grant said. "I hope you're all familiar with Senator Kendra Brown."

Right, that was it. Congress. Carrie had seen her face on television.

"Senator!" Owen boomed, a bright grin on his face. "An honor to be connecting with you today. We met briefly at a legislative forum on housing policy in your great home state of Louisiana, and it was a delight to chat with you."

Senator Brown inclined her head in recognition, a polite smile playing on her red-tinted lips. "A pleasure to see you again."

Carrie wondered how many times a day a senator had to pretend to recognize people she'd only met once.

"I'm glad you're familiar, Owen," Grant said. "I don't know if Carrie and Adam know Senator Brown, but after the call, you'll have plenty of time to get acquainted with her.

She's got an incredibly impressive resume—from her time at West Point to her military service, master's in chemical engineering, successful years in industry, and eventual run for Senate."

"In what capacity will we know her?" Adam asked, his tone bristly. He looked like a toddler whose parents had engaged in an adult conversation without him.

"We've decided that Senator Brown will be the first head of the government you establish, however you term it—president, commander, head of parliament, whatever. A George Washington of sorts."

"You're going to space, Senator?" Owen's eyes bugged out of his head.

Senator Brown nodded. "You all can call me Kendra in private while we're working together. And yes."

"Wait just a minute," Adam said. "What we're thinking of establishing is a constitutional democracy. That requires *representation*. We haven't agreed yet to anything different. The colonists are supposed to select their leader. They're already bound to a lot of Project Mars corporate rules, so it's of even greater importance that their government is left to them. Self-rule! We don't even know the senator . . . respectfully," he added as an afterthought.

"I know," Grant said. "But we like the idea of a carefully strategized first leader. And Kendra will only be serving as leader for the first class. It's only the first two years. After that, the colonists can self-govern as they wish."

"But . . . why?" Adam asked.

"Kendra brings many benefits. She has years of military service, so she is exceptional at living in tense environments and leading under pressure. Her time as Louisiana senator has prepared her to govern a large number of people and listen to different concerns. And she has a scientific background that will help her support mission needs."

She also gives the colony US government support and buy-in, Carrie thought to herself. The whole thing was brilliant.

"Importantly," Grant continued, "it is meaningful representation for the head of the colony to be a Black woman. We will make strident efforts to emphasize how much we value minority voices and how we want to elevate and amplify those voices."

There was an extended, heavy sigh. "Honestly, Grant." Adam removed his glasses and examined them in the light, his shoulders slumped. "I'm disappointed the Project has bought into this diversity mumbo jumbo. I know in some industries there's a benefit, but destroying self-rule for the purpose of mere optics, of people merely knowing that a Black woman is the leader, is preposterous. We know from 2008 that a Black leader isn't going to solve everyone's problems."

"A person can be the best fit for the job *and* Black. The two aren't mutually exclusive. Kendra is the right person for this job." Grant sat back and muted his microphone, as if he was done with the debate.

"We're going to announce Senator Brown's leadership next month," Libby chimed in brightly before anyone else could respond. "The press release will provide good publicity for your work and upcoming report. It will then offer an overview of Kendra's four years in the Marines, her master's in chemical engineering and intensive leadership program at MIT's Sloan School of Management, her half a billion dollars in profit while leading a chemical engineering firm, and all the incredible bills she has sponsored during her two years in the House and last five years in the Senate. The release will reaffirm the Project's commitment to diversity and will talk about measures Kendra herself is going to lead, like inclusivity training for the colonists. She's going to participate in recruiting efforts for the next colonist class as well. In short, we've got a whole campaign going."

"I think it's a fantastic idea," Carrie said. "I warmly welcome your leadership, Kendra, as well as your engagement as we finalize the government system. This is definitely a step in the right direction. It will make many of the colonists feel more comfortable, and you'll be a great role model for little girls who themselves want to go to space."

Despite her measured words, she barely resisted the overwhelming urge to stick her tongue out at Adam. She couldn't wait to watch the launch with Naomi knowing that Kendra was on board. She figured some of the measures the Project envisioned were just lip service or empty programs, but she hoped some of them would be meaningful. Whether or not they could change the composition of this class, the Project had managed to find a workaround to add a person of color who would benefit the colony. One person of color wasn't going to change everything. But under her leadership, she could oversee a more supportive and inclusive community. And it was better than nothing.

"Thank you, Carrie," Kendra said. "I am looking forward to getting to know you better both professionally and on a personal level." The way Kendra peered at the camera from beneath her thick dark lashes gave Carrie pause, but she couldn't decipher why.

"Same here, Senator," Owen said. "This is a good development for the colony. You have a hell of a resume."

At Adam's silence, Carrie couldn't help but chime in again. "I think I speak for everyone when I say we're all thrilled, Kendra, really. Thank you, Grant and Libby, for pulling everything together."

"Of course," Grant said. "Thanks for your cooperation and your time today. Please keep the senator apprised of any developments in your research so she can continue to prepare herself."

"Was Adam mad? Was he furious? Did steam come out of his ears?" Kim asked on the phone the next day. She had a delighted gossipy lilt to her voice, like she was lounging on her bed with the house phone, speculating who'd asked who to prom.

Carrie was, herself, not far from bed. She had curled up on the love seat in her bedroom in cozy pajamas and under a heavy throw blanket.

"Oh my goodness, Kim, the call was fantastic. He was so frustrated. He was already grumpy that he had to take thirty minutes out of his *very busy schedule*, and then for something as maddening as a Black woman? Ruining his elected democracy? I thought he'd storm off. He might have if he hadn't been so flabbergasted."

"Excellent," Kim chuckled lowly. "I'm very glad to hear it."

Carrie pulled the blanket closer to her, cozy and content. "All is well."

There was rustling on the line, then a distant yelp. "Gabrielle Taylor, I can see your light on! You think I can't tell you're reading under the covers? Put the book down, or I'll beat your little butt with it."

Carrie avoided laughing, worried she might be on speakerphone. It reminded her of her own childhood. She'd always had her head in a book, wanting to know all there was to know about everything. Her mother had been torn between letting her daughter explore and enforcing bedtime. Kim seemed . . . less torn.

A door slammed. Kim sighed, and then her voice came back on the line at full volume. "I have a little girl for you, if you want her. You can have her for free." She could hear Kim descending the stairs.

"No, thank you. Happily child-free."

"Ugh, she's going to lead me to vice."

"Drinking?"

"Worse." There was a rustle and then a crunch. "Cheetos."

"Extra spicy?"

"Just like in college." Kim crunched another hot chip. "So, with this whole Senator Brown thing. You think the Project has gone far enough then, to address your concerns?"

"Not really," Carrie said. "The installment of one Black woman can't solve the major representation problem Project Mars faces. I don't want her to be a mere token. But honestly? It's more than I expected from them. They're not going to change overnight. So we can go step by step. Having Senator Brown there is more helpful than not. She's smart, accomplished, and seems to get the diversity thing. In the meantime, I think she's going to be a fantastic leader."

"Mm, yeah. I'm sure you'd like to be under her . . . leadership."

"What are you saying? And why do I have to fend off your lewd comments every phone call?" Carrie complained.

"Senator Brown is queer, isn't she?" Kim said, ignoring Carrie's complaint. "And single. I haven't seen news of her bringing dates to any functions in ages, at least two or three years. And honestly, such a catch. Gorgeous by all measures, the world's most impressive resume, and the perfect mix of power and Southern charm."

"Maybe you should date her."

"Eh. I think I should keep Brian around. He helps me hide the good snacks from the girls."

"I'm sure the senator would help you do that."

Carrie could almost hear Kim rolling her eyes. But her voice a second later was serious. "I don't know, Carrie. There's nothing wrong with meeting women at bars, but Kendra is the kind of woman you deserve to be with. She fits in your world and you fit in hers. She's brilliant and funny and worthy of you. She wouldn't have you in a—"

"The next two words better not be *jail cell*."

"I had to bail my best friend out of jail!" Kim wailed. "I'm still traumatized, and I wasn't even the one locked up."

"Oh goodness," Carrie said. She still couldn't afford to think in detail about what had happened. The physical bruises had healed, the university had forced her into line, and she was taking what action she could. And it was working out. Plus, she hadn't seen Shauna in at least two months.

"Look. Just because Devon thought you were nerdy and boring does *not* mean you should see yourself that way. The right person would recognize you as a trailblazing theorist and devoted teacher—and they would find that sexy. I miss you and I love you and I want what's best for you. I want you to be with someone who appreciates all that you are."

"I know." Carrie was surprised by the lump that was forming in her throat. "I want an equal partner."

"Come to DC, and we can plot how you'll get into Senator Brown's astronaut pants."

Carrie groaned. "I will not be doing that."

"C'mon, you've gotta admit that Project Mars has been a godsend for your romantic life. You've got the choice between a movie star and a sitting senator. If you don't slip between Carlos's silky sheets and report back on all the details, I'll disown you."

She had a point. With the flurry of recent activity, Devon seemed like a lifetime ago. "I'm hanging up on you."

"Don't you dare."

"But I'll see you soon. I'll be in DC next month for our team meeting. Owen is hosting."

"Fantastic. I'll come visit your big fancy Project Mars–sponsored hotel room. We can chat about my newest draft journal article, which will be hitting your inbox in approximately ten minutes. I welcome your thorough edits."

Carrie glared at the phone. "More work, *and* I guess I'm not staying with you?"

"We're redoing the guest room. Gray is out. Beige is back in."

14

TWO WEEKS before her trip to Washington, DC, Carrie gathered her research assistants for another review meeting. She had learned her lesson from her battle with the conference room's coffeemaker the last meeting. She would not be fooled twice. Rather than wage war against an inanimate object, Carrie had stopped at the campus coffee shop to buy a thirty-two-ounce container of the liquid gold the shop called the Scholars' Roast. And rather than stare in hunger at the snacks her students had the foresight to bring, she had baked fresh blueberry muffins. Boo-yah. She was on her A game.

Evie sighed as she pulled open the gingham cloth lining Carrie's trusty picnic basket. "Oh my goodness, they're still warm." She looked on the verge of drooling.

Carrie pushed a stack of paper plates her way. "Fresh from the oven, and slathered in butter."

Parker pulled out a muffin and tore off a decadent chunk. "Mm. Thank you, Professor Davenport. These are good.

Although, what's happening with Project Mars is even better." They glanced beside them at Lori, who was busy pulling a thick binder out of her backpack. At Parker's words, she paused and squeezed their hand.

"Yeah." She turned to Carrie. "What do you think?"

"About Senator Brown? What do *you* think?" Carrie asked softly. She met Lori's eyes.

"I like her," Lori said.

"And . . . ?" Carrie prompted.

"I like Senator Brown's involvement because I think visibility and representation is good, even if it's the bare minimum. I don't think it's enough. We need to stage protests and engage in activism to force Project Mars to go further than they'd naturally be inclined to. Evie and I have talked about that," Lori said, nodding at Evie.

Evie swallowed a chunk of muffin and brushed crumbs off her hands. "We need to inspire enough students and concerned citizens to mobilize," she said earnestly.

Carrie wanted to take back Evie's muffin. They'd already acted! She wasn't going to chain herself to the Project Mars front door. Even if it worked, she would never put herself in harm's way again if she could help it—she wouldn't deprive her father of another Davenport. She couldn't put at risk Evie, Lori and Parker, no matter how willing they were to put themselves on the line. She knew better.

"But," Lori said after a long pause, "I think you're also right that maybe what we're doing here with the constitution is bigger and more lasting. Activism will take time. What we're doing with the constitution will last, and we need to get it done now. I want to make sure everything we write stands for our values."

Carrie hadn't realized her arms had been crossed over her chest, but she experienced a release so visceral she nearly knocked over her coffee as she uncrossed them. She breathed in deeply. "Yes. Exactly."

She glanced at Parker, who bowed their head to her. "I'm in favor of your approach, Professor."

She turned to Evie last. "Okay? We start with the constitution, and the rest can come later?" she prompted.

Evie's lips twisted in dissatisfaction, but she didn't protest. "I agree that the constitution is the most important thing right now."

"Good," she said. "Let's get to work then. We need to determine the core values and themes that we want to incorporate into a governing document. We'll start with Evie, then go to Lori, then Parker."

"Alright," Evie said, pushing her muffin plate away. "In this round of research, I studied shared values among people living in democracies. I looked at polling data in the United States and abroad to get a sense of what people find important. Most promising is that in terms of the top ten democratic values among Americans, respect and freedom were paramount. Of polled Americans, 84 percent said it was very important that the rights and freedoms of all people are respected. That comes above any other value."

"That's good. Wonder when people stopped living that value in practice," Parker mused.

"What, you don't think Americans respect each other's rights?" Lori said with a wry twist of her lips. "Probably started from day one."

"Yeah, that whole slavery thing wasn't a good look, so I'd say we got off to a poor start. But people still consider it one of the top American values today."

Evie explained that the next most important values were that elected officials face serious consequences for their misconduct, judges remain neutral, and everyone be given an equal opportunity to succeed.

"Great," Carrie said after Evie had summarized the bulk of her research. "These are basic principles that should form the basis for everything else we do."

"Are those values the same for people from other countries?" Parker asked. "Like, do other countries have different core principles?" They bit into a muffin and shrugged. "I'd be curious to see."

"Yes and no," Evie said. "Values like social justice, the rule of law, and freedom of speech are core principles across all democracies. But the importance of each value varies by country. For example, in most other democracies, equality is valued much higher than liberty. But in the US, we tend to value liberty as much as, if not more than, equality. Likewise, we value individualism over either respect for authority or social harmony. We put our own freedom and enjoyment over getting along."

"That sounds very American," Lori said with a tilt of her eyebrow. "But it's yet another thing we should change for Mars. There is no reason for individual colonists to put their own needs above the needs of the group. It would be chaos, especially when they're all relying on each other."

"I agree," Carrie said. "While we aren't trying to diminish individual rights, the needs of the group will come first. Social harmony is even more important in space. And that relates to your work, Lori."

Lori opened a binder stuffed with printed articles and extracted a page of handwritten notes. "I looked at how to shut down misogynists in space . . . or, I guess as Prof

Davenport put it, what language ensures maximum equality for women and gender minorities." She pulled her braids into a high bun as she scanned her notes. "Essentially, we need to include language that mentions equality as many times as possible to make clear we're serious about treating people right."

Lori passed out articles she'd read on feminist constitution drafting. "Look at this one by Kathleen Sullivan. Essentially, the constitution will need a general catchall provision promoting equality, plus a specific provision committing to sex equality. That's been effective before— back in 1979, the United Nations adopted a treaty called the Convention on the Elimination of All Forms of Discrimination against Women, which has both broad and highly specific provisions. Sullivan's article also explains that we need to think about whether we ban sex discrimination— which would ban discriminating against people of all genders on the basis of sex—or try to specifically mention that we want to protect women. In this day and age, although we want to uplift women, we all know gender isn't a binary. So, a general ban is better."

"That's fair," Carrie said. "While putting an emphasis on the social classes we want to protect is helpful, we don't want to be too rigid in who is a part of that class."

"Right," Lori said. She spent the next few minutes highlighting Sullivan's framework: how, in an ideal world, the constitutional provisions would keep Project Mars from discriminating based on sex and would also prevent individual colonists from discriminating against others. The provisions would also go beyond mere prevention of discrimination to list positive rights—affirmative commitments the colony government would make to assist with equality, similar to how the US Bill of Rights guaranteed certain freedoms to citizens.

"I like it," Evie said, handing the article back to Lori. "It's cool to see that scholars have already considered the best language to use to be inclusive in drafting a constitution. Is the scholarship on race pretty similar, Parker?"

"Er . . . not exactly. I'd actually like to start with a quote I think is really helpful. This is from one of Girardeau Spann's articles, titled 'Race Ipsa Loquitur.'"

They read, "The truth is that the United States is so firmly committed to the doctrine of white supremacy that any escape from the gravitational force of that doctrine seems simply unimaginable. In fact, racial inequality appears to be a constitutive element of United States culture [...]. The United States has always placed the interest of whites above the interest of racial minorities. It formally did so in the past. It tacitly does so in the present. And all indications are that it will persistently do so in the future [...]. By generating constitutional doctrines that marginalize the significance of discrimination, the Supreme Court has successfully rede-fined the concept of equality in ways that protect the contin-uing practice of racial subordination. Our cultural commitment to the principle of racial equality has proven to be more rhetorical than real."

"Damn, Parker. That was unbelievably depressing." Lori laughed.

"So much for an exciting day of constitution building," Evie joked.

"I know, I know." Parker held up their hands. "Spann's premise is that the Supreme Court helps the white majority oppress racial minorities by deeming such oppression to be something that is compelled by the Constitution. It's not light stuff."

"But it's clear where you're going with this, Parker," Carrie said. "There are a few problems. Obviously, the original US Constitution is problematic. It has provisions intended to preserve slavery. But even when it does mention equality, this country has often ignored those general constitutional principles of equality to, practically speaking, still engage in discrimination. Culturally speaking, this country has never been about fairness and equality."

"Yeah," Parker agreed. "I think our constitutional language is crucial, and we must take care in its drafting, but I also never realized how much a commitment to it in *practice* matters."

Neither had Carrie, if what had happened to her was anything to go by.

"Which is why Parker is on our team," Evie chimed in. "We need a comprehensive solution."

Carrie suppressed a sigh. "Right," she echoed. "Well, finish updating us on how we can promote racial equality in the constitution, Parker, and we'll go about dismantling systems next."

After dinner the following week, as Carrie was finalizing her research notes at her kitchen counter, a low vibration rustled her haphazard stack of papers. She shifted journal articles aside and stacked her scattered books on top of each other until she unearthed her phone. The screen flashed with an unfamiliar area code.

"Hello?" Carrie said tentatively.

"Carrie," said a soft voice. "Hi. You don't have to sound so on guard. It's Shauna."

"All the more reason to be on guard," Carrie mumbled.

"You don't have my number saved in your phone?"

"No."

"Ouch."

"Honestly, Shauna, what did you expect?"

"I don't know. So far, your track record seems to be that you can't stay mad at me for too long. Even after what happened, you still . . . well. There was that time."

Carrie closed her eyes. How was this woman so uniquely her undoing? But, she rationalized, it wasn't Shauna herself. It was this hellscape of a school year. It was Project Mars, and Adam, and her run-in with the police, and *everything* that had weakened her until she was willing to compromise her usual standards to be with—and go back to—someone totally unlike her. Shauna was gruff and direct and bold. She cut through all Carrie's blustery academic defenses, all her pompous seriousness, to physically touch and feel her way past Carrie's hard outer shell. There wasn't an awkward bone in Shauna's body, and that was both Carrie's problem and her saving grace at a time when all she wanted was to feel something *good*.

Kim was right that she deserved someone who understood her and who valued her years of study and hard work, especially since Devon had . . . not. But one word from Shauna, and all negative consequences seemed to vanish in a pink cloud of lust. Carrie liked to know and understand things, but she was willing for *this*, in the here and now, to make absolutely no sense.

"That one time was a mistake," Carrie said.

"A lot of good times involve a few mistakes."

Carrie didn't reply.

"Let's hang out again," Shauna prompted.

"I have to work," Carrie said. "I have to figure out core values for humanity to carry forward into space."

"It's just a rich person's playground anyway, right? Why invest billions of dollars into something when people here can't afford to eat?"

"It's the future," Carrie argued.

"For a select few."

"I'm literally in the process of trying to make space travel more fair," Carrie snapped. She took a deep breath. "I don't need you to get it. It's my job, and the job is unfinished, so I'm telling you that I can't hang out."

Shauna pressed on, undeterred, as if Carrie hadn't spoken. "So, what are you wearing?" she tried in a caricature of lust that still made Carrie squirm.

She tried not to say anything. But after a beat, she couldn't help herself. "You first."

"An Eagles jersey. And that's it, because all my pants are in the wash."

Oh fuck. "Sounds like very easy access."

"Mm. It's a shame you're not here to help me take it off. What are you doing this Sunday night?"

"I just said I'm busy."

"You're going to hide from me forever? Is that really what you want?"

"I do mean it this time. I'm leaving Sunday afternoon for Washington, DC."

"Is there a convention or something? Will the folks writing the Venus and Pluto constitutions be there, too?"

"No, the Pluto guy can't come. He just found out it's not a planet."

"Devastating news for him. I hope he didn't get too far in the drafting."

"Eh, this constitution writing stuff is a breeze; I'm sure he didn't strain himself too much."

"Glad to hear it." Shauna laughed, deep and throaty. "How long are you gone?"

"Only two days. Driving up Sunday morning, coming back early on Tuesday."

"Perfect, I can afford to take two days off. I got fired from the Z Mart after that whole theft thing, but now I'm at the world's slowest Italian restaurant, and they could care less when I dip out."

"What?"

"I'm coming with you."

"What?" Carrie repeated. "Shauna, no. It's a work trip."

"I won't get in your way, I promise. I'll keep myself busy during the day. I need a break from here, from life. I haven't been to DC in decades."

"I can't just . . . ," Carrie spluttered. She paused. "Are you in some kind of trouble? Something with the police?"

"No. Despite what you may think, Carrie, I'm not a common criminal. What happened before with the store was . . . I mean, that's not me. It has eaten me up since then, thinking about how it hurt you. I don't like it."

What was she supposed to do? It was a Project Mars trip. She needed to focus at night, review her notes so she could present a clear picture to the team of what needed to happen. She couldn't be distracted. And was she going to be one of those people who kept a pretty woman stowed away in the hotel room? Even if it was a tempting reward after a day of dealing with Adam, it felt like such a dirty cliché she could barely wrap her head around it. What if the team found out?

"Before you say no, just . . . don't. Don't overthink it. I need this, and you need this. Pick me up on Sunday."

Carrie let out an internal guttural scream of frustration to the heavens. But over the phone line, all she said was, "Okay."

15

ABRAHAM LINCOLN DID NOT SEEM interested in having a late-night existential conversation with Carrie as she stared up at his marble form, swatting early spring gnats away from the straw of her milkshake. She had, against her better judgment, picked Shauna up earlier that day, and the two had made good time to DC despite her driving barely above the speed limit all afternoon. She would not tempt fate twice with Shauna in her car. The journey reminded her of old road trips with her father, who loved any excuse to be in the car. He'd finish fixing up a car he'd built from scratch, and they'd head out for a few days to drive up or down the coast.

Darkness had fallen by the time they arrived in DC, and Carrie drove them on a slow tour around the glowing, illuminated monuments for Shauna's benefit. They parked near the tidal basin to throw out the remnants of their rest stop burgers and fries, and Shauna, despite the late hour, strode off toward Lincoln, leaving Carrie to follow in her wake.

Carrie had words for Lincoln, anyway. She didn't know how any leader could stare ahead at an uncertain future and make choices that would impact millions of people to come. She wondered whether he had done enough, and whether people might think she should do more, too. She remembered reading a Lincoln quote in her high school history class: "I shall, when the time comes, try to do right, in view of all the lights then before me."

Shauna spun in a circle under the domed monument, staring up at the ceiling, before looking at Carrie. "You look like you've got a stick up your butt," Shauna said.

"I do not."

"Alright, maybe you're not screaming and hollering, but you look thoughtful and tense."

Carrie sighed. "I want everything to go well with this meeting tomorrow. There's been good news lately, a bit of progress. Like how I was telling you in the car about Senator Brown. I just . . . want to be able to have faith in people and institutions again."

Shauna leaned against a stone pillar and cocked her head toward Lincoln. "Most people and institutions are a mixed bag. Good countries do bad things, and the people in them do things for their own damned selfish reasons. If I've learned anything, it's that some people and situations are shitty, but if you stop believing everything will be okay, it never will be."

"That's an optimistic way of viewing it, I guess."

Shauna shrugged. "In the worst of times, you have to pretend things will be okay. So, I choose to believe that this week will go okay."

"I'm hoping. I'll pop the world's biggest bottle of champagne once this project is over the finish line." Carrie sucked on her chocolate shake and turned away from Lincoln. She made her way down the steps, this time leaving Shauna to follow.

Shauna skipped up to Carrie and bumped their shoulders as they walked. "I'll raise a glass to that. In the meantime, maybe there's a way we can get you less tense."

Carrie glanced around them. The grounds of the mall were nearly deserted and still, quiet in the early spring evening except for a few tourists in the distance.

"We need some ground rules."

"Oh, come off it." Shauna waved her away. "I'll keep a low profile in the hotel. I only plan to do naughty things to you behind closed doors."

Owen had arranged to hold the meeting on Capitol Hill. Carrie took a cab from downtown. She drove up Constitution Avenue toward the Senate and emerged from the car in her burgundy suit amid a whole crop of dark-suited lobbyists. She rushed through the tiled hallways until she reached the door to a small conference room, flanked on either side with American flags. Her time with Shauna the previous day had distracted her indeed, to the point of arriving on time rather than early.

"Carrie Davenport," Owen said heartily as she opened the door. "Welcome, welcome!" He shook her hand with enthusiasm as if she were an old friend. To him, she probably was. The small paneled room had a conference table with room for six, and she and Owen were the first arrivals. She arranged her notes at the head of the table, opposite Owen.

A second later, an aide entered with a carafe of coffee, and Adam followed on his tail. *Guess you take the good with the bad,* Carrie thought. She let Owen chat up Adam and the aide as she poured herself a cup of coffee and added cream, wondering whether it would be unreasonable to ask for a little wooden stirrer.

"Well, anyway," Owen said as Adam got seated and extracted his legal pad, "I'm glad you're both here. I'm also glad Senator Brown could arrange this conference room for us here on the Hill. There's a lot going on today with the vote on the crime bill, and you know that Senator Appleton always has a lot to say about inner-city crime, which riles up both sides to the point that—"

"Ah," Adam interrupted. "Yes. We've all certainly had enough of talking about crime with Carrie's recent run-in with the police, and I do have a meeting this afternoon with an old friend from college who's now in the House, so if you don't mind, Ms. Davenport . . ."

Carrie blinked. *Don't kill him don't kill him don't . . .* "Delighted to kick things off. Based on our project plan, at this stage we should have all given thought to the types of values we want embodied in the constitution before we turn to the final task next month of proposing and revising draft language. Owen, as our distinguished host, if you'd like to get us started?"

"Thanks, Carrie," Owen said. "My main focus has been empirical research from bipartisan and partisan think tanks about common American values, and, at Carrie's direction, I compared those to global studies."

Owen explained his high-level takeaway that the US Bill of Rights still represented the most commonly held values and rights, with individuality, liberty, equality, and access to justice serving as broader shared values. His work fully tracked the research she and Evie had done.

"Excellent. If I may go next." Adam cleared his throat. "I studied the values espoused by the founding fathers in early American writings." Adam distributed to the group a stapled stack of papers so heavy Carrie nearly dropped it on the table. The top of the document read, "Outline: Takeaways from Framers." She flipped through the stack, noting sections on Thomas Paine, James Madison, Thomas Jefferson, Alexander Hamilton, and Benjamin Franklin. She kept her eyes glued to the document lest her face reflect her utter exhaustion at the mere idea of interacting with Adam and his scholarship.

Adam cleared his throat after several long minutes. "And that's why I concur with Owen that the views of our forefathers are largely reflected in current core American values."

Carrie jumped. She had almost zoned out through the conclusion of his explanation. "Yes. Uh. That's helpful. Thank you." She paged through her own notes. "I think it's always good to know where we've come from, although in my own studies, I was interested in ensuring that we have a modern constitution that fairly represents the incredibly diverse group that we will be sending into space. I think we can agree our country today doesn't look the same as it did two hundred years ago. With that in mind, I've prepared a short memo for you two that summarizes my research on how our constitution can best protect the rights of women and minorities, as well as the socioeconomically disadvantaged."

Adam took the single-page research summary from Carrie like she had just rubbed the page in fresh dung. He skimmed the contents before looking up at her, an incomprehensible look on his face that Carrie assumed he reserved for his slowest, most bird-brained students.

"I take issue with the nature of this memo." Adam pushed his glasses up his nose.

"Please explain," Carrie said.

"Well, right off the bat, I don't agree with the premise," Adam started. "Project Mars asked us to create a charter similar to our US Constitution that will provide a broad legal framework for the colonists to govern themselves. Period. And from the start, you have acted like American democracy isn't the unquestionable solution. You were proven wrong on that point, the tomfoolery with Senator Brown aside. And now, you're advancing some socialist, radical hippie commune that reflects the world according to Carrie Davenport, far removed from actual American values."

"That's not correct," Carrie countered. "Project Mars didn't ask us to model the charter on the US Constitution. They asked us to start from scratch and create the best possible governing structure for a space colony, whatever that government may be. We would have been shirking our duty if we hadn't considered every possible government, as I have said time and again. You're the one who couldn't believe anything other than the culture you grew up in is valid, unwilling to take your head out of the sand. But just because something is familiar and comfortable doesn't mean it's the right answer."

Adam drained his coffee and crushed the paper cup in his hand, his knuckles going white with the effort. He leaned forward in his chair so his upper body towered over the table.

"Am I the enemy, Carrie, for wanting to preserve a good thing? America used to stand for something. And then the liberals came in with their woke attitudes and gave us a list of things we couldn't say. They put diversity above all else, even above people with more merit. You go to a symposium for political science scholars, and they won't let you speak because every panel has got to have a woman and a person of color or one of the letters in that godforsaken *LGBT* acronym. Decades of research and effort sidelined for some they/them in jeans touting their poorly researched theses. I enrolled my own *daughter* in one of the country's most academically prestigious boarding schools shortly before Susie died, and she upped and got a nose piercing. She graduated college with a theater degree, for heaven's sake, and thinks living in a studio in Brooklyn with a tattooed barista is going to get her anywhere. We don't have control over anything anymore."

"Your daughter sounds lovely," Carrie couldn't stop herself from murmuring. *More likeable than you.*

"She's starring in a play about how Reagan ruined Black people. And she's playing Ronald Reagan!" Adam snapped. "We've lost control over society. No one respects our values anymore amid these culture wars. This country is indeed changing, but it's for the worst. And you want to put that in a constitution. A permanent document."

"Adam, I don't think . . ." Owen tried to interrupt. He stood to pour another cup of coffee and slid it across the table to Adam. "Here, maybe if we could all take a break and—"

"Despite all that, I was willing to acknowledge that even if you were a mere diversity hire, you had some of the degrees that might've helped you to do the job," Adam continued, before taking a sip of the coffee and wincing. "But all that changed overnight. After you were taken into police custody, it was like that single night of incarceration infected your mind. You were radicalized from one night of lost sleep. I had laughed when I first heard the police locked you up like a common criminal, but now all I'm left to do is weep for the bitter, whiny woman it turned you into." He snatched up her memo. "I weep for this misguided document."

Carrie sat in stunned, furious silence. There was a vague crunching sound; she looked down and realized she'd clutched her stylus pen so hard that it had snapped, its black and red wires peeking out.

A knock on the door pierced the silence. A second later, the door opened to the smooth-skinned face of Senator Brown, this time in the flesh, in a perfectly tailored purple suit with a skirt short enough to make eyes wander.

"My apologies for being late; I've been in meetings all morning," Kendra said. She sat in the free chair opposite Adam and glanced at her phone, dismissing several notifications before speaking again. "But I'm delighted to participate and hear what you're cooking up! Thank you to Owen for extending the invite."

Carrie and Adam stared at her like she were a literal alien who had just returned from Mars.

"Oh right, yes, I almost forgot to mention it to the team! It's our pleasure, Senator," Owen said with an awkward chuckle. "We just got done highlighting some of our American ideals, and now we're turning to a few other considerations."

"Oh?" Kendra said. "Like what?"

"Professor Davenport would have us draft a feminist, antiracist constitution," Adam said, his words coming out in practically a snake's hiss.

"What's the motivation for this, Carrie?" Senator Brown probed. Her eyebrows shot up in a "pray, do tell" look.

"Our United States Constitution was drafted by slave-holders at a time when women did not have the right to vote and slaves weren't considered people," said Carrie firmly. "They weren't trying to be fair. The language is, as a result, not always inclusive or representative. We're now given a fresh chance to include and protect all voices. Current events show that we need, more than ever, a constitution that provides the legal basis to preserve and expand citizen rights."

Kendra looked from Carrie to Adam. "Well, I wholeheartedly agree. If we'd had a founding document like that, it would make all of our lives easier here on the Hill. Well, the Democratic Caucus, at least." She winked at Owen, who beamed at her.

"This isn't how a constitution is meant to be drafted," Adam said, his tone far more patient with Kendra than it had been with Carrie. "It's meant to be a neutral document, not play favorites among a small subset of people. There's no need to add this kind of radical language."

"Surely it's not radical to recognize that not everyone has been treated equally, and that this document is committed to doing so," Kendra said.

"We can achieve equality by the colonists doing the right thing and being upstanding citizens, not by turning the document into liberal blather." Adam turned to Owen, gesturing toward Carrie's memo. "Owen, you've been needlessly silent in this debate. Come on. Think of the key players in space right now. Air force commanders. Space force guys who want to prepare for war in space. Shareholders of aerospace and defense-weapons companies. And all of those old hats in Congress who have been questioning Project Mars in the news. These are classic conservative figures who don't care whether some woman has her panties in a bunch because not everyone is cheering on her rights. They'll never approve of this kind of document! They'll call it *mumbo jumbo*, and the Project won't get the support it needs from the military. It'll delay liftoff."

Owen cocked his head, weighing Adam's words. "Well, Carrie, Adam has a point about getting military buy-in. These are old war hawks we're dealing with. Project Mars wants, and needs, the support of Congress and the military. They're launching from an Air Force base, for heaven's sake."

Carrie glared at Owen over the rim of her coffee cup. *Et tu, Brute?*

"Exactly. Quite sensible, Owen," Adam said.

Carrie's glare deepened.

Owen blanched as he faced her. "That's not to say I disagree with the premise, Carrie," he filled in quickly. "I agree it's important to recognize past injustices and make things fairer in the future. I merely think Adam has a point about the language we use being important. Er . . . what do you think, Senator?"

"To the same extent you worry about the military, you likely also need buy-in from liberal academics, the international community, the astronauts I talked to who are worried about the colony's diversity, and the whole half of Congress who would probably support a so-called antiracist constitution. I think Carrie's right, gentlemen. And to the extent that we're worried about the military, we can be cautious in framing. The text isn't some liberal mumbo jumbo like Adam said, is it, Carrie? We'll make sure they know that."

"No. It's not. It's still a neutral document. We'd use gender-neutral terminology, phrases like 'equality' and 'on an equal basis,' and the like. It's not like we're saying, 'White men get one vote and everyone else gets two.'"

"That's what I thought," Kendra said with a smile. "I honestly don't think it poses an issue, and to me this discussion is over. We're all benefitting from Carrie's perspective and expertise. If any of you have any doubts, I'm happy to put in an extensive effort to lobby my colleagues."

Carrie wanted to do backflips. She had half a notion to sweep off the materials and coffee mugs from the conference table and do a handstand right there. She would, if given the opportunity, marry Kendra and have her politically minded babies.

"Great!" Carrie said. "It sounds like there's some consensus on this issue, then."

Owen looked from the senator to Carrie, then nodded.

Adam sported his deepest frown yet, his eyebrows nearly obscuring his dark eyes. "I will decide once I read the draft language, but I vehemently disagree with the path we're headed down."

It was a start.

Carrie adjusted the plunge of her black V-neck dress, wondering whether it had been a mistake to wear a dress that revealed half her chest. After the meeting, while Owen had tried to calm a fuming Adam in the hallway, Kendra had stepped closer to Carrie, making her pause as she gathered her purse and coat. She proposed that the two meet for evening drinks at Carrie's hotel, with a sultry smile and a hand on her lower back that made Carrie think, yeah, maybe a little black dress would outperform a stuffy burgundy blazer. Now, as she stood in the elevator bank a few paces away from the swanky downtown hotel bar, she wasn't sure whether this was too much. She didn't want to look like she was throwing herself at the senator in gratitude for all her support in the meeting.

Even if that was exactly how she felt.

She had spent most of the day on the Hill, meeting and having lunch with the team before visiting the Library of Congress to ask about a rare book she'd been chasing. By the time she'd returned to the hotel room, it was early evening, and the room was empty. She hoped Shauna was off enjoying herself and hoped even more that she would remain hidden away until after drinks. It left a bitter, metallic taste in her mouth how excited she was to meet Kendra, knowing that Shauna would soon be upstairs waiting for her in the room.

She quit adjusting her dress and entered the bar. There were a handful of couples and mixed groups in business suits at little bar tables up front, still wearing name tags from whatever conference they'd attended. It took her a second to spot Kendra, seated at the secluded far end of the bar, typing what was probably a long email on her phone.

"Senator," Carrie said softly as she approached and pulled out the neighboring barstool.

Kendra's eyes trailed from Carrie's hand on the back of the plush velvet stool up along Carrie's body to her chest, and the slight smile that accompanied Kendra's lingering eyes flooded her with warmth.

"Carrie," Kendra said affectionately. "I'm glad you're here. Please, sit. And if you call me 'senator' again, I'm going to kick your butt right out of this bar."

"Okay, noted, I'll be good tonight and call you Kendra,"

Carrie said with a chuckle. "What are we drinking?" Carrie nodded at Kendra's drink.

"Old-fashioned. Can I get you one?"

"Oof, no." She flagged down the bartender and ordered a martini.

"I think tonight calls for a celebration," Kendra said, raising her glass as the bartender set down Carrie's drink. "What should we toast to?"

"You," Carrie said bluntly. "And how you saved me this morning. I honestly am so deeply indebted to you, I don't know what to say."

"Oh, I know you can roughhouse with those boys all on your own." Kendra laughed. "I already do it all day for work, though, so I'm happy to step in and lighten the load for you."

Carrie smiled and sipped her drink.

"And you were right, Carrie," Kendra said, placing a hand on Carrie's forearm.

"Hmm?" Carrie murmured, wishing her brain cells could think of something more clever and witty to say instead of shutting down at the close, warm contact.

"Diversity in space is important. There's a lot that's going to happen to make space very unfair and unequal. A lot like here. Anything we can do to make it better, we should do. I'm in awe of all the ways you've stepped up."

"It was nothing. I've hardly done anything." She took a longer sip of her drink, hiding her surprise and pleasure behind the wide brim of her martini glass. "Honestly, my biggest success has been keeping my cool around Adam."

"Are you normally hot . . . headed?" Kendra said, drawing the words out in a way that left Carrie's mouth dry despite her drink.

"Oh, um . . . no. I'm your classic professor type, level

headed and academic. I've never really been pushed to anger like this before. This whole process has driven me crazy."

"I can see why. Adam is infuriating. And he's so much more dangerous because he's not ignorant. He's prejudiced, and he knows it."

"He is!" Carrie moaned. "God, it feels good to complain about it."

"I'm always here to listen. And to the extent that there are any issues in getting your constitution written the way you want, I can maybe help, too. I can set the tone in speeches to the colonists and in any initial resolutions we may pass. Maybe we can enact some of the first laws to cover any gaps in the constitution."

"I . . . wow." Carrie felt like a stone had been removed from her chest. She could now breathe deeply and fully again, the way her whole body felt infused with air. She took an exploratory breath, and it was easy without the physical weight of stress holding her back. "I, um . . ." She placed a hand on Kendra's. "That would mean the world to me. It would finish the job no matter what happens with Adam."

"Then let's do it." Kendra cracked a smile at her, and Carrie ached to feel the actual physical contours of those perfectly lined upturned lips. "And don't say you're forever indebted to me again, because a woman can only have so many life debts." She wagged a finger at Carrie.

"I won't say it. I'll just have to return the favor one day."

Kendra's eyebrows shot up faster than a rocket. "You will?" she teased.

Carrie's whole face went hot. Was this really happening? She was in a swanky hotel bar in the country's political headquarters, sharing a drink with a famous senator-turned-astronaut. And not just sharing a drink but clumsily flirting with her, too. And that senator was going to help her with her constitution for planet Mars. None of it made sense. What made even less sense was that it had come on the tail of passing the evening with a famous movie star in a billionaire's mansion. And what was downright unfathomable was that as she flirted with a mouthwatering dark-skinned power broker, she was entertaining a woman upstairs in her hotel room, whom she'd been through hell with, who was waiting to help her de-stress.

The whole thing, indeed, made her head spin. Devon, and his disappointment and disinterest in her, seemed a million light years away. She was still a bookish professor, and she was still more concerned with her research and writing and students than anything else, but in the last few months those things hadn't mattered. Because she had, with some fantastical aligning of the stars, grown powerful. Almost . . . sexy. And wanted. And in her new power and bravery, she'd managed to make a difference.

"You mentioned you have to roughhouse with all those insufferable congressmen," Carrie said, changing the subject. "What's the wildest thing you've said to any of them?"

"Well, if you can keep a secret, I'll tell you a story of blackmail and general mayhem," Kendra said with a wink. "Get me a little drunker, and you'll get the full scoop."

"I better buy you another drink, then."

They ordered another round of drinks, and Kendra regaled her with stories from Washington, of clandestine hotel-room meetings and thinly veiled insults traded at constituent barbecues.

"That's why I want a wife who isn't in politics," Kendra said, laughing around a burp as she finished a bawdy story about nearly getting into a fistfight with a Wyoming senator at a bar the night before a vote. "I don't want her to know any of this stuff about me."

"Or pull the same stunts on you," Carrie joked.

"Exactly. I need someone professional and brilliant and focused who will keep me in line." She looked Carrie up and down. "And someone who photographs well."

Carrie's head was spinning again. She glanced around the bar. They were still tucked in their secluded corner, no one daring to sit next to their intimate huddle. Her eyes skimmed the swanky silver clock near the entrance. It was already ten.

"I feel lucky to have enjoyed your company for so long. You must have very busy evenings as a woman who is so in demand," Carrie said.

"I do, usually. I have to return a few phone calls tonight and wake up early for a breakfast meeting tomorrow."

"I should get you into bed, then. Er, I mean, let you get to bed."

"Either way, darling," Kendra teased. "Let me walk you upstairs, like a real Southern lady should."

Kendra paid, and the two made their way to the elevator. Carrie liked the way Kendra's arm brushed hers as they walked; not too forward, but initiating body contact none-theless. The elevator arrived, and Carrie pressed the button to take them to the fourth floor.

As the doors opened again to the long hallway of rooms, dread suddenly slowed Carrie's steps. What would happen at the door, when Kendra bid her goodbye? Would Shauna hear their conversation outside? Would she smell the other woman on Carrie's clothes? What even gave Carrie the nerve? She had—begrudgingly, but still—welcomed Shauna onto the trip. They weren't together, and Carrie didn't owe her anything, but bringing another woman to the room was beyond rude.

Kendra stepped ahead of her down the hall, in charge even though she didn't know where she was going, and Carrie nearly cursed at the sight of the senator's tapered legs beneath her skirt. Kim was a little bit right. Kendra understood her, and she could help her with some of her toughest professional challenges. This was the kind of woman she was meant to be with.

Carrie was in a bind.

She quickened her pace and stepped in front of Kendra when they were still five doors down from the hotel room.

"This is good here," Carrie said softly. She wrapped her arms around the other woman's waist before she could say anything, and Kendra leaned readily into her embrace. "Maybe we can get together next time I'm in Washington. Before you go to space and everything."

"We better."

Kendra's eyes were dark and lusty when she pulled away, and Carrie tried to ignore their draw. She leaned against the door that was not hers as Kendra returned to the elevator, sparing a lingering look back at Carrie as she pressed the button and stepped in. The moment the doors closed, Carrie let out an enormous breath of relief.

16

"THERE YOU ARE!" Shauna said as soon as Carrie swung open the door to their hotel room. Shauna was flopped on the bed on her tummy, her slender legs sticking up in the air. She wore slightly worn, gray cotton shorts and a loose tank top, her blond hair spilling over her shoulders in loose waves as she cocked her head at Carrie. "I was beginning to think you'd returned home without me."

Carrie pressed her fingers to her chin. Her lips still trembled in anticipation of kissing Kendra, a need unfulfilled, her body still tingling with desire at the sight of the other woman's dark eyes seemingly undressing Carrie with just one look. She felt like her lust must be written all over her, a physical marker like a scarlet *A* on her chest.

"Oh, no, I could never do that," Carrie mumbled. She averted Shauna's gaze as she slipped into the bathroom and firmly shut the door. She peeled off her low-cut dress, wondering what had even made her wear it in the first place. What was she doing? God, Shauna was sprawled on the bed, expectant and sassy. Why had she put herself in this bind?

She knew, from the moment Kim had clued her in, that Kendra was the kind of person she'd been craving for ages. Why torture herself by inviting Shauna? She jabbed her toothbrush into her mouth so hard her cheek ached as she brushed away all remnants of the drinks she'd had. The fluffy hotel bathrobe hardly felt luxurious against the taint of guilt on her skin.

"Ah," Carrie said as she returned to the room. Her minty-fresh teeth had slightly restored her courage. "Well, how was your day? Did you do anything fun?" She sat on the bed a few inches from Shauna's outstretched leg.

"I had a very good time," Shauna said. "I climbed to the top of the Washington Monument and scoped things out, then people-watched along the Mall during lunchtime. Checked out the Air and Space Museum in the afternoon. Cool space stuff, but way too many kids."

"They do tend to get in the way." Carrie smiled.

Shauna rolled onto her side so she could better face Carrie. "How was your day, Professor?"

"It was good. Great, really. The team met to discuss the values we want enshrined in the constitutional text. Adam started to balk at my efforts to make the document more inclusive, but Kendra—er, Senator Brown, or, um, Kendra. Yeah. She really pulled through and convinced Adam to stand down, at least for now. So, everything went really well."

Shauna leveled her with a long, evaluating look. "You seem really grateful to the senator."

"I . . . yeah." She pulled at a loose thread dangling from her robe. "I truly could not have gotten through today without her," Carrie said, her voice barely above a whisper.

"And you want her. Badly."

"What?" Carrie yelped. "No! I mean, she's a sitting United States senator. She's way out of my league. Brilliant, charming, powerful. I don't know how I could possibly date her. And you don't have to worry that—"

"Carrie. Please. We're not together." Shauna rolled her eyes. She slid off the bed and reached into the minibar to pour herself a vodka tonic. She swirled the drink in one of the hotel glasses and faced Carrie, resting her back against the TV stand.

"Okay. Yeah," Carrie said slowly. That was good news, she thought.

"Look, I have something to tell you, though." Shauna took a sip of her drink. Her blond lashes obscured her eyes as she stared down at the hotel glass. "I don't think the senator can be trusted."

"Excuse me?" Carrie narrowed her eyes at her. "She's a public figure. Everyone loves her. What could you possibly know that the public doesn't?"

Shauna let out a serious, heavy sigh that was entirely unlike her. She knocked back the rest of her vodka tonic. "Earlier this evening, I went down to the hotel bar. Before you'd returned home for the day."

"What happened to keeping a low profile?"

"You can't just lock me up like . . ." Shauna burst out in anger. She shook her head and squared her shoulders. A second later, her voice returned to the eerie calm from a moment before. "I needed a drink. I sat at the far end of the bar, where I thought I wouldn't be seen. There was a Black woman there in an expensive-looking suit, and it wasn't hard to pick up that this was your beloved senator."

Carrie thought back to an hour before, when she'd been

tucked away with Kendra in the exact same spot. It had certainly been dark and secluded. "And you . . . what? Flirted with her?"

"No! I just sat there, trying to play it cool. And I did a pretty good job, because I went unnoticed enough that I could overhear part of her phone conversation. She was talking in a low voice to someone who sounded like a man. And she was saying how she's still on track to push Project Mars in the right direction, and how with her new role as commander, she'll have more authority to pass laws to get the job done."

"What job?"

"I don't know exactly, but she said that if they're careful, in a few years the money will be raining in. And she mentioned something about being sure they'll be able to extract what they need."

"Extract what? Come on, Shauna, what kind of joke is this?"

"Carrie, I'm serious. I started doing some research on my phone, and I think this could have something to do with space mining. Like, the whole thing about getting minerals and precious elements and stuff from up in space. I found an article on how a lot of people in the international community are wary about it. But maybe she's not. Maybe she wants to—"

"No. Stop. Just stop." It was the conspiracy of a crazy woman. Nothing like that could be true. It couldn't be. Kendra had saved her just hours earlier, had put her weight behind Carrie's efforts to uphold an inclusive and equitable constitution. And, honestly, it had been her last hope. After years of being disappointed by politicians, institutions like the police, and the failure of the law to protect citizens like her and people who looked like her, something was finally happening. She was making change, and Kendra was helping it to happen. The first politician she actually felt she could trust. She wouldn't let this ruin her recent success.

"You have to believe me!"

"This is absurd." Carrie stood and paced a few feet away from Shauna. She stopped and faced the other woman, her hands nearly shaking in anger. Had Shauna seen the two of them sitting together? Was she making this up to get back at her? "You're jealous! I met someone who is smart and talented and worthy of me. But the second I show an interest in someone else, suddenly she's secretly planning to steal precious metals from outer space. Do you hear yourself?"

"Oh, fuck you!" Shauna slammed her glass down on the TV console so hard the entire wooden surface shook. "You sit up there in your pristine academic tower and think you're better than everyone, with all your smarts and fancy degrees and tweed blazers. But you're not better than other people, Carrie. And just because you've read a lot of books doesn't mean you're better than people like me. Especially not when it comes to things like this. I know what I heard. I know what I saw. And whether you think I'm only good to sleep with and discard before we can have a meaningful conversation, whether or not you're embarrassed by me because I'm not a powerful, brilliant senator, I am trying to help you avoid disaster. Kendra can't be trusted. So, spare me the fucking condescension, and take a closer look at that senator you love so much."

Carrie felt hot, like a branding iron had scorched her flesh, like her blood had been left on the stove until it threatened to bubble over the top. Everyone she knew and trusted had turned on her. She reached behind her and grabbed one of the fluffy down pillows from the bed.

"Fuck you, Shauna," she said. She threw the pillow across the room, where it hit a defenseless Shauna in the chest. "I've given all I have to this project! And all you can do is fuck it up! You've ruined everything, every time. I'm not going to treat a con artist like a knight in shining armor. Enough. I'm done with this."

"What?"

"You heard me. Get out. I don't want to see you tonight."

"It's nearly eleven, Carrie. What would you have me do?"

"I don't know. If you're so smart, figure it out."

Shauna picked up her glass again like she was ready to hurl it at Carrie, but she rolled it in her hands before setting it back on the TV console, her movements jerky, like her brain had intercepted her physical instincts at only the last second.

"I heard Kendra tell the guy on the phone that she'd meet him tomorrow for breakfast at Dauphine's. Maybe you can find a way to be there. See if you believe me then." She spared a final glare at Carrie before she opened the hotel room door and left.

Carrie sat on the bed and read emails. She scrolled through university announcements and early Easter shopping discounts and questions from her students until the messages blurred and she realized angry tears had fallen onto the screen. She threw her phone across the bed. Shedding her robe, she slipped under the comforters and pulled the duvet over her, curling in so tightly on herself she resembled a knot. And she cried.

An hour later, a vibration pulsed near her foot. She fumbled on the bed for her phone. Through red eyes, she made out Kim's name on the screen.

"What are you doing answering my call? It's nearly midnight. I was going to leave you a voicemail about getting together tomorrow."

"Oh."

"I got a flat tire earlier today and Brian insists on taking his car to work, so I don't know if I can get together for breakfast because . . ." Kim trailed off. "Wait. What was that?"

"Nothing."

"Are you crying, Carrie Davenport?"

"No."

Kim paused, and her voice lowered. "Do you want to talk about it?"

"No." She didn't know how she could possibly explain to Kim all the ways she'd fucked up and the stupid amount of trust she'd put in complete strangers.

"Okay. Let's just cry, then. I've had a hellish day, too. We can just cry for a bit."

Carrie laid her head back on the pillow and closed her eyes. Tears flowed until a little wet spot formed on the fabric, damp against her cheek. *Stupid stupid stupid*. The words played in her head on repeat. A million academic degrees, and yet, here she was. When the pillow was firmly drenched, she pulled back and looked at her phone, realizing Kim had been silently commiserating with her for nearly twenty minutes.

She pressed the phone to her ear. "I don't want to keep you up."

"It's okay. I'm up."

"No breakfast tomorrow?"

"That was before I knew you were at the edge of the cliff. I'll take an Uber. We can catch up."

"Actually, there's something else I think we need to do during breakfast. Have you been to Dauphine's before?"

17

CARRIE MET Kim three doors down from Dauphine's fifteen minutes before they opened and hours before she really wanted to be awake. She had walked the few blocks from the hotel to the restaurant with bleary eyes worn from crying and sleep loss. She'd only been standing at the street curb for a minute before a black car pulled up. The door opened, and out slid Kim, clad in a black turtleneck, black skinny jeans, and black Louboutin stilettos.

"You're taking this spy mission very seriously," Carrie said, stepping up to Kim and pulling at the end of the black silk scarf wrapped around Kim's head. She had the incognito look of an international superstar trying not to be recognized.

"My best friend sets me to a task, I'm going to show up ready to deliver." She reached into her oversized handbag and pulled out a travel mug. "Coffee. Spiked, because we both need it."

Carrie accepted the mug with the same reverence and

delicacy as when she'd first held Naomi the day she was born. The thermos contained sweet, sweet salvation.

"Thank you. For this, for everything."

"Eh, don't mention it. I'm excited to see whether the senator is as sexy in person as she seems on TV. And to see whether she is in fact a con artist with nefarious intentions in space, or whatever."

"I really hope not. Everything in me hopes not."

Carrie glanced at her watch. Five minutes until the restaurant opened. She took an even deeper gulp of coffee.

"Carrie," Kim said under her breath, nudging her best friend in the side. "Look."

She immediately followed Kim's gaze to their right. Down the street, at the end of the block, a blond woman shuffled slowly their way. Dread turned Carrie's limbs to lead despite her recent caffeine jolt. Her heart pounded as she walked down the block to meet the woman. She stopped when she was still two paces away.

"Shauna."

"Good morning."

"What . . . what are you doing here?"

"Whether or not you were going to show up, I wanted to know for myself what Kendra has up her sleeve. Figured I needed to get here when they open so I don't miss her."

She was dedicated to the cause. Guilt flooded Carrie like a burst dam. If not to help Carrie, then solely out of her own stubbornness, Shauna had made her way to the restaurant to get to the bottom of what was going on.

"Where did you go?" Carrie asked in a low voice. She glanced at Kim, who was pretending to look at her cuticles. "Last night."

"You mean, after you invited me to come to DC and then

kicked me out of the hotel room, knowing I was penniless and knew no one here?"

Carrie gulped. "Um. Yeah."

"I sat on a park bench for a few hours. Wandered a bit. Haven't slept much."

Carrie, quite frankly, could've died, the guilt stabbing so forcefully at her heart. She turned her head away, too ashamed to even look at Shauna. A movement slightly behind her caught her eye. A white-clad waiter was setting up a chalkboard outside the restaurant. Kim coughed loudly.

"Hi," Kim said, pushing around Carrie to stretch a hand out toward Shauna. "We haven't been formally introduced, but I noticed you in jail when you got Carrie beaten by the police. I'm Kim Taylor."

Shauna raised an eyebrow. "Charmed."

"Likewise. Look, I hate to rush this reunion, and obviously Carrie treated you quite poorly in all her stress and angst, but I do think we should come up with a game plan so we're not standing here missing Kendra's entrance."

"I agree," Shauna said. "Both that Carrie's an undeserving motherfucker and that we need a plan of action."

"Great. I brought two super-high-tech voice recorders my husband, Brian, used to use for his failed podcast. Let's put one in my purse and one in your pocket, Shauna? That way we can record whatever we hear, and if God is good, maybe we'll catch a faint wisp of audio."

"What about me?" Carrie asked. "I don't get one?"

"Now that Shauna is here, I don't think you should even go in at all. If Kendra spots you, she'll instantly clam up. It's not worth the risk."

"So, you two are going in without me?"

Kim looked at Shauna, the two looked back at Carrie, and they nodded in unison. "Yup."

"I'll call you so you can listen in," Kim offered.

"Let's stand over by that bus stop and pretend we're chatting or something. And then when Kendra arrives, we can get a table and hide behind our menus," Shauna said. "Order breakfast so we don't look suspicious for staying so long." *And because I'm starving,* her eyes practically screamed as she glared at Carrie.

"Good. Excellent. We can hash out any final details there."

"After you, Kim Taylor." Shauna offered Kim a mock bow, and they made their way to the covered bus stop at the other side of the restaurant door.

Carrie stood on the street, looking at her best friend and the woman she'd fucked over last night, wondering what had just happened.

It didn't take long for Kendra to arrive. Although Carrie was much farther away from the restaurant, seated on a bench out of sight from the door, within ten minutes, an incoming call from Kim had her phone buzzing.

"We're in," Kim said. "I've got my earbuds in. And whew, does Shauna have a mouth on her."

A chair scraped against a wood floor, and cutlery clinked against plates. Other than that background noise, Carrie couldn't hear anything for a few minutes. She glanced anxiously around, wondering what was happening inside.

"I'll have the 'hearty Southern breakfast' with scrambled eggs, a side of biscuits and gravy, and an order of beignets. Might as well add a mimosa while you're at it."

Carrie nearly rolled her eyes at Shauna's excessive breakfast order. So be it. Shauna deserved it, and Kim was paying.

"Listen," Kim whispered a moment later.

There was a crackle. "Reggie, you know damn well that it'll be a good six months before the colonists trust me. I can't push forward with getting a regulation passed until they do. It's like you've never seen a government in action, Jesus."

Carrie nearly growled. The line was so staticky and faint. She wished she could be inside where she could hear Kendra with her own two ears. "Can't you move closer?" She complained to Kim.

"No."

Before she could complain again, the line cut out. Carrie held her phone out and stared at it in disbelief, like it might explode at any second. If it did, it would've matched how she was feeling inside. She could kick something. After a few moments of glaring up and down the city block, freshly warmed by a dawning sun, she huffed and trudged two blocks down to the McDonald's. A McMuffin it was.

A half hour later, Kim texted her. *Come sit with us. I got you a fruit plate.*

Carrie balled up her empty fast-food wrapper and headed back to the restaurant. Kim and Shauna sat at a table in a quiet corner with at least six empty plates crammed onto the small tabletop. She didn't see any signs of Kendra.

"I was right," Shauna declared as soon as Carrie sat down. Carrie looked at Kim.

"Shauna was right," Kim said quietly. Her gaze was soft and sympathetic. She reached out for Carrie's hand.

"Explain."

"She . . . well, she came in and sat with a white man in his early sixties. I've never seen him before," Kim said.

"Rich," Shauna chimed in. "A big-baller kind of suit, expensive haircut, overpriced cologne."

"Right. And I'll just cut to the chase. She seems to have a vested interest in serving as the first leader of the colony. From what I've just read online, the international community is opposed to private companies mining other celestial bodies for resources because those bodies aren't meant to be co-opted by any one country."

"That's true," Carrie agreed. "The Outer Space Treaty is clear that no country can claim sovereignty over part of a celestial body like Mars. It doesn't address exploitation of resources from mining or private property rights over what's been mined. In other words, it doesn't tell us whether countries and their resident companies can own and sell what they've mined. But many scholars think doing so would violate international law—whether it's a country or a private company exploiting the resources."

"Senator Brown seems . . . less opposed to the idea. Probably because, if what we heard is right, there's a potential six-trillion-dollar industry on the line."

Carrie stabbed a blackberry with a fork and let it burst on her tongue. She thought about the little bit she'd heard before the phone connection dropped. Kendra wanted to pass regulations through Project Mars.

"You think . . . hmm. You think she wants to legalize mining on Mars?" Carrie chewed her blackberry and ate another, her mind whirling. "If she's head of a new government on Mars, she could argue they're establishing a new legal regime that permits mining. Let a few private companies extract resources and send them back down to Earth."

"Not a few companies. Just one," Kim confirmed. "We haven't figured out which one, but Senator Brown must have a boatload of stock in it. She stands to personally profit."

"Why wouldn't she tell me that?" Carrie mused.

"So you would change whatever document you're working on and take away all her powers? Are you dumb?" Shauna retorted.

Carrie started in on the rock melon. Everything was always happening. Since the project had started, there hadn't been a single moment of peace, a quiet moment of research, or a project participant she could fully trust. Life should've been easier than this. She wished there were a Pause button, where she could alert the universe that she was overloaded and would split into two without a break or some respite from the string of overwhelming events.

She swallowed a large bite, took a deep breath, and looked Shauna in the eye. "I'm sorry," she said. "It seems like you may be right. I wanted to trust the senator, but maybe I was blind to all the ways she was tricking me. Misleading the project. You were absolutely right."

"I was right, and you were a shithead."

"I know," Carrie said. "I was."

"Alright," Shauna said. She drained the last of her mimosa. "You're my ride home, anyway. Just . . . don't do it again. People have been shitty to me my whole life. I thought we could be friends. I need a friend, if I'm going to try my hand at settling down someplace. I want it to be you."

"We can be. I think I'll need it, too."

"We got you, Carrie," Kim jumped in. "For whatever you want to do next. Brainstorming how to take Kendra down before she goes to space? Planning a kickass outfit to do so? Ice cream? I'm on it."

Carrie sighed. "I think the first step is for me to go home."

"Okay! That's a start. And then we'll regroup later. You've gotta confront Kendra about what she's up to before she goes to space. At the very least."

"I suppose." Carrie sighed again. "And more research, I think. Into the company, and Project Mars. I'm curious, too, whether US law would trump any regulations Kendra passes. The team hasn't fully addressed that yet."

"Great! So that's something to do."

"I guess. For now, I think I'll just have a bit of a cry when I get home."

Although she had wanted to be a teacher from the very first time she'd seen her mother standing at the front of a class, being a professor came with one big downside: No matter how tired or distracted or unenthusiastic she felt, class was an unshakable constant. Her students were paying thousands of dollars per class period; the world would literally have to be on fire for her to miss a single session. It unfortunately meant that, despite the soul-crushing revelations at breakfast, Carrie had gunned it back to North Carolina and plastered a smile on her face to teach later that afternoon.

The smiles cost her energy and the sheer will to live. She returned home directly after class and locked the doors and shuttered the windows. Then she donned her ratty ten-year-old bathrobe, slippers, and bonnet, and sat on her couch for what she hoped was for good. The afternoon slipped into evening and then night. Carrie beckoned the darkness, welcoming an end to a horrific day. Luckily, the universe took pity on her, and she fell asleep on the couch, slippers and all.

She awoke to the ping of her phone. A new email. Carrie groaned, sat up, and rolled her stiff neck. She was getting too old to sleep on the couch, without her trusty memory foam mattress. She was no longer the young hopeful creature she'd been only a few years ago when she'd met Devon. She was a certifiable dinosaur.

The email was from Anna: *Are you coming in today?* She looked at the time: 10 a.m. She'd shuttered the windows, but enough light still peeked out from between the slats to signify that it was indeed morning. She'd normally be on her third cup of coffee by now. She typed out a quick reply: *No.* A second later, her phone rang with a call from Anna, but Carrie immediately silenced it. *Not even for office hours?* Anna emailed back. *No. Pls cancel. Tell students class this afternoon will be via video call.* It felt like cheating to move class online—dangerously close to breaking her cardinal rule of never skipping class. But it would have to do, for today, if she was going to salvage her sanity.

Carrie spent the rest of the day on the couch. She took a momentary respite from potato-ing to comb her hair, throw on a blazer, and teach for an hour, using an exact copy of her notes from last year and hoping the students wouldn't notice she hadn't talked about a new Supreme Court case that had been decided a few months ago. They had Google; they could figure out the law had changed a bit. Speeding through class only got her closer to where she wanted to be: back on the couch, in her robe, with Chinese food for dinner and a comically large bottle of vodka that had her feeling very much like Annalise Keating, Victorian house and all.

Lights flashed outside the front windows around 8 p.m.,

followed by the abrupt jingle of the doorbell. Carrie stumbled to the door to peek out of the peephole, squinting because she hadn't bothered to turn on the porch light. She found Anna standing on her doorstep with a brown paper bag. Carrie looked at the bag longingly, but then down at her robe.

"Give me two minutes!" she called out to the door and sprinted upstairs. She threw on a sweatshirt and sweatpants —hardly a step up from her robe—and ran back downstairs. Anna still waited patiently at the doorstep, clutching her paper bag.

"Anna, hi," she said as she swung open the door. "How unexpected. Come in."

She led the way to the living room, which reeked of Chinese food and liquor. Anna sat on the wingback chair slightly away from the mess and set her package on the coffee table.

"You've never missed office hours," Anna said bluntly. "Let alone class. I thought I'd see what was up." Her gaze swept over the mess of the room.

Carrie sat on the couch opposite her. "I didn't miss class. It was a video call."

"Mm." Anna didn't comment further.

"Where's Waverly? I didn't know you could leave her on a weeknight."

"She's in the car, duct-taped to the back seat."

"What?" Carrie screeched. "You can't leave a toddler in the car—it's still cold at night and—"

"Relax." Anna rolled her eyes with a small smirk. "She's at her dad's house tonight. I'm not an idiot. I sent her off because I was worried about you."

"Anna," Carrie said, her voice soft. "You didn't have to do that."

"Well, I've done it. Because something is wrong, and I want to know what." She reached into the paper bag and pulled out a bottle of tequila and a handful of limes. "Although it looks like you've already gotten a head start."

"Only a little bit." If that was how one could define an evening of vodka on the rocks.

Carrie cut the limes in the kitchen and brought them back on a tray with salt, two lowball glasses, and a reheated plate of egg rolls. She poured two moderate shots of tequila.

"Although I'm worried about getting fired for getting you more drunk than you already are . . . bottoms up, I guess." Anna clinked her glass to Carrie's and downed the shot. She coughed, then settled back into the chair. Her fingers toyed at the fringe of a gray throw blanket draped over the armrest, and then Anna pulled it onto her lap and settled beneath it.

"You look cozy," Carrie said, with a raised eyebrow.

"I'm ready for story time." Anna smiled sleepily. She rested her temple against the side of the chair. "I don't get to hear stories now that I'm the chief storyteller. Nor do I get to drink much."

"I can imagine it's hard being a single mother," Carrie said. "But I know Waverly loves having you as her mommy and—"

"You're getting sidetracked," Anna complained. "I want to know what's wrong with you. Did something happen in DC?"

"No one can be trusted, Anna." Carrie sighed. She poured herself another shot, not waiting for Anna to join her. "Not the police, who are supposed to keep us safe. Not the university and all their efforts to silence me. Not Kandace Pinkney, who acts like I'm a discredit to the race even though I'm trying to do something meaningful. Not Adam, nor Owen, nor anyone at Project Mars. Nor anyone in Congress. I'm not even sure I trust myself anymore. It's all gone to shit."

"Got it. Main thesis: There's not a single person you trust."

Carrie peered at her. "So far I think you're okay," she amended. She could count her father and Kim—and potentially Shauna—among that crowd, too.

"Probably only because I came bearing tequila." Anna poured herself another drink but left it in her glass, cradling it in her hands. She eyed Carrie, who squirmed under her gaze, trying not to sway too much. "You can't stay like this forever," she said. "You'll have to go back to class eventually. Finish your Project Mars report. Grade exams."

Carrie shook her head, noticing the world blurred a little each time she moved. "No. I can't. I'm just . . . I'm done."

"You can't be done. Your students need you. I need you, if only so I can stop making excuses to all your office hours attendees. I don't think you can just give up."

"I really think I can. Adam can finish the report, and they can find a substitute for my classes. I truly don't know how I could leave my house again."

"Carrie," Anna chided. "What's happening here?"

Tears flooded her eyes before she could even blink. These probing questions were too . . . probing. She had just wanted to sit in her house by herself and cry. The crying part, at least, was happening, although her heart broke to know that Anna, in all her patience and kindness, had to suffer through Carrie's endless tears. She was an independent, resilient professor, for heaven's sake. Today, though, she just couldn't be.

"There's too much on my plate," Carrie said thickly, her throat tight and raw. "I can't do it all. Somehow it has fallen on me to fix everything, and lord knows that's not a role I've ever wanted to take on. This isn't right. I can't step up and do everything and be the person everyone wants me to be."

Her eyes were wet and sore, cramped like she'd been reading for hours. She poured herself another shot and downed it despite her raw throat. Tears and insobriety blurred her vision. She hung her head so Anna wouldn't see the mess she'd become.

"Carrie," Anna said. Unshaken by Carrie's own doubts, Anna's voice was confident. "You can do this. I believe in you. I've seen you accomplish extraordinary things. That doesn't mean you have to do it all. You deserve a break from the weight of other people's expectations. But to the extent that you will eventually accomplish whatever you want done, I have full faith that you can."

Carrie didn't respond. Anna's words touched some deep and insecure part of her, but she didn't know if she could abandon the safety of simply sitting and letting the tears fall. Anna didn't interrupt for several minutes. Finally, she stood and approached the couch, then sat on the cushion next to Carrie. She pushed the tequila bottle farther away on the coffee table, slightly out of Carrie's grasp.

"What happened in DC?"

Carrie kept her gaze trained on the floor. "Senator Brown is not who I thought she was." In halting words, Carrie recounted what they'd overheard at breakfast and the possibility that the senator had disingenuous intentions.

"Do you think Project Mars is in on it?"

"I'm dying to know," Carrie admitted. "I want to know if they're complicit."

"Well, when we get back into the office, we can do some research or try to arrange a call with them."

"Maybe," Carrie said. Finding out she had poured her heart into supporting Project Mars, only to support their efforts to pillage natural resources from another planet, might just break her for good.

Anna took a long look at Carrie's face. "One last drink, and then I'm distracting you with photos of Waverly at the park. She completely destroyed the other toddlers in an impromptu sandcastle-building contest. I've got the mud and sand all over my car to prove it."

Carrie cracked a small smile. "An engineer at work. A true woman in STEM."

Carrie wondered whether it was possible for skulls to explode. Her head felt heavy, impossible to hold up, and there was a throbbing at her temples that left her desperately pressing her fingertips to her forehead. She sat on the couch and stared at the offensive tequila bottle from last night, wishing her death glare could cause the bottle to tremble and shatter instead of her head.

Her living room smelled of alcohol and takeout. She gathered the plate of egg rolls and glasses and threw everything into the kitchen sink. Outside the kitchen window, birds flitted and danced in the morning light around the bird feeder she'd installed at the corner the deck. She wondered how they could be so joyous and energetic and industrious at a time when her life felt like a mosh pit of despair. *Ugh.* She retreated upstairs to shower, scrubbing her skin to wash off the stench of alcohol. In a steamy soapy mist, she emerged from the shower moderately clean, though she couldn't shake the stench that radiated from the inside out. No matter. No one was going to smell her anyway.

She donned an old T-shirt from her days in law school and slipped into bed, pulling the covers up to her chin. Under the weight of her comforter, she was safe.

She spent the remainder of the week in her cocoon. She had nailed the routine: Wake up, eat leftovers, sit on the couch, drink, then go back to bed; she ditched the shower because it cut into her fog. She went to bed Sunday night dreading the following morning, when work and students and obligations would again clamor for her attention and go unaddressed. She'd have to remove her bonnet, which was slightly damp from sweat that had accumulated from a weekend of nightmares. She'd have to comb the knots from her hair and scrub the plaque and stench of alcohol from her teeth and quit spiking her coffee in the morning, and she'd have to put on clothes that weren't made from age-worn, holey fabric. None of that seemed appealing, or even possible.

When her phone rang Monday morning, Carrie stared at it in mild revulsion, wishing the world would stop creeping in.

"I'm not going to ask about class," Anna started, not bothering with pleasantries. "This is different. Your research assistants stopped by first thing. They said they've been emailing you to no response. They want to meet with you tomorrow or Wednesday about all the work they've done."

"I can't," Carrie whispered. She rubbed at her eyes, dislodging a thin layer of crust from around the rims.

"Lori nearly knocked down the door. They're pretty insistent. And excited, I might add. They sound like they've been working hard and have something to show you. Something that will bring about change. This is a good thing."

"Is it?" Carrie asked. *Nothing good ever lasts.*

Anna paused, and when she continued, her words were fast and sharp. "Look, I'm not your mother, and I'm not going to tell you what to do, but I'm also not going to participate in this much longer." Anna huffed. She could feel the other woman's embarrassment through the phone.

"I know," Carrie said quietly and let the phone slip from her ear and plop onto the comforter.

But later that afternoon, while she was still semidressed after conducting her class session via video call, a knock on the door startled her hazy daydreams about returning to bed. Anna was nothing if not persistent, although Carrie wasn't sure her liver could take another night of tequila. She hastened from her office to the front door. When she swung it open, the shock knocked the breath from her body.

"Daddy."

18

HER FATHER WAS CLEAN SHAVEN, dressed in a neat flannel shirt and soft pants, his eyes dark and piercing as he gazed at her. Under his gaze, she could feel her sore muscles from having lain in bed for so long, could taste the residual alcohol on her breath. Her bare, unpolished toes scrunched up against the spring chill at her doorstep.

"How did you . . . ? How—"

She finally looked beyond his face to her driveway, where a man in a blue jumpsuit was removing two suitcases from the back of a bright-yellow passenger van. CAROLINAS MEDICAL TRANSPORT was etched in blue lettering on the side.

"You made your own way up here?"

"Your assistant called me. Anna. Said you might need a little help. She used your credit card to get me here so I could see for myself what was going on."

So much for letting Anna into the most vulnerable moment of her life. Anna knew full well she could get fired for using Carrie's credit card without her permission. And that Carrie barely trusted anyone these days and was quick to judge.

And she loved Anna all the more for it.

Anna had put her job and their friendship on the line to do what she thought was right. To do what she thought Carrie needed even though Carrie had refused to voice it herself. She loved Anna for wanting her to be okay and for recognizing that, rather than improving, Carrie was on a rapid decline. Nothing she could do would ever repay Anna for her foresight and care.

"You gonna invite me in?"

"Oh my goodness!" She leapt forward and helped guide him inside. She led him to her living room, cursing at the debris littering the expensive Victorian furniture. "Here, let's get you settled on the couch."

There was a clatter back at the archway leading to the living room. "Good afternoon, ma'am," the driver said. He had deposited the two suitcases in the hallway and lugged a breathing machine behind him. "Where do you want this set up?"

"I'm going to make a bed in the office," she said. "I have a folding cot there, but I'll have a proper medical bed delivered tomorrow if I can. I trust you're going to be here awhile?" She eyed her father. He nodded.

"The office it is."

She got the cot made up, her father's comfortable clothes unpacked, and the breathing machine plugged in. She settled him on the couch, then rushed upstairs to shower and do all the normal human care activities she'd been neglecting for days. Her pores seemed to cheer in victory as she worked cleanser and moisturizing cream into her skin and the bags under her eyes. She fluffed up her hair, which had curled into a dampened afro, then changed her mind and stuffed it into a wig cap and threw on her emergency wig.

"Dad," she greeted him thirty minutes later, freshened and ready for the inevitable confrontation. Without leaving the couch, he'd gathered all the debris from the surrounding cushions and coffee table and pushed it to one little corner of the table. A little hotspot of incriminating evidence. She sat on the opposite side of the room, settling in an armchair near her father's knee.

His eyes flicked from the mess to her face. "When we talked at Christmas," he began slowly, his voice measured, "I knew something was wrong. I knew you had too much on your plate. And I worry that maybe something I said made you think you had to change the world all in one go."

After days of tears, none came to her now. The well was dry. Instead, she sat and studied her hands in her lap. "Mm," she said, not adding much to the conversation but not knowing how to explain.

"I take it there are new developments in your work?"

"Mm," she said again.

"Carrie Davenport, did your mother raise you with nothing to say?"

"No." She sighed. "You're right. The first problem is work." She recounted the newest challenges working with Adam, the efforts to draft inclusive constitutional language, and her shock and frustration at Kendra's false friendship and betrayal . . . leaving out the more intimate details of what had passed between them. "This whole time, I've done all I can, and it has either gotten messed up or it's not been enough. I'm tired. I wasn't built for this." As she said it, she realized she could sleep for a million years, even after all the sleep she'd gotten the last few days.

"Mm," her father said now, mimicking her, his tone unimpressed.

"What?" Carrie said with a start and, for the first time in days, a small smile. "No lecture about how my mom was a hero, and I'm letting her down by not rising to the occasion?"

"Nope. You and your mother are really different, baby. Don't get me wrong, you have an incredible number of things in common. Your dedication to helping others learn, to understanding tough problems. Not to mention your smile and love of food and drink and life. But your mother was quick to act. Patient with her students, but hotheaded with everyone else. She would leap into fights without thinking, and I'd have to come in after her with my fists raised."

"I don't remember that," Carrie admitted.

"That's because she never laid a hand on you. She loved you more than life itself."

"Yeah." Carrie smiled.

"What I'm saying, though, is that she solved problems in her own way. She leapt out onto the picket line and devoted her body to the cause because that's how she approached most things. She got in the car and went and did it without a thought. Middle of winter, and she was out there." Her father had both a smile and a frown, his face twisted with dueling emotions at the memory. "So, that's what you've gotta do."

"What, go and picket? I don't think so." She shot him a side-eye.

"No! The opposite. You've gotta react in a way that's 100 percent true to you. Your talents, your personality. The solution is to *be you*."

"Be me?" It sounded like words etched on an inspirational coffee mug. "How would that ever help this situation, me sitting quietly in my house, afraid of conflict? Because that's what I want and plan to do."

"Think harder. What are you good at?"

"Cooking."

"Do you get paid six figures to do that?"

"Oh. You mean teaching?"

"Carrie, use those degrees, girl, and get on the same page as me. You're a writer! You write fancy journal articles and book chapters, and you've got this Project Mars report coming up. What's that phrase they say? You write like you're running out of time."

"Oh." She paused. She did write relentlessly. She wrote because academics had to publish to get the job and keep it. She wrote because she constantly uncovered new connections between areas of the law, and whenever there were no more articles left to read, she filled the gap by writing her own. She wrote because it meant organizing her thoughts and helping others to understand complex ideas more easily.

"You're tired because you thought you had to jump up and solve this problem the way your mother would. But you're faced with a unique problem, and the solution is you. Your talents, your strength. When you start doing it your way, and stay true to you, I promise it will be easy. And your house won't reek of liquor." He waved his hand in front of his nose, like the smell had only now caught up to him.

She didn't know what to say. Maybe this was what he'd meant from the start, back at Christmas, when he'd said she should step up. She hadn't realized it at the time, but he was right. Changing the world couldn't be done using just one tactic. And there was something she was good at, something she could contribute. Something that would make a difference. Those efforts hadn't been successful so far, but maybe it would only require a bit more elbow grease doing what she did best. Even if her world and the people in it were shitty.

"Okay, Daddy. First, let me make us some coffee."

Before she went to bed that night, Carrie closed her bedroom door and sat on the edge of the bed, her cell phone clutched tightly in her hand. She didn't want to call, but she couldn't take any next steps without knowing the truth. And, if she waited until morning, she might lose her nerve. With a trembling breath, she scrolled through old emails until she found one with Libby's signature block at the bottom, phone number and all. She dialed.

"Hello?" Libby's bright voice answered on the fourth ring.

"Libby. It's Dr. Davenport."

"Carrie! I'm surprised to get a call from you so late."

"You know me, always hard at work!" Carrie laughed a little too loudly at her own joke that was not even a joke.

"Well, what can I do for you?"

"Tell me the truth. How long has Project Mars been planning on mining resources from Mars?"

A brief silence. "Well . . . of course we have to use some of the materials on Mars to build the habitat. It's too expensive to transport heavy building supplies up there, so we're using soil and sand to 3-D-print building blocks for our residences, as you know. There's a lot of good information about this on our website—"

"Not building materials. Precious minerals. I know that you plan to engage in space mining."

"That's not at all the mission of Project Mars."

"Senator Brown told me about your side mission. All that extra money you're hoping to cash in on."

Libby's voice lowered, hushed and deliberate. "What did she say to you?"

"She told me everything. Your little scheme, your partnership with other private entities, how you've installed her in a leadership role so she can exploit the self-government system, all of it. My own research confirms it," Carrie lied.

The line was silent for long enough that Carrie could hear her grandfather clock in the hallway. She leaned forward in anticipation.

"You can't say anything to anyone."

Carrie nearly dropped the phone. This couldn't be.

"What the actual fuck, Libby? All this corruption doesn't sicken you? Or are you as greedy as Beau and the rest of them?" Carrie said.

"No," Libby said urgently, her tone still low. "Carrie, please. Listen to me. Project Mars is not involved. This is not a Project Mars thing. It is still an incredibly important endeavor. The work we're doing is good and will alter the course of human history."

"This can't be happening," Carrie said, almost to herself. "You're ruining the government I'm working so hard to create." All her months of hard work, all her hopes that they were building a better society, and yet something nefarious was happening right under her nose.

"Please, don't get upset. We all have to stick together. I need you to stay silent."

Carrie chewed on her bottom lip, weighing her words. "Whatever may be going on, and whoever is involved . . . what you're doing is wrong. I should be running straight to the press with this."

"Carrie, no! I'm telling you . . ."

"But I won't, on one condition."

"Anything."

"I need data on Project Mars and Perpetua. Internal data on diversity and inclusion. Statistics, personal anecdotes, anything you can send."

"That's it? What is this, some kind of academic article?"

"For an article, yes."

"Fine. Just don't implicate Project Mars in anything broader. We're working toward something good here, Carrie. I hope you see that."

"I certainly see the bigger picture now." She hung up.

It was time for things to change.

19

WHEN CARRIE ENTERED the suite of faculty offices the next day, the room smelled of roses. Fragrant, floral, with the hope of summer soon on its way. She rounded the corner to Anna's desk, and all she could see was a cornucopia of yellow. An enormous vase of yellow roses towered over Anna's desk, completely obscuring the small woman behind the forest.

"Is my assistant back there?" Carrie called.

"Mmpf," came a muffled sound. Anna stepped out from behind her desk, a tentative smile on her face. "I like the roses. Does that mean I still have a job?"

"There are like a hundred roses here, Anna," Carrie joked. "You definitely still have a job. And my utmost thanks."

She headed toward her office and waved Anna in to join her, depositing her tote bag stuffed with reading materials onto the floor.

"First. Thank you. Sincerely. For knowing that I was offtrack and knowing the one thing that would restore my hope."

Anna inclined her head in recognition. "I'm happy to help. Does that mean you're back?"

"I'm back. But you're not."

"What?"

"Take the next three days off in recognition for all your hard work. Spend the time with your daughter, if you like. Take a road trip, go to the beach, whatever. On me. Just do one thing first? I need to get the research assistants in here."

When Evie, Lori, and Parker entered her office that afternoon, she didn't have anything to offer them. No tea, no coffee, no baked goods or English pastries she'd handcrafted in her kitchen. She had not done any new research in the past few days, and the bags under her eyes were barely hidden by concealer.

But it didn't matter.

Evie entered with a stack of books so tall Carrie could barely see her tiny freckled face. Lori had a tote bag with sports drinks, a party-size bag of chips, and three packs of cookies. Parker held a thermos of coffee and a smile so hopeful and enchanting it lit up their serious, studious face. They all managed to find a seat in her office, with Evie camped out on the floor with her piles of books, her back against the love seat where Parker and Lori had seated themselves.

Carrie pushed her swivel chair slightly out from behind her computer screen so she could better address the scholarly camp in her office. "I heard you all have been trying to get in touch with me," Carrie began. "I'm sorry." If she dwelled on the past few days, she put herself at risk of crying again, and surely she would shrivel up like a dehydrated prune if she shed any more tears. She pressed forward. "The constitutional team had a, um, productive last meeting in DC, and we're ready to go from deciding on values to writing the text itself. Have you had time to think about that at all?"

"It's done!" Lori proclaimed. Her arms shot up with such victorious energy that the newly opened bag of chips threatened to spill.

"What?"

"Well, not the entire constitution, you'll have to write a lot of the mundane provisions and the all-important preamble. But Parker, Evie, and I wrote five core provisions that will achieve the diversity elements we talked about."

"You wrote them already?" Carrie asked, stunned. While she had been underground, buried in a hole of darkness and despair, her students had been reaching toward the sky, pens in hand.

"We put them all in a section titled 'Equality Among Space-Goers' to separate them out and make clear their importance," Evie said.

"And I have a couple of recommendations on how to incorporate this language into other sections, too. In case the colonists go crazy and try to repeal that section, the language will be laced throughout," Parker added.

Carrie had a wild, distracting flashback to one night a few weeks after Kim had given birth to her first daughter. Kim had been so exhausted and hopeless with postpartum depression she could barely lift her head as Carrie came in the door, and Brian was pulling longer and longer shifts at the hospital. Carrie had tried desperately to get Gabby to stop crying, whispering lullabies and rocking her even though she had no clue how to hold a baby. It hadn't worked. After an hour, they'd given up and split a bottle of wine and blasted eighties music from the speakers, dancing around the living room. They'd both belted out, "I believe the children are the future," lifting Gabby up high as they danced. The baby had promptly burped, yawned, and knocked out in sleep, and they'd danced in victory, whisper singing about how the next generation would save the world until cramps pricked at their sides.

She felt like that now. Breathless and giddy, with full faith that the next generation would change the world for good.

"Let's see it, then." She held out her hand for whatever paper they would hand her.

"Ahem," Evie said. "We had kind of imagined a dramatic reading."

"Ah. You were drunk when you wrote this?" Carrie asked, deadpan.

"The whole plan sounded good at 2 a.m.!" Evie whined. "And, erm, a beer or two might have been consumed."

"Everything sounds good at 2 a.m.," Carrie joked. "But don't let me stand in the way of *Mars Constitution: The Musical.*"

Lori stood and grabbed Parker's thermos as a microphone. "Article Oneeeeee," she sang in a drawn-out dramatic alto. She cracked a smile. "Just kidding. Anyway, envision that you've just written a great preamble, there are some administrative articles, and now this one gets inserted. 'Equality Among Space-Goers.'"

Lori cleared her throat. "Paragraph one. 'All human beings are born free and equal in dignity and in rights.' Period."

Carrie nodded. "Hard to argue with that."

"I thought Lori was smart to start with this one because it is unequivocal and all-encompassing, and it will give a future court a broad textual hook to uphold more rights in the future," Parker said. They shot a lingering, appreciative smile at Lori.

"And it distinguishes between humans and aliens, in case things get freaky up there," Evie said with a conspiratorial wiggle of her eyebrows. She grabbed one of Lori's energy drinks and took a sip.

"My turn," Evie sang. "Paragraph two. 'The government shall not unfairly discriminate, directly or indirectly, against any individual or class of people on the basis of race, color, sex, gender identity or sexual orientation, national origin, rank or work position, ability, socioeconomic status, or any combination thereof.'"

"Gotcha." Carrie turned the words over in her mind. "And why this provision?"

"We need to call out specific classes of people to ensure they specifically are protected. All the worst ways this country has discriminated in the past, we need to protect in the future," Evie responded.

"I agree." Carrie blew out heavily. "It's great. We can maybe add a clause about how that list is not exclusive, so other aspects of identity can be included later."

"That sounds good," Parker said. "We'd talked about that, too—how protecting certain groups of people might leave others unprotected, so I'm glad we can add to the list." They nodded, almost to themselves. "Anyway, I drafted the third article, although I'm not sure it fully captures that—"

"Parker," Carrie interrupted. "I know it's perfect. Let's hear it."

"Third," Parker said. "'Recognizing that, historically,

discrimination has unduly prevented the exercise of equal rights of certain societal groups on Earth; diminished access to equal opportunities in education, employment, health care, and political participation, among other sectors; and that this discrimination was fundamentally wrong as a denial of equality, the governing body of the Mars colony condemns discrimination and commits to taking positive steps toward preventing discrimination in the future.'"

"It's a beautiful tribute, Parker." Carrie nodded. "We have to acknowledge where we come from."

"Paragraph four, building on Parker's excellent points," Lori said. "'The above notwithstanding, the Mars colony governing body may take positive steps to increase equity by supporting historically disadvantaged groups for colony participation, leadership positions, and work assignments.'"

"I like it. We may need to be sensitive in our wording, but—"

"But we gotta get what's owed to us!" Lori finished for her. "Hell yeah."

"Right," Carrie said. *I guess.* Maybe not the words she would've used, but close enough.

"And last but not least," Evie said in a stadium-announcer voice, "'The Mars governing body is empowered to enact additional legislation in support of these goals of equality and inclusion and shall have the full power of the law to enforce these provisions.'"

Carrie sat back in her desk chair and swiveled so she mainly faced the window, too overwhelmed to even comment on all they'd done. It was harder than it looked, to write meaningful text that would stand the test of time.

"You don't like it?" She heard Lori's voice from behind her.

Carrie swiveled back around abruptly. "Can I give you guys a hug? Would that be wildly inappropriate?"

"A hug would be heavenly."

She pulled her assistants into a group hug, tight enough so that no one would look back and see the tears pricking at her eyes. *God, not the crying again.* But could she help it? They'd done something big, and lasting, and better than Adam or Owen alone could've written. The same students who had faced their own burdens at a young age, who had already been touched by the country's injustices, had paved the way for the colonists to live in a society that truly valued freedom and equality. The draft spoke to their collective experiences and all the experiences they didn't want the colonists to face. All the ways life should and would be better.

Now it was her turn to carry that same sense of fairness forward throughout the Project Mars endeavor. It was time to stop hiding in the shadows.

Carrie's "spring of big things" continued for the rest of the week in a burst of good-weather, good-vibes energy. She made healthy spring-vegetable soup and homemade bread for chicken-salad sandwiches and scoured the farmers' market to make eggplant Parmesan so she and her father could sit at her dining room table and feast. Feast, and plot.

Oh, they plotted. Project Mars had organized a big publicity campaign launch for later that month, which would be the perfect time to call attention to the company's activities in an op-ed. She was ready to reveal as much as she could in an exposé. She wrote drafts and read them aloud to her father, the same way she used to read chapter books to her mom after school. He offered feedback and helped her strike the right balance—not too apologetic or wimpy, not too aggressive that no one would act. Ten days after he'd turned up on her doorstep, as they cut into gluten-free pound cake with a heap of strawberries and low-fat cream, the draft was starting to feel right.

Her father pushed his plate aside and shifted around stacks of papers until he found a stapled report underneath one of her books.

"I don't think I've looked at the actual data yet. This is what Libby sent over?"

It was indeed what Libby had sent over. Carrie knew Libby would be twisting her hands after their late-night phone call, wondering whether Carrie would spill the beans about the illegal mining side hustle. As she developed her plan, she'd let several phone calls from Libby go unanswered, which could only have deepened Libby's unease. It was to her advantage. After the meeting with her research assistants, she'd called Libby back and demanded even more specific categories of data—any complaints staff had made about the Project Mars corporate culture, and statistics on their hiring trends.

She had done a thing. *Blackmail* might have been one word for it. But Libby was desperate, and so was she.

"This data is going to be helpful," her father said as he looked up from a report, his reading glasses perched on the tip of his nose. "We're cooking up something good here, baby girl."

"Yeah?"

"Yup." He took his glasses fully off now, cleaning them on the edge of his shirt. "But tell me, you're not giving up on one thing for the sake of the other, right? You're not letting them mine and pillage other planets for the sake of improving the culture and diversity? I'd hate to see us take one step forward and two steps back."

Competing goals vied for her attention. The podcaster Kandace Pinkney had been right: They couldn't let space become a white segregationist escape. Space was meant to be a shining beacon of discovery and opportunity for all. Improving the diverse makeup of the colonists mattered as a first step toward representation. And the culture on Earth certainly needed to change so that those in power recognized and actually cared about the experiences of minorities. But on the other hand, none of that would matter if space was another "manifest destiny" colonization of virgin lands where the colonizers exploited the resources of other planets only to benefit the rich. Something had to be done about the mining scheme, too.

"It won't be easy, but I have a few ideas," she said. A slow smile spread on her face, and she shot him a conspiratorial look. "You'll see in the next draft."

He winked at her. "Alright then. Now, you talk about the grievances of the astronaut class, how the colonists themselves are feeling the effects of the Project Mars culture. Is there any documentation of psychological harm?"

"You think it'll help?"

"A lot."

"Hmm. Libby said they scrubbed a lot of that data." That probably wasn't something she could get.

She fetched a stuffed file folder from her home office and brought it back to the table. She flipped through newspaper clippings and handwritten notes, not entirely sure what she was looking for, until she found a business card with a tiny cartoon astronaut and a phone number. One corner was frayed and bent from when she'd shoved Michelle's card into her purse at Beau's mansion. *Perfect.*

She took a final bite of pound cake and set down her fork as a wave of nerves battled against her desire to finish the slice. Once she released the draft to the world, there would be no going back. She'd make an enemy of one of the world's biggest and most influential companies, a US senator, her constitutional design team, and a whole host of people she didn't even know. It would put everything at risk—her involvement with the constitution, her paycheck, her reputation at the university, and her future as an academic. All of it.

"Stop stressing and finish this pound cake," her father chastened. "If you don't, I'm going to eat it all, and we both know that's a bad idea." He touched her hand. "You've done the right thing, baby. It's like fireworks. Yeah, you're going to blow something up, but it will be an amazing sight for all the world to see."

20

I<small>T WAS</small> a regular Tuesday in mid April, five weeks before the constitutional design team was slated to deliver the first draft of its final report, three weeks before final exams for her students, and about a week before Project Mars launched its major publicity push, with celebrities across the country promoting the company and its vision for the next few planned missions.

Carrie sat at her desk on campus, with her finger poised over the mouse, gathering the courage to press Send on the email over which she'd agonized for the past hour. She'd had too much help and support not to take the leap. Her father had spent countless hours with her, refining the draft. She'd managed to get ahold of Carlos Martinez, who had enthusiastically connected her with a reporter at *The New York Times* who covered all things space and culture. Not to mention the time Anna had spent proofreading it and Kim talking her from the ledge. The time was now.

With a wince and a quick tap of her finger, she clicked Send.

Tuesday, April 19, 2033 | 7:02 a.m.
From: carrie_davenport@law.briaruniversity.edu
To: Katie.Shaw-Singh@nytimes.com
Cc: Libby@journeytomars.com; Grant@journey-tomars.com
Re: Time-Sensitive: Op-Ed For Publication Tomorrow 4/20

Katie, as discussed, please find attached an op-ed titled "Racists in Space: Project Mars Has a Race Problem, and Humanity Is Doomed Until It's Solved" for publication in tomorrow's edition of the New York Times and online. I will let you know by today at 3 p.m. whether there are any changes to the piece. If you do not hear from me before then, please immediately publish online. Thank you for the opportunity to spread the message on this issue.

Sincerely,
    Dr. Carrie Davenport

racists in space

Project Mars Has a Race Problem, and
Humanity Is Doomed Until It's Solved

Project Mars, the billion-dollar endeavor seeking to establish a human colony on Mars, marks a new chapter for humanity—but it certainly won't be representing all of humanity on Earth. The Project has selected a narrow subset of primarily white astronauts to send to space, cutting out many qualified, nonwhite candidates and closing the door to representation in worlds beyond. As the Keith L. Giddings Professor of Law at Briar University and the Chair of the Project Mars Constitutional Design Team, I have spent months thinking about what fairness and equality look like in space. From my exhaustive research, I can tell you: This isn't it.

The space industry has never been diverse. Only 24 percent of aerospace employees are women, only 6 percent are Black, and 8 percent are Hispanic. While Hispanic Americans represent about 16 percent of the population, only 7 percent are STEM workers, and while Black Americans make up 11 percent of the workforce, only 9 percent have STEM jobs. The problem has existed, and continues to persist, despite Project Mars.

But Project Mars makes things worse by leaps and bounds. Project Mars leadership is not representative of the average American. The company is run by Beauregard Ball, a Southern white billionaire whose family spent decades using their political power to attack minorities and queer, particularly transgender, Americans. The Ball family has invested in private prisons, conversion therapy, anti-Muslim media, and Blue Lives Matter propaganda. Beau himself has mocked labor unions by defecating on their flyers and was videotaped throwing wads of cash into the dirt at a remote village in Kenya to laugh as elderly residents scrambled on the ground for stray bills. He is privately a frequent user of the n-word and was also privately quoted as questioning what was really "so bad" about slavery. In Perpetua meetings, Beau has quite publicly misidentified prominent Asian employees. And at Project Mars, diversity is worse than even the pitiful national averages. Only 27 percent of employees are women—as in, not even a third of the company—and a mere 2 percent of the Project's STEM workers are Black and 5 percent are Hispanic. Internal employee data reflects that the average Hispanic employee lasts only six months—in other words, the workplace is so toxic that these employees are forced out in less than a year. Including Asian Americans, the total minority workforce winds up at only 15 percent. The remaining employees are overwhelmingly white, coming from elite schools and affluent upbringings, with many devoted to maintaining an aggressive dog-eat-dog culture. A yearly company event is the "Joust," which requires participating employees to go topless (even female employees), pay a $10,000 buy-in, and hit each other with wooden swords until one party gives in, with the losing party literally losing their job with the company. The winner gets the privilege of claiming any employee's work product as their own for three months and a private outing with Beau.

Project Mars has done extensive work to make sure its first colonist class has the best of the best. The colonists have intimate training sessions with former astronauts, study physics with Nobel Prize–winners, and see the same physicians as the president. But it has treated its minority astronauts no better than Martian dirt. Project Mars did a covert study on whether white astronauts are genetically superior. The answer (unsurprising to those who aren't racists) is no. White people are not any better suited to space. In fact, melanin helps protect against harmful radiation, one of the greatest dangers in space.

Two years ago, the five racial minorities in the first colonist class approached Project Mars with a report detailing pervasive mistreatment. They described being called racial slurs, being artificially ranked at the bottom of the class despite testing higher than most counterparts, and enduring physical hazing in training locker rooms, including one man being stuffed into a locker, breaking his clavicle. Project Mars stole confidential medical records from therapy sessions those astronauts had with Project Mars psychologists and destroyed them because they corroborated the experience and the impact: severe psychological harm for a group of pioneers needlessly and cruelly bullied. Their complaints remain unaddressed.

The company did make some inroads with their announcement one month ago that Black US senator Kendra Brown would command the first colonist class. Senator Brown, a celebrated veteran, is an incredibly talented leader. Unfortunately, her talents include orchestrating nefarious profit-seeking schemes. Sources reveal that Senator Brown has links to a company called United Resource Enterprises, which plans to privately mine precious minerals at the colony or beyond, which would undoubtedly violate the Outer Space Treaty by co-opting space resources for the gain of an American company. This is unacceptable. Project Mars must ensure the senator denounces all ties to space mining.

Space mining aside, the installment of one person cannot solve a massive problem. Mars will soon become a rich person's playground, and it's going to look very white and male. This is wrong.

It's wrong because of the historical legacy of white people pillaging land that is not theirs and profiting off of resources that don't belong to them to the detriment of nonwhite communities.

It's wrong because the experience of the current colonists matters. We are taking a group of human beings who have already been mistreated and sending them thousands of miles away in a vulnerable state and to a high-risk environment. No government system written into the Project Mars constitution can make up for abject human cruelty, as hard as the constitutional design team may try.

It's wrong because we have known for decades that more diverse teams yield better outcomes. Diversity does not mean less qualified talent or worse performance. Companies in the top quartile for racial and ethnic diversity are 35 percent more likely to have financial returns above the national industry medians. That same success applies here. It's even more important for science, which relies on group problem-solving and where unique perspectives improve mission success. Think of the Sally Ride tampon story —where NASA asked Ride, the first American woman in space, if she needed a hundred tampons for a six-day mission.

It's wrong because it deprives Black and brown scientists, researchers, writers, explorers, and the like access to one of the most momentous and unfathomable human endeavors: living on another planet.

The exclusion of diverse voices in space will soon trickle down to everyday people—impacting all of us —as commercial space travel proliferates, and people who look like me are routinely denied a seat on the spaceship.

I have lived this—in the steady uphill battle earning my degrees, and in untold microaggressions in my professional life. But as those closely attuned to North Carolina news cycles may know, this past fall I experienced a more brutal, physical, cataclysmic event. An instance of racial violence. The experience, as much as I initially tried to write it off, changed me. It opened my eyes to an undeniable reality: We must change the culture at the top so that individuals—police officers, politicians, and astronauts alike—eschew racism and acknowledge that they can and must do better in treating people fairly.

The grand irony of the situation is that most Americans say they value diversity. Eight in ten Americans say it is at least somewhat important to have racial and ethnic diversity in today's workplaces. A quarter of people think this sort of diversity "is extremely important," and another quarter think it's "very important." Separate studies also show that the majority of people think space travel should be open to all. This isn't some far-fetched liberal ideal. It's something we all want—and need.

What's standing in the way? Beauregard Ball, and his complete inaction on an issue critical to the future of humanity. Either because of laziness or indifference or an actual intent to keep Mars white, Beau has not stepped up despite knowledge of the issue. But he could still act. The colonist class needs to be diversified, immediately. Project Mars needs to implement binding policies that commit to minority representation in space. And after this trial phase, Beau must commit to making Project Mars colony participation equitable and inclusive by offering a set number of affordable seats on initial journeys. This he must do, at the very least.

AFTER SHE WATCHED the email zip off, Carrie stared at the blank screen. Then she navigated to her "Sent" folder and stared at the message again. The boldness of her piece left a cold sweat threatening to seep out from her pores. Would it be the biggest mistake of her life? She sat there for twenty minutes in a daze, unable to look away. Then, with a sharp ring on full volume, her cell phone rang.

"Carrie, what the fuck?" Libby snapped as soon as Carrie answered. "I thought you were going to write an obscure little academic piece about the meaning of diversity in our lives, not go straight to the fucking *New York Times*." Libby sucked in a huge breath and let out a huff of air. "This is not what we agreed to. You promised you'd stay silent on the mining."

"I didn't break our agreement," Carrie countered. "Read it again. I never implicated Project Mars in any space mining. I only mentioned Senator Brown's involvement. The ball is in Kendra's court."

"Oh, fuck off. This is why people hate lawyers. It's a technicality, and you know it."

"Things need to change, Libby; surely you can see that."

"No, I don't," she snapped.

"Libby, I . . ."

"I never thought you had it in you," Libby interrupted, her tone shifting from angry to bewildered.

"I do," Carrie said simply.

"Well, you've unleashed a shit show. I forwarded your email to Beau, and he's livid. He called me screaming. I'm getting a string of angry texts as we speak."

"I'm sorry it had to be this way," Carrie said. "But this is important, Libby; you know that. And I'm not wrong. Have you read the article?"

"I had the pleasure of my heart literally sinking into my stomach as I skimmed it. I'm rereading it now."

"What is Beau going to do? He's gotta step up somehow."

"Shit." A string of muffled curse words followed as Libby apparently pulled the phone away from her ear. "I can't even read all his messages fast enough."

Carrie sat quietly, waiting for Libby to push through her morning fog and the wave of Beau's anger.

"He's coming."

"What?" Carrie asked. "What does that mean?"

"Where are you right now?" Libby asked. "At home?"

"No, I'm on campus. At . . . at Briar." Carrie stumbled over her words. Was she understanding correctly? Did it mean . . . ?

"Stay there. Be prepared to meet in about five hours."

Libby hung up.

Carrie stared down at her lap. She had on an oversized sweater blazer and comfortable stretchy pants, assuming that she'd just have a phone call with Libby or Grant, or at the most be on video. She could practically feel the bags under her eyes from the string of sleepless nights when she'd stressed about the article draft. Now, it was a little over seven hours from being published at 3 p.m. If Beau arrived by 1 p.m., they'd have just two hours to hash it out before her article made its way into the world.

"Oh my god," she said out loud. "Anna! Get in here ASAP!"

Despite Libby's admonishment to stay in place, after she and Anna had a moment of silent screaming and panic, Carrie leapt into her car and sped home. Despite everything she'd said about him, she still couldn't meet Beau in lounge pants. When she skidded into her driveway, two other cars were parked on the grass in front of her home. She dashed inside and was met by voices in the living room.

"Carrie! How was it?"

Kim and Shauna sat on the couch next to her father, sharing morning coffee. Shauna was drinking out of Carrie's Society of Black Professors mug, and Kim and her father were sharing a throw blanket. The different pieces of her life had somehow meshed together, and Carrie could barely comprehend the weird picture it all made.

"Er. How . . . what are you all doing in my house?"

"Carrie. We knew that you were sending out the article today," Kim said. "We weren't going to leave you alone in all that turmoil. I drove down super early this morning."

"You came all the way here?"

"Girl, lucky you, because I can't miss any more classes for your behind. This better be wrapped up in time for me to make my evening seminar." Despite her words, Kim stepped forward and wrapped Carrie in the tightest of hugs.

"Kim told me what was going on," Shauna said. "I want to know what PM says. And how Kendra is going to respond."

"Thank you for being here," Carrie murmured.

"So?" her father prompted, interrupting the greetings. "Any response yet?"

"Beau is coming. To Briar."

"What?" Kim screeched. "A billionaire is coming to campus?"

"Good girl." Her father nodded.

"'Good' my ass. You cannot meet Beauregard Ball looking like that, Carrie Davenport. Upstairs, now. Thank god I brought my makeup bag with me, or we'd have to throw a paper bag over your head. Are you even sleeping?"

With a sharp glint of sun on metal, a blue object appeared high in the midday sky. The breezy day whipped wind through Carrie's freshly pressed curls as she stood next to her camp: Anna, President Farrington, and Cameron, the university's director of communications. She'd had Anna send the article to Cameron after finding out Beau would be coming. Although the university was furious with her, their main focus was damage control. Fine by her; she had bigger fish to fry.

They stood at the center of Briar's giant turf football field, staring upward, as the helicopter made its descent. Behind her on the bench where the team's players normally sat, Kim and Shauna huddled together to watch the scene. Kim would not be shaken from the notion of meeting one of the world's richest and most powerful men.

The wind whipped even fiercer as the helicopter sank onto the grass. The engine cut, the door slid open, and three figures emerged: Beau, clad in jeans and a Sonics T-shirt; Libby, her eyes glued to her phone even as she plopped out of the helicopter in stilettos; and a lithe young woman Carrie didn't recognize, with bone-straight blond hair.

Carrie stood with her arms crossed over her chest as the trio approached. Beau sidled up to Carrie, his eyes squinting against the gleaming sun, until his nose was inches from hers.

"Carrie Davenport. You've caused a big fucking problem."

Carrie, in the face of an angry billionaire who had flown across the country to chastise her, smiled. "Good." She raised her chin. She refused to feel guilty.

President Farrington seemed to choke on air beside her.

There was a pause as she regained her breath. "Mr. Ball," she said briskly after she had recovered, "it is an honor to welcome you to Briar's campus for the first time." Her lips pressed together. "Circumstances aside. Please, if we could convene in the president's suite and adjoining conference room, we'd be delighted to—"

"No, no." He smirked. "I'd like to speak directly to the troublemaker herself. Libby, you join the, uh, university lady and await the others. Carrie, Mandy, let's go."

Beau strode off in the opposite direction, crossing the football field, with the blond closely on his heels. Carrie scrambled forward to keep up with his relentless pace. He clipped away with a tight, jerky stride, swift despite his short legs.

"You know where I was supposed to be?" he called over his shoulder as Carrie trailed him. "Flying to Saudi Arabia to crash failed Mars rover vehicles into each other on the sand dunes. Adult bumper cars." He raised two exasperated arms in the air. "Now I won't get to try them until tomorrow."

She managed admirably to keep her mouth from popping open. Naomi, at age five, seemed to have more grace than Beau when she didn't get her way.

They reached the opposite end of the field, where a tall archway led past the stands, toward the football team's locker room. Although he couldn't have known where he was going, Beau slammed open the two doors, emblazoned with a blue snarling wolf, and strode down a brief hallway into the team's empty locker room. Gold trophies lined the walls behind glass display cases in the richly decorated changing room, and two long wooden benches framed rows of large gleaming metal lockers. As Beau reached one of the benches, he spun on his heel.

"Mandy, juice me."

Mandy had an impossibly small backpack hanging from her shoulders on thin straps. She pulled it around to her front and extracted a slim can. "A jolt of energy you can't even imagine." She winked at Carrie as she handed it to Beau. "Illegal in six countries. You want?"

"Erm, no."

Beau ran a stressed hand through his hair and took a long gulp of juice. "The editor wants to run the piece," he said to the mostly empty room at large. "Can't be swayed by money. Thinks there's something there."

"Hmm. Too bad you can't just buy the paper," Carrie suggested.

"I tried that. That con artist Bennet won't sell it to me. Thinks the whole thing is hilarious. Like he doesn't have the same fucking problem. His senior leadership looks like a Klan rally."

"A pity."

Beau crumpled his now-empty can with rough, impatient hands and tossed it to the ground with a clatter of aluminum. He hopped up onto the bench so that he towered over Carrie and Mandy, his shoes squeaking on the shiny wood. "It's ridiculous, is what it is. I'm the least problematic guy out there."

"Right," Carrie said, deadpan.

"Everyone loves me." He spread his arms wide.

"You sound like you're two seconds from saying you have a Black friend," Carrie joked.

"I do!" Beau said and then, picking up on her sarcasm, glared at her. "This isn't a joke, Carrie."

"Okay. Then get off the bench and talk to me."

He hopped down with a heavy thud, apparently disturbed

that Carrie seemed to have taken the upper hand in the conversation. His eyes scanned the room.

"Hand me that trophy," he said to Mandy. "The big gold one."

She looked at him and back at a gleaming two-foot-tall trophy sitting in one of the display cases. Her fingers pulled at the handle, but the glass door wouldn't budge. She turned so her back was to the case and rammed her elbow into the thin glass pane. With a shatter of broken glass, the case yielded. She reached past the wreckage to pull out the trophy. She wiped stray glass shards off her shirt before handing it to Beau. Carrie realized, with the pretty girl's effortless strength, that she must be both assistant and body-guard. And maybe something else, too.

Beau didn't blink at the wreckage. "What does a trophy mean, Carrie?" He waved the shining gold trophy above his head.

"You tell me."

"It means a win. Trophies are for winners."

"And that's you?"

"It's you, too. You got this prime spot designing the colony constitution. But yes, mainly it's me. Project Mars has been winning awards left and right. Do you know why?"

She raised an eyebrow.

"PM is about innovation. Before us, the world's best aero-space companies were talking about merely visiting Mars, and we came up with cutting-edge technology that was unimaginable to even the top minds in space. We're not sending a handful of astronauts to Mars; we're sending a whole damn colony, all at once, and all signs show we're going to pull it off. Decades before anyone thought it was possible. That's a scientific marvel. And that's the priority.

Innovation. Creation. Exploration. Growth." He jabbed his finger at her. "You're messing with that."

"How am *I* the problem?"

"Because spending time on this little diversity problem you've created means my team can't concentrate on keeping our astronauts safe. You're ruining the vision."

She resisted the urge to huff in annoyance. "I think you're ignoring the big picture. Your astronauts won't be safe *because* of the psychological harm they have already endured and will continue to endure. Your mission won't be lauded when it's a vehicle of injustice. And you won't be able to innovate when your toxic company culture turns away the brightest minds—because we all know there are talented people of color being excluded."

"Carrie, come on. Tell me how I can get rid of this problem. Money? I'll transfer a million into your bank account right now." He nodded at Mandy. "Where's my phone, babe?"

"Obviously not money," Carrie said before Mandy could extract Beau's phone from her little bag. She could almost hear Kim's voice in her head, saying, *Take the money now; ask questions later!*

Carrie sat on one of the benches. "Tell me about your Black friend."

He scowled. "Stop mocking me."

"I'm serious. Sit down and tell me about someone you care about."

He plopped onto the bench and cradled the enormous trophy to his chest. "You know who I really like is Justice Donalds. He'll rule pretty much whichever way we want after a few rides on the PM jet. He really gets the plight of today's CEOs."

She leveled Beau with her best glare. "I don't mean the Supreme Court justices you buy off."

He shrugged. He set the trophy on the bench beside him and eased forward so his elbows rested on his thighs.

"Someone you care about," she prompted again.

He glanced at her. "From the way you keep nagging me, I assume you've read the gossip about Mikayla."

She considered giving him a blank "Mikayla who?" stare as if Anna hadn't already filled her in on what the tabloids had reported. But she was aiming for a candid conversation, and she couldn't cut through Beau's blustery defenses if she faked her way through it, too.

"I've heard about Mikayla, although I'm aware that not everything that's online can be trusted."

He sighed. "Mandy, baby, can you let the others know we'll be there in fifteen minutes? And juice me before you go. Mango Breeze, no more of that Fruit Punch bullshit."

She pressed another slim can of juice into Beau's hand and trailed her fingers along Beau's shoulders as she departed. The locker room door opened with a squeak and closed again with a sharp clack.

"What happened to you and Mikayla?" Carrie prompted.

"You know the deal. High school sweethearts. Madly, madly in love. Until my parents found out. It went badly for both of us."

"So, that was the end."

"No. A lot of people think that, but no. We dated for years. She'd sneak into my dorm room in college and read until I got back from class. She would make microwave mac 'n' cheese for dinner. She would fall asleep on the ratty couch in the garage while we built Perpetua."

"She lasted until Perpetua?"

"Yup."

"But you didn't marry her."

"No. She thought it was fairly ridiculous how much we had to sneak around. How my family could still be so closed minded in this day and age. She didn't want to be treated like that anymore. She married this light-skinned Black guy, moved to the Houston suburbs, had one older son early and then two other kids down the road, and became a really kick-ass pediatrician."

"Why does it matter that her husband is light skinned?" Carrie stated the question that most piqued her curiosity, then covered her mouth with her hand. It wasn't like her to voice her internal musings. Especially not tangential ones.

"Because her son . . . No, you're right, it doesn't matter." Beau shook his head.

Oh. *Oh.* She'd had a son right after leaving Beau. A man she'd loved but whose family had rejected her for years. Then she'd married someone close enough to her son's skin tone to be believable.

"This thing with race . . . it's personal for you," she said slowly. "You didn't stand up enough to keep Mikayla. And now people are accusing you—well, *I* am telling you—that you're not doing enough, once again."

"I'm accountable to a lot of people. I wouldn't be where I am now without my family and their support."

"Sure, but you can't be beholden to your family forever. Your choices affect all of us. And I can't imagine you're building the kind of future Mikayla and her family would be proud of."

"Don't talk about what Mikayla would want," he snapped. "This whole thing . . . it's not fair. When Kendra said she wanted to go to space, I was more than happy for it to happen. It was an amazing solution. And I asked Mikayla about it, and she was happy."

"Why did she care?"

"Kendra's her half sister."

"Your former love interest has been hiding in plain sight as a senator's sister?"

"Most people don't know they're related. They don't look alike. By all accounts they're both the only children in their families."

"So, you sent Kendra to space to please Mikayla."

"I didn't send Kendra anywhere. She's her own woman, and she was really motivated to go. Anyway, I'd think you'd be happy to have a Black woman space commander. Yet here you are, ungrateful."

"Representation in space is good. But appointing a single person of color to a leadership position isn't enough. Especially if that person puts her corporate interests first."

"Is this about the mining?" Beau nearly growled.

"I don't know, is it?"

"Look, you have no proof on any of that. And I won't have you drag Kendra's name through the mud. If only for Mikayla's sake, you've gotta take Kendra out of the article. Leave her out of it."

Carrie wasn't sure what to say. She needed the publicity of the article to keep Senator Brown in check. Without it, no one would know of Kendra's true intentions, or even the potential hidden intentions of Project Mars. Exploiting space would ultimately only oppress more people; the same way other discoveries of natural resources on Earth had harmed local populations, from fracking to diamond mines.

"I can't do that," Carrie said quietly.

"Excuse me?" He blinked as if returning to himself, and

the distant reflective look in his eyes morphed with a flash of black. His face twisted and flushed, as though the Mango Breeze had fueled him with a dark energy. "I can make life miserable for you, you know. It's not all free money and begging—that's just a courtesy. I didn't come here to tell you about my ex. I'm here because you've made problems for me and my bottom line, and because you pissed me off." He stood and paced the length of the bench.

She looked Beau up and down. High strung, red faced. But most important, nearly a foot shorter than her. She could probably take him if his anger sparked, now that Mandy was gone.

"I'm glad you told me about Mikayla. Not that you should only care because it'll affect someone you love. This isn't a 'what if it were your sister or your son' kind of issue. This affects her, and me, and everyone. Your company included."

"I'm not talking about this anymore. Fix the part about Kendra." He banged his fist on the nearest locker. Carrie jumped.

"You don't run a billion-dollar company for nothing. Negotiate," she pressed him. "Tell me what I get in return."

21

WHEN CARRIE and Beau swung open the door to the conference room overlooking Briar's campus fifteen minutes later, the room vibrated with angry energy like a beehive of on-edge adults. The conference room tables had been set up in a U shape, with the open end facing a large projector screen and a small food table near the door. The left side of the U shape seemed to be the Project Mars camp. Libby sat on the table with her legs crossed as she barked at four young aides camped out on the floor in front of her. The aides sported the characteristic orange Project Mars T-shirts, their thumbs rapidly tapping their screens as they carried out her commands. On the right side of the U-shape was Carrie's camp. Kim had a glare on her face as she observed the room, making comments to Anna, seated on her left, and President Farrington, on her right. The university president, for her part, huddled over a plastic plate of blueberries, practically on the brink of tears, as if she could physically see the river of funds from conservative donors drying up. She got little support from Cameron, on her other side, who was defending against a verbal assault from a feisty Shauna, who had grabbed Cameron's tablet and was waving it in the air to punctuate her words. On the projector screen, someone had pulled up a video call with Adam, Owen, and Grant, who were muted to the room but seemingly in the midst of their own argument.

Beau's eyes scanned the room, then flashed to Carrie, like *This is your mess, now fix it.* She raised an eyebrow right back at him.

"Libby!" he snapped.

She hopped off the table. "B-Ball is in the building! Everybody quiet. I'll unmute the video call, but you all need to zip it, too."

The room silenced to the quiet of a library, and all eyes turned to the CEO and the professor.

"I'll start," Carrie said. She addressed the room, her voice growing louder. "Today I sent an op-ed to the *New York Times* for publication. I did this not to harm Project Mars or anyone involved, but because I truly believe that there are issues with how we're approaching the important endeavor of the first humans living on Mars—from the culture of Project Mars itself to the values we're carrying forward. After discussing, Beau and I agreed that the article will no longer state that Senator Brown is involved in space mining, provided he agrees to changes of his own on some of the other issues. We need your help designing those changes."

"The article will be revised prior to being issued. I don't know why we have anything else to discuss," Beau muttered.

"You know we do," Carrie said. "We all care about making sure Project Mars is a success, and being inclusive is a part of that journey."

He sighed. "What do you want?"

"Why don't we talk about the colony government?" Carrie suggested.

She jumped as a loud voice chimed in from the video call.

"Mr. Ball, please," Adam implored, leaning in close to the camera so his face dominated the screen. "Please don't let Carrie's guerilla tactics undermine a foundational and lasting document for your colony. This document should be based on tradition and long-held American values, not the latest liberal cause complaining about so-called historic injustices that have nothing to do with the present. We need to be looking to English scholars and the great history of this country, not—"

Beau pressed his fingertips into his temple, squeezing his eyes tight. "Please, just . . . shut up. For a moment. You talk a lot."

Adam's head snapped back like he had actually been slapped, and his mouth gaped. Carrie heard a muffled cackle from the side of the room and narrowed her eyes at Kim's attempt to cover up her glee behind a paper napkin. Beau ignored Adam's glare as he paced at the front of the room.

"No," Beau said firmly, responding at last to Adam's outburst. "There's no reason to have a Mars charter that doesn't value everyone equally. I can get behind that."

"Owen?" Adam prompted, his tone venomous.

Owen shrugged and nodded. "The language will be fine," he said, his voice quiet for once instead of booming. "It's probably the right thing to do."

"Great," Beau said. "Are we all set?" He shot Carrie a weary look.

"What about changes at Project Mars?" Carrie reminded him.

"Putting aside the fact that it's not your business, this little diversity issue isn't meant to disrupt our productive company culture. We've done enough."

The constitution was a win. Beau had silenced Adam once and for all, and the colonists would have good legal protections in place going forward. But she had to finish the job.

"Let's take a five-minute break, and then we can wrap up. Come on, you haven't even had any juice in the last half hour," she teased. At some point, Beau would tire of her mocking him, but she couldn't help it.

She headed toward the food table and, most important, the coffee carafe. With her back to the room and before anyone could accost her to either scream at her or, she hoped, give her the hug she desperately needed, she unlocked her phone and navigated to her email drafts. Beau was tiring of their negotiation before she had even achieved all her concessions. It was time to start the second phase of her plan and gain more leverage. After only a second of hesitation, she opened the email with "Draft B" attached and typed a short message to remind the editor of their agreed-upon backup plan. *PUBLISH NOW,* she wrote in all caps. She clicked Send and ensured that the email zipped off to *The New York Times.* Then, she made herself a coffee.

Anna came up to her first.

"Everything okay?"

"Everything is good," Carrie said, taking a large gulp of coffee. The warm drink settled her. Premium roast. "Beau didn't beat me up or anything. Not that I don't have a height advantage."

"That's not spiked, is it?" Anna joked.

Carrie cracked a smile. "Too soon. And no, not this time."

She chatted with Anna as she watched Libby out of the corner of her eye. Libby had found Cameron, and the two were in conversation in hushed voices in the corner. Her heart nearly stopped as Libby's phone pinged. Then pinged again. Libby held up her hand to interrupt whatever Cameron was saying. From across the room, her wide eyes found Carrie. With that one lingering, incredulous look, Carrie thought her stomach would drop out of her body. Libby took a jerky step toward Carrie but stopped, swiveled in the opposite direction, and made frantic taps on her phone.

Then Anna's phone buzzed right in her periphery.

"What's that?" Carrie asked.

"Probably just a random news alert," Anna said. She unlocked her phone. "Oh. Whoa."

"What is it?"

"A post from Carlos Martinez."

"You get news alerts from Carlos?"

"Well, I was already obsessed with him before you even met him, and then once you did, I set up push alerts on his Lune posts so I could see his sexy, benevolent face every day. This, though, is not a thirst trap. It's . . . well. It's you."

Carrie grabbed the phone from Anna. Carlos had shared a post that Katie from *The New York Times* had posted on Lune two minutes ago. A snippet from an op-ed titled "Racists in Space: Progress Has Been Made, But Project Mars Company Culture Has a Loooong Way to Go." Carlos had commented above the post, *You tell 'em, Carrie! A must-read.*

"Wow, Carlos is already spreading the word. That's perfect."

"You and Carlos knew the article would go out early?" Anna asked at Carrie's lack of surprise.

She nodded. Her secret backup plan.

She was so engrossed in his repost that she missed Beau and Libby striding up to her in tandem.

"The article wasn't supposed to go live until 3 p.m. It's 2 p.m., Carrie," Libby said. Beau stood behind her as if waiting for his mom to chew out the manager.

"It's not the same article," she said. "We agreed the article would no longer accuse Kendra of being involved in space mining. The changes reflect that."

Draft B had kept everything the same except she'd swapped out the paragraph on Kendra.

The company did make some inroads through their announcement one month ago that Black US Senator Kendra Brown would command the first colonist class. Senator Brown is a celebrated veteran and brilliant leader. One of the best parts of her new role is her commitment to doing the right thing. She plans to prohibit any sort of mining of precious minerals at the colony or beyond, which could potentially violate the Outer Space Treaty by co-opting space resources for the gain of an American company. Though some Americans want to proceed down that path, thankfully Senator Brown has privately stated to Project Mars leadership, and will soon publicly announce, that she rebukes that approach. Rumors suggest she imminently plans to sell her entire interest in United Resource Enterprises, a company notorious for aggressive lobbying efforts to line the pockets of billionaires with resources stolen from space. The senator's moral resolve is commendable.

"This is not what Beau meant when he said to revise the article," Libby said through gritted teeth. "I want you to make my impossible job a little bit easier."

"I want that, too. But there's work left, and you know it. You both know it."

As if on cue, a Project Mars aide jumped up and bounced nervously at Libby's side. "Um, you know how you asked me to monitor social media activity?" His voice wavered and his hands shook as he held out his phone to Libby. "I'm not sure if this is newsworthy or not, but Alana Rodriguez just reshared Carlos Martinez's Lune post. You know, the actress who was on *SNL* last night. The post is about Project Mars being really whi—"

"I got it, Harper," she snapped at him and scrolled on her phone. "Damn. All these celebrities are tuned in for the media blitz next week."

Over the course of the next ten minutes, Carrie's stomach turned as phone after phone buzzed with incoming news alerts and activity. On her own phone, she scrolled and saw that a Chinese American CNN news anchor had posted, *I'm glad to see this. My cousin was forced out of Perpetua six months ago.* Further down her Lune feed, the head of the country's preeminent professional society for Black engineers wrote, *About damn time.* Then it was a congresswoman from California, and a teenage pop star whose song played nonstop on the radio, until finally, somehow, with alarming speed, the head of NASA reposted the snippet. Carrie stood next to Anna, unsure of where to put herself or what to do as chaos unfolded around her. The eye of the storm.

Beau sat on one of the conference room tables, but every few seconds he jumped up as if bitten by mosquitos, unable to settle. The multiple cans of juice only seemed to fuel his restlessness. His face grew so red she wondered about his blood pressure, and before long a bead of sweat dampened his temples.

"What are they saying now?" he demanded of Libby.

Libby bit her lip. "People are sharing issues they've had with Perpetua and Project Mars. Some of the former employees are getting pretty close to violating their nondisclosure agreements. The stories are bad press. The whole point of the media blitz was to keep the investors happy right before we announce projected expenses for the third colonist class. We don't want to rattle them."

Grant, who had been silent throughout, spoke up from the video call. "Look, Beau, let's hear what the demands are. It could be cheaper overall than upsetting the investors."

Beau started pacing again, his stride jerky. "Does anyone actually care how a few disgruntled employees are feeling?"

"Apparently, they do," Libby said. "The article already has ten thousand reposts."

This was her moment. She made her way to the center of the room, into the cavity created by the U-shaped tables. Kim rose and stood at her side. Shauna perked up, and Cameron had her phone out as if she was already plotting how to recraft anything Carrie said into a benign public statement.

"Let's start with the astronaut class," Carrie said simply.

Beau huffed. "We've already got five astronauts of color in the first colonist class. Plus, we've already budged on that by adding Kendra."

"Has anyone at Project Mars come forth with an idea for

how to increase diversity in this first class? Has anyone even half mentioned to you a potential idea?"

"No."

"That seems far fetched." She surveyed the PM aides camped out on the floor of the conference room. A young woman stared directly at her. Carrie raised an eyebrow.

"What is it?" she said softly.

"Kwame just posted about it. A few minutes ago. He's an astronaut in the second class." The woman held out her phone for Carrie. His post read, *There are fourteen people of color in the second class. We're more qualified than anyone and ready to go.*

"What does this mean?" she asked.

Another aide, this time a man in his mid-thirties, clarified, "The astronauts in the second class are highly trained and slightly more representative. There has been talk at PM that some of those astronauts should be put on the first mission to balance out the numbers and improve the experience."

"Hmm," Carrie mused. "Internal talk, you say?" She glared at Beau. "Sounds like the kind of thing a CEO should know about."

A voice cut through the silence. "You can't employ people and then fail to take their legitimate criticisms seriously. Let alone punish them for it. You all sound like shitty bosses." Carrie's heart stuttered at Anna's words. The other woman had an indignant look on her face, and it made Carrie feel as if Anna had physically hugged her.

"Add four more astronauts of color to the first mission," Carrie demanded. "Get their permission, give them the training to succeed, and give them the proper media attention as if they'd been in the first class all along."

"Just Kwame," Beau said.

"Four. With a promise to treat them well."

"Carrie—"

"I would like to work with Kwame," Libby said. "And some of the others, too. You could add Crystal, and Kashmala, and Julian or Sonia. They're all terrific, and the media loves them."

"You know all the second class by name?" Beau said with a start.

"These are people. Who care a lot about space and about your project, Beau."

He sighed. "Fine. Three astronauts. Kwame, Crystal, and Sonia. If they want."

Carrie breathed out as if she'd been holding her breath underwater and had finally kicked to the surface.

"Woo! More concessions!" She heard a cheer from the back and nearly rolled her eyes when she realized it had come from Shauna. She caught Libby's eye, and she could almost read the question *Who the hell is that?* in her raised eyebrow.

"And how about an apology to the current colonists for how they've been treated?" Carrie tried.

"Fine," Beau ground out.

A new voice spoke up. Kim Taylor, her ride or die. "You have no formal diversity-and-inclusion program at PM. How about putting in a person of color as the head of a new DEI role?"

"I'm sorry, but who is this?" Beau said. "And are you nominating yourself for the role?"

"Hell, no. I'm a tenured professor at one of the nation's most prestigious universities with a famous daddy and a few million in the bank. I don't need your little job. I do have a cousin, though—"

"Ahem, let's just go ahead and agree to a DEI department and legitimate money toward a diversity-in-STEM program at PM," Carrie interrupted before Kim could subject her unsuspecting cousin to the lion's den.

"We'll have to carefully tailor the program," Grant spoke up in warning.

"Then do so," Carrie replied. "Your company will be better off when you recruit widely and incorporate new voices and innovative ideas into your work. Having a range of voices in the room doesn't mean hiring less-qualified employees. It strengthens you."

The room had grown warmer. Bodies pressed in closer as the onlookers and aides struggled to hear what had been agreed to. She was in the center of her own cocoon of people making change, though maybe *cocoon* was the wrong word. *Hornet's nest* was more like it.

"If I may, Carrie." A throat cleared, and someone waved on the video call to gain attention. Owen, looking contemplative and hesitant. "Don't mean to add to the burden, Mr. Ball, but have you considered putting in a whistleblower protection program at PM? A lot of corporations use them to cover their asses—pardon my French—so it makes good business sense. But it's good people sense, too. Those astronauts who were brave enough to come forward about how they were treated deserve protection. There needs to be some sort of compliance oversight."

"Uh . . ." Beau said. He looked as though he'd forgotten Owen's name. "Um, yeah. We can do that, buddy."

"Thank you kindly."

Beau jutted his chin and surveyed Carrie with a long assessing look.

"Happy?"

She looked around the room at Shauna, with her defiant, eager glare and her penchant for standing up for what she thought was right; Anna, who had voiced her support as an employee and a friend; Kim, the world's best friend, who had traveled to and fro to always be fearlessly by her side; and the aides who had spoken up even though it may have put their jobs at risk. She thought of her research assistants, who weren't in the room to see the changes but who she thought, who she hoped, would agree that some progress, however infinitesimal, had been made. And she thought of her parents, who had thrown themselves body and soul into the fight for racial justice and inspired her to contribute in her own way. She would return home and tell her father all that they had accomplished.

They hadn't solved the country's race issues or its war on DEI. Maybe it would still be the case that another professor, driving at night, would be stopped and hurt by the police. Maybe there was still an engineer at Project Mars who'd face microaggressions at work, who would have to list her degrees to justify her employment there. She couldn't solve racism for good. What she could do, though, was try. Take action instead of doing nothing. At a critical moment where humanity would benefit from a fresh start with newly crafted laws and values, she'd made an effort. She hoped society would be all the better for it.

"It's a start," she said. "I hope you'll be proud of the changes you've made. You're on the right side of history."

There was a small snort, and she looked at the screen. Adam was still on the call, sitting stiffly in his office chair.

"What?" she said, with an edge in her voice. "Am I wrong?"

He shook his head. "No, unfortunately not, Dr. Davenport. History does seem to be heading in that direction."

Forward, she thought. Whether or not Adam was on board. With the work of the people in this room, with their efforts, with their *care,* and with the voices and support of everyone online sharing their stories, they could get on the right path. Toward justice.

epilogue

IT WAS AN HOUR BEFORE DAWN, when the sky above was still a subdued inky indigo. Soon, fledgling rays of sun would peek over the horizon to warm and brighten the earth.

But, before then, the sky would glow a fiery orange.

Carrie sat on a metal bleacher in a clementine-colored Project Mars T-shirt. On her left, Naomi's hand was tucked into hers, the small brown hand warm and a little sticky from a strawberry Pop-Tart. Her goddaughter grinned pink from frosting as the space-themed cover band started to play a new song. Kim grinned as she handed Carrie a flask behind Naomi's back.

"Only ten more minutes!" Kim stage whispered. "Drink up."

Only a narrow grassy bank separated their bleacher seats from a wide swath of dark water. A few hundred feet off, across the bay, a silver launch pad steamed around the body of an enormous rocket. The multistory rocket towered above the hundreds of onlookers clad in T-shirts and jeans on Florida's coast, awaiting a rare moment in history: the launch of the first colonists to live for any period of time on Mars.

"Don't be stingy with that flask," Shauna said on Carrie's other side. "It's a big day. Calls for being a little tipsy." She took the flask from Carrie and took her own swig. With Carrie's help, Shauna had started as an assistant team manager for Briar's football team. She had a whole set of superstitions on game days that included never drinking beforehand; only after they'd won and she'd taken care of the team would she even consider a sip. Today, though, was a different kind of special occasion that called for libations.

Slightly off to the side, illuminating the swaying reeds on the banks, a stadium-style LED screen projected Libby and two other newscasters hosting live programming in the crucial final moments as the crowd awaited the launch. Libby paced back and forth in a neon-orange dress on a platform overlooking the launch pad. The other two women reported from the Project Mars studio. The cameras couldn't hide the slight sheen of sweat on their brows or the way Libby kept glancing up at the launch clock. It reminded her of the prior year when she and Kim had watched Libby on television for the final supply landing, safe from their respective couches. Only this time, it was showtime. This was it.

"We've got an incredible crew of colonists here, don't we, Libby?" said one of the three women. "We've got Will Reynolds on board, our chief engineer, who actually helped develop some of the technology that makes today's launch possible." The screen split so that an image of a white man with a blond crew cut appeared.

"He's accompanied by a host of talented engineers, like Sonia Gomez. Not to mention other fan favorites like Crystal Wan, whom you all probably know from her viral videos on botany." Replacing Will's image, the screen flashed with a picture of a Hispanic woman with her black hair pulled back in a tight bun, posing beside an Asian woman in an orange Project Mars space suit. *That right there,* Carrie thought. *I did that. We did that.*

"That's right," Libby agreed, her voice almost a shout to be heard over the mechanical humming near the launch pad. She waved a hand behind her, gesturing back toward the steaming rocket. "And we're extra excited that Kwame Mensah is sitting right behind me, ready for launch. I'm sure many of us have come to love his Wednesday story hours as he explains various aspects of our mission to kids at home. It's our sincere hope that he'll continue to inspire future generations of space-goers."

"He's an inspiration," the third newscaster agreed. "Although, truly, we can't end today's program without high-lighting one of the visionaries launching tonight, our formidable commander, Kendra Brown. With her impressive military background, years of leadership, and advanced scientific degrees, you couldn't ask for a better leader to shepherd us into a new world."

"I'm told Kendra has a special token she's bringing up with her this morning, is that right?" the first newscaster asked. "As the first leader of the colony government, she's bringing up a leather-bound copy of the constitution. And not our constitution here in the United States. Project Mars has created its own charter for the colony that draws from the best legal minds in the country, premised on shared core values and centuries of proven history. It's a marvel, isn't it?"

"It's beautiful," Libby said. "I've read the preamble enough times that I have it memorized." She stared at the camera, her eyes piercing through the screen. There was a moment of silence, where the only sound was the water lapping at the banks and the mechanical whir of technology. "'We, the people of Earth, recognizing the great heights humanity can and will reach, while not forgetting historical injustices on Earth, endeavor to create an equitable, compassionate, and just society on Mars, governed by the colonists and the rule of law.'"

Carrie mouthed the words along with Libby, words she had toiled and stressed over and rewritten until each word ceased to have meaning. Words she had talked to her research assistants and her father and Kim and Owen about until they would rather talk about the weather than hear her circle back to a prior draft or tweak "just one word" one more time. The words filled her soul and made her feel light enough to float to Mars without a rocket. As Libby got to the final phrase, tears pricked at Carrie's eyes. The colonists, living under the rule of law—her laws.

A hush fell over the audience at the poetry of her words. "Beautiful," one of the newscasters agreed as Carrie fought to keep tears from spilling out of her eyes.

There was a downward tug on her hand.

"Auntie Carrie," Naomi said. "Lift me."

She gave her goddaughter the tightest hug possible, squeezing all her love and pride into the embrace. Then she pulled Naomi onto her back so the little girl could see above the majority of onlookers. They watched the newscasters explain for the final time features of the rocket. After only a few more minutes, huge white numbers appeared on the screen below a live feed of the launch pad. Her stomach fluttered so fiercely she was on the verge of doubling over with her hands on her knees just to catch her breath. Mission control started their final checks as the numbers counted down, flashing as they neared one minute.

Shauna slipped her hand into Carrie's on one side. Her most improbable friend and confidant, who didn't need to understand any of Carrie's world to care about her. Including the things she cared about, if the tears in Shauna's eyes were anything to go by. Kim rested her hand on Carrie's shoulder, patting Naomi's little hand resting there, and bit her lip.

The white numbers reached their peak: *3 . . . 2 . . . 1.*

Somehow, impossibly, the heavy rocket full of hopes and dreams and rapidly beating hearts rose a few feet off the ground in a blaze of orange fire. It lifted until it was at eye level and then rapidly gained speed, blazing up into the sky until they had to crane their necks back to see it. A blue-and-gray vapor trail clouded behind the rocket as it arched toward Earth's atmosphere and beyond. Within minutes, the rocket had disappeared into the clouds, already farther than any group of colonists that size had ever gone. The colonists had departed for a new world.

acknowledgments

To Marie Brown, thank you for being my first agent and champion. I have been touched by your faith in my writing and the stories I wanted to tell.

Kimberly, thank you for your editing genius! You have handled my stories and characters with such care and have helped me craft meaningful narratives. I appreciate your thoughtfulness and willingness to go above and beyond. And to Anna, thank you—you are unmatched!

To my parents, you have always encouraged me to shoot for the stars. Thank you for being role models, for listening to years of hopes and dreams, and for your support.

Paula, you are a source of inspiration for all writers. I can only hope to follow in your footsteps one day and to pave the way for the next generation as you have.

To Tayari, not only do you have a gift with words but you are also gifted at helping aspiring writers find their own voices. Thank you for helping me shape my characters and share their stories with the world.

Thank you to Erin, Mallika, and Kiana for reading the novel in its infancy, and for encouraging me to believe that this out-of-the-box story about racism and a Mars constitution could actually be something. I also deeply appreciate the words of encouragement and insight as part of the broader writing journey, with thanks to Elizabeth and Claudia.

I am struck by Octavia Butler's words in the reader's guide to her novel *Parable of the Sower*. She expressed her hope that readers "will think about where we seem to be heading—we the United States, even we the human species. Where are we going? What sort of future are we creating? Is it the kind of future you want to live in? If it isn't, what can we do to create a better future? Individually and in groups, what can we do?"* I hope that readers of *Arc of the Universe* will contemplate these same questions as we consider our future on Earth and in space.

---

* From *Parable of the Sower*, p. 341, by Octavia E. Butler, copyright © 1994. Reprinted by permission of Grand Central Publishing, an imprint of Hachette Book Group, Inc.

about the author

Nikki Alexander crafts stories that represent the many facets of the Black community. She strives to tell the stories of successful Black women navigating difficult environments in ways that are unexpected in light of traditional narratives, at the same time exploring themes that will appeal to any reader—moral dilemmas, high expectations, and romantic relationships in the face of career and family pressures. When she's not writing, she enjoys tap dancing and attempting to keep her temperamental houseplants alive.